ASSASSIN'S
WEB

A DARK WEB THRILLER

Richard T. Burke

Richard T. Burke

Other books by Richard T. Burke:

The Rage
Decimation: The Girl Who Survived
The Colour of the Soul

Assassin's Web
A Dark Web Thriller

Richard. T. Burke

First Edition: August 2019

Richard T. Burke

First Printing: 2019
ISBN: 978-1916141704
Published by RJNE Books

www.rjne.uk

For my daughter, Emily.

You will always be the apple of my eye.

Richard T. Burke

Contents

Assassins did have a certain code, after all. It was dishonourable to kill someone if you weren't being paid.

Terry Pratchett

One kills a man, one is an assassin; one kills millions, one is a conqueror; one kills everybody, one is a god.

Jean Rostand

Day Five: Friday, 31st July, 2020

Every fibre of my being screamed at me to run and hide. Instead, I sat at one end of the tatty, beige sofa, digging my fingers into the armrest. The room lay in darkness, lit only by the open screen of the laptop resting on the cushion beside me.

A week ago, my biggest problem had been retaining control over a group of boisterous teenagers, buzzing with excitement on the final day of school term. Now, a mere seven days later, every television and newspaper in the country displayed unflattering photographs of my face. I found myself the most wanted man in England, accused of vile offences against children and a string of horrific murders. And as if that wasn't bad enough, a killer was on his way here.

Outside, the tail end of a summer storm was passing over. The branches of the huge oak tree writhed in a frenzy of motion, back-lit by the last vestiges of daylight that penetrated the grimy windows. A strong gust of wind set the garden gate rattling on its hinges. The irregular clink of metal on metal carved through the blustery night, sounding like a prisoner frantically trying to escape his chains.

I pushed myself upright and peered around the edge of the open curtain. Distracted for a moment, I studied the haggard reflection in the dim light from the computer display. The grey half-moons beneath my eyes contrasted with the paleness of my complexion. My skin sagged; exhaustion stared back at me from every pore.

Focusing past the surface of the glass, I inspected the swaying foliage, seeking any hint of human movement. My gaze snapped to the right, drawn by surreptitious motion at the periphery of my vision. As I peered into the darkness, the black shape of the neighbour's cat sprang into the air and over the fence between the two properties.

My heart thundered against my ribcage, pounding out a jagged rhythm. I clasped one hand in the other to still the trembling of my fingers and resumed my search. Nothing else stirred beyond the tumult of the storm.

Without conscious thought, my gaze strayed to the spot at the corner of the lawn where I caught the last glimpse of my sister, Elena. Even though she had vanished over two decades earlier, the events of that night remained seared in my memory. Over the course of the intervening period, I had always held myself partially responsible for her disappearance. Maybe my current situation was God's punishment for not doing enough to save her.

Pushing the familiar sense of guilt to the back of my mind, I scanned the deep shadows once more before returning to my seat on the sofa. As I lowered myself onto the sagging cushions, the laptop screen turned off, plunging the room into darkness. In a flurry of panic, I reached for the keyboard and stabbed randomly at the keys. The photograph of Elena wearing a red cardigan on her first day of school filled the display, once again illuminating the walls in its dim glow.

"I don't think they're coming," I said aloud, more to reassure myself than because I believed my own words. My voice trembled with anxiety.

The killers who were tracking me had already murdered six people. The true number was probably higher, but those were the ones I knew about. My only crime was to be in the wrong place at the wrong time. That and the note. In hindsight, I wished I had left the damned thing unread—or at least ignored its contents.

But I hadn't. They say curiosity killed the cat; my curiosity had come within a whisker of killing me. During the past week, I had used up most of my nine lives. Tonight, I prayed my luck would last long enough for me to survive until the morning.

I strained my ears to pick up the crunch of footsteps on gravel but failed to detect anything above the fury of the storm. The hiss of the wind in the leaves built to a crescendo as the gale strengthened. Somewhere in the distance, a loose door slammed shut. Moments later, the sound repeated in a series of thunderous crashes.

I glanced at my watch: twenty to ten. My heart wouldn't take much more of this. Were they going to come? If they didn't arrive soon, there was a distinct possibility my blood pressure would finish the job for them.

Any hopes I might have harboured of postponing my ordeal vanished when an unfamiliar rattle came from somewhere inside the house. I held my breath and angled my head to one side, attempting to identify the source of the disturbance. A muted click originated from the hallway, followed by a thud. Somebody cursed in a low whisper.

In the dim glow cast by the laptop screen, I watched the door handle turn. My actions of four days earlier had finally caught up with me.

My executioners were here.

Day One:
Monday, 27th July, 2020

Four Days Earlier

The man pushed through the heavy, oak front door and headed towards the alarm panel. On his way, he dropped the two shopping bags at the foot of the stairs.

"Hey, watch that," came his wife's voice from behind.

The man rolled his eyes but said nothing. He had long since learned there was little to be gained by arguing with her. One bag contained a purple, Analeena designer handbag, hand-crafted from crocodile skin. The other held a Dolce & Gabbana evening dress. Between the two, they had cost more than most people earned in a year. And neither was in the least bit fragile.

Something wasn't right; the beige box should have been beeping. Instead, it remained silent. He peered at the status display: *System Disabled*. He could swear he had set the alarm. The car had been waiting outside, and they were running late. Perhaps he had forgotten the final keypress in the last-minute rush.

A flashing red light in the top right corner of the fascia caught his attention. He lowered his head and squinted at the embossed text: *Broadband*. That must mean the Internet connection was down—again. Living in the countryside had its attractions, but the poor quality of the telecommunications services certainly wasn't one of them.

"I'm not getting any Wi-Fi," his wife said, confirming the diagnosis. It seemed the problem affected more than just the alarm panel. She had dropped the two bags she was carrying by the door and was staring at the screen of her top of the range iPhone. "The 4G is down too," she added. "How am I supposed to keep in contact with my friends?"

She marched over to the mahogany hall table on which the landline telephone rested. Furrows creased the smooth skin of her forehead. She picked up the handset. Moments later, she slammed it down. The frown deepened. "That's out too."

The man felt his blood pressure rising. He was already imagining the conversation with the hapless call centre operator. So much for guaranteed data rates.

"Useless tossers," he said. "I'd tell them what I think about their crap service if any of the damned phones in this house worked. I'll walk down the road in a minute and see if the reception is any better from there."

"Well, I'm going upstairs to get changed. Can you bring my shopping up?" She turned and headed up the stairs without waiting for a response.

The man watched the tautness of her calf muscles, the curve of the thin dress over her perfectly shaped bottom and the bounce of the blond curls. When she was out of sight, he took a deep breath and shook his head. *What the hell was I thinking when I married her?* She was fifteen years his younger and undoubtedly attractive to look at, but she seemed to take pride in being high maintenance. The most irritating part of it was the way she treated him like her personal manservant.

The marriage was not yet in its third year, but already he was no longer receiving his conjugal rights. A month ago, she had announced she was moving out of the master bedroom into one of the guest rooms. He had only agreed to take her shopping in London that morning because if he did so, she hinted that she would spend the night with him in the super King-sized bed. It would have been considerably cheaper to hire out a top-class escort for the week.

Maybe he should insist on a face-to-face inspection of the wares. Amongst the girls arriving in the country over the following days was an exquisite brunette. She claimed to be eighteen, but most of them lied about their age. Little did she know she would be performing more than just modelling assignments.

She would be unhappy for a while but would soon get over it; they all did when their 'manager' explained the options. The problem was the women talked to each other. Word would get back to his wife, and the consequences would be dire; he'd be lucky to wake up with his private parts still attached to the rest of his body.

Once the phone lines were working again, he resolved to call his lawyer and ask how much it would cost to get a divorce. In the meantime, he needed a stiff drink. He strolled down the hall to the expensively furnished kitchen. Of course, she didn't cook. That would be beneath her. If they wanted to eat in, he called up a chef from an agency to prepare the food.

He opened the door of the drinks cupboard and pulled down a bottle of thirty-year-old single malt whiskey. Leaving the bottle on the polished, black granite of the work surface, he shuffled to his right and grabbed a cut crystal tumbler. He held the glass beneath the ice maker attachment on the double size refrigerator and pressed the button. The grinding of the motor mingled with the clink of ice cubes.

He returned to the bottle and sloshed in a generous measure, then used a finger to stir the contents. The ice cubes crackled as the amber liquid worked its way between the fissures. With a sigh of contentment, he raised the glass to his lips, inhaled the earthy aroma and took a sip.

As he put down the tumbler, he sensed movement behind him. Before he could turn, a powerful, gloved hand grasped him by the hair and pulled his head back. Another hand drew a razor-sharp knife blade across his throat, severing his windpipe and jugular vein in one stroke. A gout of blood splashed against the clean, white walls. A drop landed in the glass, swirling in an inverted, red mushroom cloud as it sank slowly through the amber liquid.

~

The assassin held the man upright until the flow turned into a dribble. Then he gently lowered his victim to the ground, taking care not to step in the expanding pool of crimson. The target's eyes remained open, his face still etched in a rictus of shock. He wiped the steel edge on the dead man's light-green designer jumper.

He placed the weapon on the work surface and retrieved the compact camera from his shirt pocket. The sudden flash left a floating, white afterimage on his retina. He took two more photographs and, after checking the quality of the pictures, padded towards the staircase.

As a general rule, he didn't like killing women. The contract only specified the man should die, but it wouldn't be too long before she discovered the body. Despite the phone lines being out—the work of a mere few seconds for a professional operator—the remote location meant he would be unable to put sufficient distance between himself and the crime scene before she ran down the lane to call the police from a neighbour's house.

No, she had to die, too. It was a shame to snuff out something so beautiful, but self-preservation came first. This was a job, pure and simple. Regrets were for amateurs.

He picked up the weapon and crept up the stairs, holding the knife blade out before him. With a bit of luck, he wouldn't need to use it; he planned to finish her with his bare hands. His heart beat faster at the prospect. The last few seconds were the most fascinating. Some struggled right to the end; others gave in quickly, seemingly resigned to their fate. Either way, looking into somebody's eyes as the life faded from their body was an intimate and exhilarating experience. The buzz it created was almost sexual in nature.

Despite his careful movements, one of the steps creaked.

A voice called out from behind the partially open door of the room straight ahead. "Thanks, Babe. Just put them on my bed, will you?" Her words carried the hint of a Russian accent.

The assassin paused for a second then continued his progress to the top step. Despite the loss of surprise, he now knew her location. He approached the wedge of light penetrating the doorway and bent down to place the knife on the deep, shag pile carpet. Straightening up, he gently shoved the door all the way open.

She had her back to him, studying her reflection as she applied a layer of mascara. Her gaze rose, and their eyes met in the mirror above the sink. A slow smile curved over his face. The brush stopped in mid-stroke. She frowned in confusion as her brain struggled to take in the presence of the grinning stranger in her house. It was only when he moved towards her that she turned and screamed.

The assassin took two long strides. His hands closed around her neck. There was little chance of anybody hearing her cry for help given the remote location, but all the same, he preferred to keep things quiet. He angled his head away as her fists flailed at his face. She lifted her leg to knee him in the groin, but he sensed the sudden movement and adjusted his position to the side. The intended blow glanced off his thigh.

"Bitch," he muttered, tightening his hold.

She staggered, unbalanced by her attempt to escape the steel-like band around her neck. Her mouth opened, but little more than a gurgle emerged. He stared into her eyes, studying the flecked, pale-blue irises as the light behind them slowly faded. Moments before the end, he allowed her lungs to fill one last time, then leaned in close and inhaled her final breath. Even when all movement had ceased, he maintained his grip for several more seconds.

Eventually, he lowered her body to the ground. A shiver of excitement ran through him. He placed a finger against her neck and checked for a pulse, marvelling at the warmth of her skin. She had seen his face, so he couldn't risk the possibility that she was still alive. In his line of business, witnesses could result in the premature end to a career and a lifetime in prison. Nothing.

He performed a final check of the room. The woman's body lay on its side, one leg angled awkwardly beneath the other, exposing a band of white underwear where her dress had rucked up. His gaze lingered for a minute. Even in death, she was beautiful—way out of her husband's league. It just showed what money could buy. The assassin shrugged. It was a shame, but he wouldn't lose any sleep over this murder.

Satisfied that everything was in order, he backed out of the bathroom, retrieved the knife and headed down the stairs. Unlikely though it was the man could still be alive, years of experience had taught him not to underestimate the human instinct for survival. He entered the kitchen and surveyed the body once more. Nothing moved other than the slowly expanding puddle of blood.

With a final backward glance, he closed the front door and strolled along the long, curved driveway. He was yards from the imposing, stone gateposts when he detected a shift in the shadows in the woodland to his left. Ducking behind the granite column, he watched as a rambler emerged from the footpath and ambled along the lane past the entrance. The new arrival seemed preoccupied, his eyes downcast instead of taking in the scenery around him.

The assassin frowned. Had the man seen him emerge from the house? He showed no interest in his surroundings, so the chances were he hadn't witnessed anything incriminating. The killer waited in his hiding place until the hiker disappeared from view.

The man was lucky. He would never know how close he had come to joining the other two victims.

It is often possible to trace a complex sequence of events back to a few seemingly insignificant triggers: in my case, the decision to set out on a walk at that particular moment, the flash of white catching my eye amidst the greenery and stooping to pick up the scrap of paper.

It was the first Monday of the school summer holidays, and six weeks of glorious free time stretched out ahead of me. The build up to the end-of-year examinations had left me exhausted as I tried to cram the critical facts into the brains of my reluctant students. It would take a few late morning lie-ins followed by lazy days for me to recover my energy.

When I drew back the curtains shortly after midday, the sun was already blazing high in a sky of cerulean blue. A storm was approaching across the Atlantic. The forecast was for rain to sweep in from the west later that afternoon, so I wanted to make the most of the opportunity while it lasted.

I strolled into the kitchen and placed a slice of bread in the toaster. While I waited, I picked up a holiday brochure from the work surface and flipped through the pages. The pictures depicted photogenic people engaged in a variety of water sports against a background of golden, sandy beaches and impossibly blue seas. I had saved several thousand pounds and intended to blow it on a package that offered windsurfing lessons. The costs would be eye-watering during school vacation, so my intention was to book at the last minute to save some money.

A metallic clack drew my attention back to the present and my empty stomach. After slathering the hot toast with butter, I wolfed it down and deposited the dirty plate on top of the pile of washing-up from the previous evening. Knowing my rushed meal wouldn't keep me going for long, I stuffed a breakfast bar in my pocket and ambled into the hall where I dragged my walking boots out of the cupboard.

Within a few minutes, I was strolling along the narrow pavement. The distant buzz of a lawnmower rose and fell in the gentle breeze, mingling with the crackle of a bonfire from a neighbour's garden. A haze of smoke drifted over the hedge, permeating the air with the acrid scent of burning leaves. Despite the indirect signs of activity, the road was deserted.

Within a quarter of a mile, the rows of houses and their tidy gardens gave way to open countryside. A sign on my left indicated the route of a footpath snaking up a slight incline through a gently swaying crop of wheat. I clambered over the wooden stile and followed the trail of cracked, bare earth cutting across the field like a scar. The heads of the plants encroached on the path and swished against my trouser legs as I strolled up the shallow slope.

As I crested the rise, I paused for a moment. The dark line of the footpath meandered down the hillside through a patch of woodland towards a narrow country lane. Three huge mansions, each occupying a plot of several acres, lay on the far side. The locals referred to the road as Millionaire's Row although its real name was Mill Lane. The last time one of these properties had come onto the market two years earlier, the asking price was over seven million pounds. What did people do for a living to afford that sort of money?

I ruffled my shirt to provide some much-needed ventilation and ambled downhill towards the temporary respite of the trees. A metal gate set in the hedge signalled the route ahead. Beyond the barrier, the path continued into the mottled shade of the small copse. A high-pitched screech originated from somewhere overhead. I shielded my eyes from the harsh glare and gazed upwards, picking up the distinctive outline of a red kite as it wheeled over the treetops.

I lifted the latch and passed from sunlight into shadow. Turning back, the bare earth of the trail I had followed described a wavy line through the undulating sea of wheat. The low drone of insects mingled with the rustling of leaves as the upper branches swayed in the light wind. I drew in a deep breath and exhaled slowly. The musty scent of damp soil and decaying vegetation filled my nostrils.

The first pangs of hunger fluttered in my stomach. I remembered the breakfast bar and removed it from my pocket. In my eagerness to open the snack, I pulled too hard. Part of the wrapper split from the rest and slipped through my fingers, spiralling away towards a clump of brambles at the edge of the path. My instinctive reaction was to retrieve it.

As my eyes tracked the trajectory, an incongruous patch of white caught my attention. I snatched up my own litter and shoved it back in my pocket. Under normal circumstances, I would draw the line at picking up somebody else's rubbish. I'm not sure why I reached out for this scrap of paper. It might have been the neatly folded, rectangular shape. Perhaps it was the whiteness and the fact it had clearly not been there long.

Whatever the reason, I closed my fingers around the edge and tugged it free of its prickly embrace. I hesitated before reading the contents. I remembered being taught from an early age it is wrong to read a letter without the owner's consent. Maybe everything that followed is cosmic payback for ignoring that one important lesson.

The faint outline of writing showed through the paper. Curiosity got the better of me and I opened the fold. Two lines of text ran across the page in a neat handwritten script.

dfwetefg.onion/login

user23956 / pw76TgRwe

The words *login* and *user* provided the obvious clues. These were the details for accessing a website. The first part looked like a web address although it wasn't in any format I recognised. The second line seemed to be a username and password. But what was the purpose of the site?

I contemplated returning the note to its hiding place. What if the owner realised he or she had dropped it and retraced their route, searching for it? I cast anxious glances both ways along the path, refolded the sheet and placed it in my back pocket.

I continued my walk, trying to enjoy the scenery during the short bout of good weather before the rain set in, but the note was never far from my thoughts. As soon as I arrived home, I headed towards the study and my computer. There, I pressed the power button and waited for the machine to boot.

After an interminable wait—not helped by an operating system update— the password box popped up, and I typed in my four-digit PIN. When the desktop eventually appeared, I grabbed the mouse and opened a browser window. I tapped out the characters in the address bar, frequently referring back to the handwritten note as I did so.

My finger remained poised over the enter key. I hesitated for a second then pressed down. Almost immediately, the screen updated to display a message stating that the page was unavailable. Not ready to abandon my efforts at the first challenge, I typed the text into a search window: a single result. I clicked the link and waited ... and waited.

Thirty seconds later, a Russian website opened. The site contained a series of hyperlinks, each starting with the first five letters I had typed followed by three more, ranging from *AAA* to *ABD*. I selected one at random. A new page popped up giving me the option to register the jumbled sequence as a Gmail, Yahoo or Hotmail email address.

I returned to the search window and removed the slash and the *login* part of the string. This time, two results appeared, both linking to the same website I had just visited. As a last resort, I deleted the word *onion* and tried once again, only to receive the same list of hits. Whatever the letters signified, they didn't relate to an active site on the Internet.

Feeling slightly let down, I rocked back in my chair. There was someone I knew who might offer advice, but I was reluctant to phone him. The situation was complicated.

For several minutes I debated with myself whether to make the call. In the end, I grabbed my mobile and scrolled down the list of contacts. The ringtone rang out six times. Just when I expected an automated message, there was a click.

"Percy, this is a nice surprise."

My brother-in-law, Jamie Saunders, was the only person I knew who still used my schoolboy nickname. My real name is Alex Parrott. As a child, everybody at school, even the teachers, called me Percy. Perhaps unsurprisingly, my sister Cathy, who is two years older than me, was known as Polly. She and Jamie met at University and married within a year of finishing their degrees.

After fourteen years of marriage, they had separated a few months ago, which went some way to explaining my reluctance to contact my sister's estranged husband. Cathy and their daughters, aged six and eight, left the family home and moved in with my mother.

Jamie ran a web design business and knew everything there was to know about computers. Despite the breakdown in relations with my sister, we remained on good terms. If anybody could explain the meaning of the cryptic note, it was him.

"Hi, Jamie. How are things?"

"Oh, ticking along. I have no idea where Cathy is if that's why you're phoning."

"No, it's not that. You two haven't made up your differences, then?"

There was a slight pause before he replied. "I think she's set on a divorce. She told me I love my computers more than I love her. At least you can turn off a computer when you've had enough. The hardest part has been the impact on the girls."

I already knew the answer from talking to my sister, but I asked anyway. "Are you seeing much of them?"

"I normally have them over on a Saturday night. They certainly know how to apply the emotional blackmail. They always turn on the waterworks when I return them to their mother's on a Sunday afternoon, begging us to get back together. It takes everything I've got to not burst into tears myself. She's the one who moved out though."

I had heard both sides of the story and knew neither half was blameless. Jamie might have spent more time with his work than his wife, but my sister had a stubborn streak the size of the Grand Canyon. Keen not to get embroiled in the rights and wrongs of the separation, I changed the subject.

"How's the business doing?"

"Things are going well. I seem to spend half my day on the phone talking to prospective customers who tell me they're about to become the next Google or Facebook then expect me to create their website for free. We've taken on a couple of new programmers recently, but we still haven't got enough people to accept all the work that comes our way. It doesn't feel right turning clients away, but I don't want to grow it too quickly. You can never be sure whether there's another recession around the corner."

"I'm glad to hear it's a success."

There was a pause as we both considered how to bring the conversation back to the real reason for my call.

Finally, Jamie accepted the challenge. "I'm assuming you didn't just phone me for a social chat."

"Actually, I wanted to ask your advice about something computer related."

"Oh. Has your machine broken down?"

I could detect the disappointment in his voice. He had commented on more than one occasion that, as a technical expert, friends and family expected him to provide free support.

"No. I ... um ... came across what looks like a website address, but my browser doesn't seem to recognise it."

Jamie's tone brightened. "Are you sure you didn't mistype it? Did you try Google?"

"Yeah, but there were no useful hits. The bit after the full stop is one I haven't seen before."

"What is it? You're aware triple X sites are to do with porn, I assume."

I ignored his poor attempt at humour. "It ends in onion, followed by a slash and then the word login."

He laughed. "Has your supply of wacky baccy run low? I have a contact who might be able to help. I didn't know you were into that sort of thing."

"What sort of thing?"

"The dark web, of course."

"I'm sorry, Jamie. You'll have to enlighten me."

"Dark websites all end in onion. You can't access them with a normal browser. You need to use special software called Tor."

"How do you spell that?" I asked.

"T. O. R. Just make sure you download it from the official site. It's something like Tor project and it ends with an *org*. There are quite a few pages out there containing versions riddled with spyware, and that defeats the whole object of remaining anonymous."

"I'm sorry to be a bit dim, but can you start at the beginning?"

Jamie sighed. "I'll give you the concise version. There's plenty more on the normal Internet if you're interested. All web traffic passes through servers, the first of which is at your service provider—companies such as BT, Virgin or Sky. When the request from your computer reaches its target, that server responds by sending back responses in the form of a web page.

"That's fine unless your activities are somewhat ... nefarious, shall we say. If the site you are visiting is illegal, it's easy for the authorities to listen in. The dark web circumvents all of that. I'm no expert on the inner workings, but the Tor software scrambles the packets of data and routes them via a random set of machines that forward the information to its destination, at which point it all gets put back together. The same happens in reverse to display the page on your computer.

"In essence, whilst somebody can listen in to the raw data stream, they can't decipher the contents or work out where it's going. The Tor browser effectively encrypts and decrypts your connection, making it impossible to see what you're accessing or uploading."

"Is everything on the dark web illegal?"

"Not necessarily. There are several reasons to encrypt your web traffic, the most common of which these days is because you want to purchase an illicit substance, for example, drugs. Sites like Silk Road popped up to service the demand although the FBI shut them down years ago. They use crypto-currencies such as Bitcoin to pay for goods so payments can't be traced easily either.

"The other main application of the darknet is to exchange information. It's a good solution, for example, if you live in a totalitarian state and don't want the authorities listening in to your online activities. I read somewhere that Facebook runs a dark website for exactly that purpose. The criminal elements have less salubrious reasons for using it, such as the sharing of child porn."

I took a moment to think before I asked my next question. "So, nobody can listen in if I install the software you mentioned?"

Jamie hesitated. "You should be okay. Obviously, you have to download it from a regular website before loading it on your machine. I've heard rumours that the government monitors downloads of the installer, but it's not illegal to do so. If you were worried about that, you could always go to an

Internet café rather than using your home connection. Do you mind me asking why the sudden interest?"

I had already prepared an answer in case he asked this exact question. "I caught a lad in my class passing a note to one of his mates. It contained the address of a website. He wouldn't tell me what it was about, so I thought I'd check it out for myself."

"Do you think this boy is into drugs or is it something worse?"

"I'm not sure. I want to get the facts straight before I take it higher."

"Anyway, isn't it the school holidays? The girls were pretty excited about having a few weeks off when I saw them last weekend. Cathy was complaining about having no time to herself for the rest of the summer."

"You're right, but I thought I should get a better understanding of what I'm dealing with before the new term begins."

"Well, I'd be careful. As the name suggests, there's some disturbing stuff out there. I hope for your sake it's nothing too serious."

We chatted for a few more minutes, but my mind was on other things. If only I had heeded his advice.

Richard T. Burke

Twenty-five years ago: Tuesday, 7th February, 1995

*E*ach night, my mother chose a different child's room for the bedtime story. That evening, it was my turn. A large promotional poster for the film, Home Alone, dominated one wall, featuring the iconic photograph of a terrified Macaulay Culkin with his hands held to his face. I identified myself with the boy who had single-handedly bettered the two burglars trying to steal from his family's house. The videotape had played the spider scene so many times that horizontal lines distorted the picture. A variety of model cars and aeroplanes lay scattered across the carpet despite my parents' frequent requests for me to keep my bedroom tidy.

"What would you like me to read tonight?" my mother asked, turning a blind eye to the mess.

The question was redundant because my younger sister's answer had been the same every night for the past few weeks.

"Magic tree," Elena yelled.

My mother raised an eyebrow and peered over her glasses. "Are you sure you wouldn't prefer Charles Dickens or Leo Tolstoy? Maybe a bit of Shakespeare?"

My sister giggled. "No, I want the magic tree book."

"The Magic Faraway Tree by Enid Blyton it is then."

Elena clapped her hands and snuggled up to me. I put my arm around her. She squirmed for a few seconds until she had made herself comfortable.

"Is everybody ready?" my mother asked.

The bedtime story had become something of a ritual. In truth, at the age of nine, my literary interests were more advanced than the books that interested my six-year-old sister, but I still enjoyed hearing the stories, especially when my mother put on the funny voices as she read to us. Cathy considered herself too old to partake regularly, but occasionally she joined us too. Tonight, she stayed in her room, listening to music.

"Hey, Cathy," Elena shouted in her high-pitched voice. "The story's starting."

We waited for a second or two, but there was no response.

18

My mother shrugged and opened the page at the bookmark. "It doesn't look like your big sister will be joining us. If we're all settled, I'll begin."

Elena listened, wide-eyed, as my mother read. I glanced sideways and watched her expression of rapt attention. After five minutes, Cathy appeared in the doorway.

Elena patted the mattress on the opposite side. "Come on, Cathy, it's the magic tree."

We squashed up until all three of us were sitting abreast with Elena sandwiched in the middle.

My mother waited until we had stopped fidgeting. "Just like the three children in the book."

"I'm obviously Joe," I said.

"I'll be Beth," Elena announced.

"Who does that make me?" Cathy asked.

"Frannie," Elena and I replied in chorus.

Cathy shook her head. "I'm not sure if that's good or bad. Let's hear it then."

My mother resumed the story. Ten minutes later, the chapter ended.

"But I want to know what happens next," Elena said.

"You'll have to be patient and wait until tomorrow night."

Cathy lowered her feet to the carpet. "Or read it yourself."

Elena considered her sister's suggestion for a moment before replying. "No, it's too hard for me. Can I look at the pictures though?"

My mother plucked her from the bed. "Nice try, but it's time to go to sleep now, young lady. Maybe tomorrow. Give your brother a kiss."

I stood on the mattress and offered my cheek. Elena's lips gently touched my skin. I rubbed vigorously at the spot she had kissed. "Ugh."

Elena squealed with laughter.

"Don't forget your sister."

Cathy repeated the act, reducing Elena to a fit of giggles.

"Come on, you little monster," my mother said, fondly. "That's enough messing about. Let's go and brush your teeth." She carried Elena to the door, pausing to allow for a final goodnight wave.

That was the last time my mother read aloud to us. It was also the last time I saw my baby sister alive.

I replaced the phone in my pocket and looked down at the notes I had made during the conversation with my brother-in-law. If I was going to pursue this any further, I would need to download the Tor browser. But did I want to discover where the link led? It wouldn't bother me too much if the site sold drugs. I considered myself fairly liberal minded. Provided it didn't adversely affect anybody else, I had little interest in what people got up to in the privacy of their own homes.

But what if it was child pornography? There was no question in my mind I would report the matter to the police immediately. I considered anything involving the exploitation of vulnerable children as morally indefensible. As a teacher, I had witnessed first-hand the devastating impact of sexual abuse on a victim. Thankfully, it had only happened once during my teaching career, but it was a traumatic experience for all concerned.

The more I thought about it, the more convinced I became that I should find out what I had uncovered before deciding how to proceed. For all I knew, the page might be perfectly innocent. The first step was to do some reading. I set about learning everything I could about the dark web. Many of the details went beyond my limited technical experience, but the gist of it was as Jamie had explained. I soon discovered that Tor is an abbreviation of *The Onion Router*, the different layers of protection analogous to the skin of an onion. The extension on the link now made sense.

I spent plenty of time researching the legality of using the dark web. Whilst not against the law in itself, the tools provided access to a network of sites, many of which involved the sale of illegal goods. One page advised that Internet Service Providers monitored usage of the Tor browser, which might, in turn, invite attention from their support team.

That decided it for me. Despite having no lessons for six weeks, I needed the Internet to access my staff email account and to prepare for the following term. I didn't want to risk losing such a vital resource. The school provided me with a laptop. It was even more underpowered than my desktop machine, but it was just about capable of running a browser. I would find a place with free Wi-Fi and connect to the dark web from there.

~

The Café Corner occupied a spot on a pedestrianised road on the outskirts of the Basingstoke main shopping centre. It offered reasonably priced drinks together with free Internet access. As I pushed through the door, the first thing to strike me was the contradictory image of the place. The wall-mounted television screens, currently displaying a twenty-four-hour news channel, belonged in a sports bar that advertised live football matches. Other aspects of the decor landed somewhere between wine bar and homely tea room, the contradiction summed up by the gurgling coffee machine at one end of the counter and the beer taps at the other.

Clutching the laptop bag under my arm, I ordered a medium-sized Americano and carried the white mug to a table in the corner. The location ensured there would be no unwanted observers. After all, I had no idea where the link would lead. The nearby mains socket provided another advantage. Without an external supply, I would be lucky if the battery lasted over ten minutes.

I inserted the plug in the wall and pressed the power button. The speaker emitted a strangulated beep as the agonisingly slow boot process started. While I waited, I scanned the other customers. At four-thirty on a Monday afternoon, the place was quiet.

Two tables away towards the front window, an exhausted-looking woman cradled a drink between her hands. Several overflowing bags of shopping lay at her feet. Meanwhile, her three-year-old child played with a sugar sachet until it popped open and deposited the contents over the tiled floor. She snatched the empty wrapper from the child's fingers without saying a word and moved the container holding the rest out of reach. Before the infant could complain, she rummaged in her bag and shoved a cuddly toy between the tiny hands.

Ten feet away on my right, a man in his early twenties hunched over his phone. Sensing my attention, he glanced up briefly then refocused on the handset. At the adjacent table, an elderly couple leaned towards each other, their heads lowered in conversation.

After what seemed an age but was probably only a few minutes, a short sequence of notes announced the laptop's readiness. I hurriedly muted the sound, typed in the password then opened the wireless connections. *Cafe Corner Public* headed the list with a signal strength of four concentric rings. I transferred the Wi-Fi security code printed on my receipt and clicked to connect.

Seconds later, I had initiated a browser search and was perusing the results. The first hit pointed to the *torproject.org* website. I remembered Jamie's advice to use the official site. This looked like the one. I navigated through the options until I came to a page with a large purple button labelled, *Download Tor Browser*. After a moment's hesitation, I tapped the touchpad.

At fifty megabytes, the file wasn't particularly big. It still took over five minutes to complete the process. No sooner had it finished than I clicked the *Run* option. After selecting the language as English, the installation progressed without issue. Within moments, I was staring at a window welcoming me to the Tor browser. I removed the scrap of paper from my wallet and placed it on the table in front of me. My half-full cup of lukewarm coffee sat forgotten as I unfolded the note.

I carefully transcribed the text to the address bar. My pulse raced as I debated whether to press the enter key. I drew in a deep breath and held it. Did I really want to do this?

I exhaled and stabbed my finger down onto the keyboard. I'm not sure what I expected, but the untitled white dialogue box requesting a username and password came as a surprise. My world shrank to a bubble around the laptop. I tapped out the characters and clicked the OK button. At first, nothing happened.

After a brief delay, a predominantly monochrome form using a grey palette filled the display. A menu bar occupied the upper area of the screen. It offered two options: *Current Jobs* and *Your Jobs*. The blue underlined text revealed I was looking at the former. A rectangle of black lines took up the rest of the page. It was empty apart from a button containing the word *Newest* at top centre. I stared at the blank box in confusion. What did it all mean? I clicked the button. The text inside the shape updated to *Oldest*, but everything else remained unchanged.

I dragged the cursor to the *Your Jobs* menu item and tapped the touchpad. The page followed the same layout as the first. This time, however, the central part of the screen contained several lines of text. My eyes darted over the rows of data.

STATUS: AWAITING CONFIRMATION
LOCATION: RG27
CONTRACT AGREED: 24th JULY 2020
DEADLINE FOR COMPLETION: 29th JULY 2020
AGREED FEE: £7250
FULL DETAILS HAVE BEEN SENT TO YOUR SECURE INBOX.

It may seem obvious after the event, but at the time I had no inkling to what the contract referred. From the limited information available, it was clear the entry related to a commercial agreement. The deadline was two days in the future. My first thought was that it had something to do with the purchase of a property. It had been many years since I had bought my house with the money left by my father in his will, but I remembered having lengthy discussions with my solicitors about the exchange of contracts and completion dates.

The location was obviously the first part of a postcode and matched the area where I had found the note. Could this be a new system for the secure transfer of funds? It struck me as strange that there was no company logo on the site, but perhaps this was a prototype user interface. The reference to jobs also seemed peculiar.

I was so engrossed in my thoughts I failed to notice the member of staff hovering by the table. She was in her early twenties with long, mousy-coloured hair and a stud through the side of her nose. Even in her flat shoes, she was taller than average, maybe five foot eight or nine. She had a slim build, and I couldn't help noticing that the blue and white striped uniform hugged the contours of her body.

"Hi, Mr Parrott. How are you?" She smiled revealing a slight gap between her front teeth.

I immediately lowered the laptop lid, but I guessed she had already seen the page over my shoulder. "Oh, hello, um ..."

"You don't recognise me, do you, sir? I'm Molly, Molly Gunther."

Now it came back to me. She was a former pupil. I had last taught her over seven years earlier. I vaguely remembered her as an unexceptional student, keen to please and hard-working but possessing no real affinity for the subject.

"Of course I do, Molly. It's good to see you."

"Doing some work for school, sir?"

"Something like that. And call me Alex. You're not my pupil anymore."

"Right ... Alex. I just wondered if you wanted a refill. We're not supposed to do this, but because you were one of my favourite teachers, it's on the house."

"That's very kind of you. Another Americano would be great. Do you work here full time?"

"Yeah. I'm going travelling with my boyfriend in a month or two, so I need to earn some money. Although don't tell the manager. I haven't told him I'm leaving yet."

"I wouldn't dream of it."

"My boyfriend said he'd pay for everything, but I don't want to go running to him like a child every time I want to buy something."

Unsure how to respond, I replied with a noncommittal, "Okay."

She smiled broadly. "Well, I'll get your coffee right away." She strolled back to the counter and set to work on the machine.

I reopened the lid of the laptop and studied the screen once more. Another idea occurred to me; perhaps it was a site for people searching for a tradesman to undertake home improvements. I remembered my sister describing a website she had discovered where individuals tendered for work, and the lowest bid won the job—a Dutch auction. But if that was the case, why hide the page away on the dark web? Could it be an attempt to avoid tax?

My relief at discovering the site was apparently neither a haven for paedophiles nor a drugs marketplace was tempered by the realisation I had no real idea what I had stumbled across.

The feeling would last until I watched the news that evening.

T he drive home was uneventful, which was probably just as well given that my thoughts were elsewhere. I had two main theories, but neither of them fitted the scant amount of information I had gleaned from the website. I was no expert on the subject, but the page didn't appear to be a commercial site.

Part of me felt disappointed that I had failed to discover anything interesting. Maybe if I revisited when there were some active jobs, I would get a better idea what it was all about. I debated with myself whether to share what I had found with my brother-in-law, Jamie. After all, I had already asked him about the dark web aspect, and his experience of business websites was far wider than mine.

I turned into my road and spotted the figure of Mrs Owens. She ran the local Neighbourhood Watch scheme, but I suspected it was all a front for keeping an eye on the activities of the other residents. If an unfamiliar vehicle parked anywhere on our quiet, residential street, she could be relied on to record the number plate in the little notebook she kept in her pocket. As usual, she trailed behind her tiny dog as it sniffed at the foliage beside the verge. The animal provided the excuse she needed to patrol the local vicinity.

I waved as I passed by, giving her a wide berth. She stared in my direction but failed to return the gesture. She had apparently not yet forgiven me for the faux pas committed by my nieces a few weeks earlier. They had been playing in my garden. Seeing my neighbour walk past the front gate, Zoe, the younger of the two, had asked in a loud voice, "What make is that lady's rat dog?"

Out of the mouth of babes. Even now, the memory brought a smile to my face. As my sister was fond of saying, the girls were all fact and no tact.

I glanced at the dashboard clock as I swung into my short, paved drive: five thirty. I didn't feel much like cooking. That's one benefit of being single; I could choose when and what I wanted to eat. A quick omelette would keep me going for the rest of the day.

I let myself in through the front door and made my way into the kitchen. There, I turned on the hob to its hottest setting and grabbed a couple of eggs and a slice of bread from the cupboard.

As I cooked, my mind turned back to the website. Perhaps it was time to forget the whole thing. Part of me still felt guilty at snooping into this other person's business. The more I thought about it, the more it seemed like an invasion of privacy. How would I feel if somebody poked into my affairs? I had used my concerns about criminal activity as an excuse and allowed my curiosity to get the better of me. I decided there and then I would take it no further.

A loud clack came from the toaster. Seconds later, I carried my meal of omelette on toast into the lounge. I turned on the television as a suited male presenter announced that the programme would transfer to the local area news.

The picture switched to a middle-aged woman sitting behind a desk. She smiled into the camera. "Welcome to the news in the south."

Her smile disappeared, replaced by a sombre expression. "Police are tonight investigating a double murder in the village of Dalton, close to the town of Basingstoke."

The fork stopped halfway to my mouth. I lifted the tray off my lap and deposited it on the coffee table, all thoughts of food forgotten. My fingers scrabbled for the remote control. I increased the volume without taking my eyes off the screen. A map of the south of England expanded to fill the display. The red dot at the centre showed the village where I lived.

"A police spokesman said a member of the public discovered the victims, a man and a woman, late this afternoon. Both had suffered multiple injuries. Their identities are being withheld until relatives have been informed. More now from our reporter on the scene, John Samson."

The view switched to a man standing in front of two police cars. He held a furry, cylindrical microphone in front of his chest. A large house loomed in the background. I immediately recognised the location; it was the lane I knew as Millionaire's Row, less than a hundred yards from where I had found the note.

The reporter spoke in a gravelly voice. "Yes, Moira. Police were called at four-thirty this afternoon when a cleaner discovered the bodies inside their property at this quiet, rural spot. We have little information about the victims' identities, although we understand that the dead man was a local businessman. Police are searching the premises and the immediate surrounding area. They do not currently have any suspects. I interviewed Chief Superintendent, Mike Chalmers, earlier today."

The picture showed a balding man in a dark blue uniform with a microphone held towards his mouth.

A voice came from off-screen. "What can you tell us about this case, Chief Superintendent?"

"This was a vicious attack that took place in the victims' own home. We are particularly interested in speaking to anybody who may have witnessed anything unusual or suspicious in the vicinity of Dalton during the last twenty-four hours. All calls will be treated in the strictest confidence. I'll be issuing a further statement at a press conference tomorrow morning. Thank you." The policeman turned away from the interviewer.

The shot returned to the reporter. "We'll keep you informed of any updates as we receive them. Now, back to you, Moira, in the studio."

The woman glanced down at her notes then raised her eyes once more to the camera. "If you have any information relating to this case, no matter how insignificant, please call the helpline number displayed at the bottom of the screen."

A series of white digits beginning with 0800 overlaid the picture.

"In other news ..."

I stabbed the rewind button on the remote control and watched the segment a second time. I paused the playback when it reached the telephone number. Pushing myself upright, I staggered into the kitchen, my head spinning. I snatched up a pen and a pad of paper I kept in a letter rack by the central heating boiler and transcribed the digits.

This was one possibility I hadn't considered before, but it all made perfect sense now. I had no idea how much it would cost to arrange a death, but seven thousand pounds seemed a remarkably small amount to end two lives. By themselves, the words on the website were inconclusive but coupled with the location where I had discovered the scrap of paper, the logic was inescapable; it appeared the killer had accidentally dropped the login details for the page on which the contract for the murder had been placed.

My first reaction was to reach for my mobile, but something made me hesitate. I wanted to be sure of my facts before contacting the helpline number. When I had looked at the website earlier that day, the status was marked as awaiting confirmation. The fact they had reported the deaths on the news should be evidence enough for the person who had placed the contract. I didn't know how the site worked, but it was reasonable to assume the job status should now be set to complete.

Before making the call, I had to convince myself I wasn't jumping to the wrong conclusions. The only way to do that was to check the page again. I could have returned to The Café Corner, but I was so shaken I didn't feel up to driving, and I needed to know immediately. I hurried back to the kitchen where I had left the laptop bag. My heart thudded in my chest as I sank onto the sofa, plugged in the mains charger and pressed the power button.

The computer seemed to take even longer than usual to boot. When the desktop finally appeared, I dragged the cursor to the Tor Browser icon and stabbed frantically at the touchpad. The note containing the login details was still in my wallet, so I removed it and straightened it out on the surface of the table while I waited for the program to start.

With trembling fingers, I copied the text into the address bar and hit the enter key. "Come on," I muttered. The little dot rotated around the circumference of the circle in the upper left corner for several seconds. I expected the bland login box to appear. Instead, I received an error message: "Unable to Connect."

My eyes darted over the letters at the top of the page. Had I made a mistake transcribing them? Everything looked correct. In mounting frustration, I deleted the line and retyped it, carefully checking each letter as I did so. A short while later, the same message reappeared. I started up a conventional browser window and confirmed the Internet connection was working. "Damn," I yelled, slamming my palms on the keyboard.

Was my Service Provider blocking access? I remembered what Jamie had said about their ability to detect usage of the Tor Browser. It seemed logical to conclude they might also prevent the data from reaching its destination.

I tried to organise my thoughts. As I saw it, three options were open to me: I could return to the café and try again from there, I could call the hotline without confirming the site was still active or I could contact Jamie and ask him to check the link. I wasn't quite ready to drag my brother-in-law further into this. Nor did I want to make a fool of myself by calling the police with no real evidence.

That just left the first option.

T he promised rain came down by the bucket full, and the wipers worked hard to keep the windscreen clear. The drive through the torrential conditions passed in a blur, both physically and metaphorically. I parked in a pay and display car park near Basingstoke town centre. I had no loose change so chose to risk it. Surely no traffic warden in their right mind would be out in the downpour, and I didn't intend to stay long.

By the time I reached The Café Corner, my feet were soaked through. A trickle of water dribbled down my neck as I lowered the hood of my cagoule under the cover of the doorway. The windows were fogged up. A wave of warm air rolled over me as I pulled the door back, the bell barely audible above the clamour of voices. It wasn't yet dark, but the place had a different feel about it. For one thing, it was far busier. As my eyes swept the room, I spotted only two spare tables. Moments later, a young couple moved away from the counter and settled down at the nearest. Desperate to obtain some answers, I made a beeline to the remaining empty table.

Shrugging off my wet coat, I draped it over the back of the chair and sat. There were no plug sockets in range of the charger, so I would just have to hope the battery lasted long enough. I removed the laptop from its carry bag and pressed the power button, waiting impatiently as it began its laborious startup sequence.

While my computer booted, I surveyed my fellow customers. Most were in their twenties or early thirties. The hubbub of conversation rose and fell. A loud peal of laughter erupted from the far corner where three men holding pint glasses studied the screen of a mobile phone. My gaze wandered to the counter. Molly stood beside the coffee machine with her back to me as she adjusted the dials. The hiss of steam brought a sudden silence in the background chatter before the sound level increased once more.

Finally, the display sprang into life. With dismay, I noticed that the power bar was already down by a quarter. As I started the Tor browser, it suddenly occurred to me that the wireless code might have changed since earlier that day. My eyes dropped to the Wi-Fi icon. To my relief, it was green with four rings.

I pulled the paper out of my wallet and hurriedly transcribed the letters. As I was about to press the penultimate character, Molly's cheery voice broke into my concentration.

"Hello again, Mr P—I mean Alex. I don't see you for seven years, and suddenly you're here twice on the same day. You must really like this place."

"Hi, Molly. I've just got some urgent work to finish up."

"Is there no Internet at home then?"

My gaze settled on the power icon. While I watched, the number displaying the remaining percentage changed from seventy to sixty-nine. "No, I've been having problems with my phone line, and I need to get this done tonight."

I could sense her studying the screen from over my shoulder. The *Tor Browser* text at the top of the page was unmistakable in its distinctive green and purple font. My finger rested on the enter key, but I didn't press it.

Finally, she shrugged. It was obvious she had been hoping I would continue. "Can I get you a drink? I can't do another one on the house I'm afraid."

I needed her to leave. "Yes, please. An Americano again if that's okay."

"I'll be right back."

My eyes followed her towards the counter. When I faced the screen once again, the power bar indicated only sixty-five per cent remaining.

My pulse rate increased as I pressed the key. Once again, the wait icon began its hypnotic rotation pattern. Surely it hadn't taken so long the last time I was here. Fifteen seconds later, a yellow warning triangle accompanied the "Unable to Connect" message. I needed to confirm the problem didn't lie with the Internet connection. Restarting the browser, I clicked the hyperlink to DuckDuckGo on the Tor start screen. During my earlier research, I had learned that it was a search engine without any of the tracking features included in the mainstream sites, such as Google or MSN. The page immediately opened displaying the image of a duck's head with a green bow tie around its neck above an empty text box. The link was working fine. That could only mean the site owners had taken it down.

Damn! I slammed the lid of my laptop in frustration. A handful of my fellow patrons glanced in my direction before resuming their conversations. I sat resting my head between my hands as my brain whirled through the options. My conscience wouldn't allow me to keep the information I had obtained to myself, but I still felt the need to talk things through before going to the police. My brother-in-law, Jamie, was the obvious candidate. He already knew a small part of the story.

I was returning the laptop to its carry case when Molly returned carrying a tall mug of steaming hot coffee. I had forgotten about the drink I had ordered.

"Finished so soon?" she said. "That was quick. Anyway, that'll be three ninety-nine please."

I rummaged in my wallet, withdrew a five-pound note and handed it to her. "Keep the change."

"Thanks, um ... Alex." She smiled down at me. "Maybe I'll see you again in another couple of hours."

Despite the seriousness of the situation, I couldn't help smiling in return. "That's me done for the day. It was nice seeing you."

She turned away then hesitated. "My boyfriend spends a lot of time on that Tor thing."

So, she had seen the screen. I didn't know what to say, so I responded with a non-committal, "Right."

She stood awkwardly for a second longer, then raised a hand in a half wave as she returned to the serving area. "'Bye, then."

I took a sip from my coffee. My gaze darted to the counter. Molly had disappeared through the door into the kitchen. I placed the laptop bag on the floor, grabbed the raincoat off the chair and shrugged my arms into the damp material. Leaving the unfinished drink, I headed towards the exit and the teeming rain.

Whether it was due to the contradictory thoughts spinning through my brain or the prospect of having to navigate my way back through the inclement weather, I'm not sure. Whatever the reason, as I hurried through the door, the laptop bag slipped my mind.

Richard T. Burke

If anything, it was raining even harder as I made my way through the drenched city centre back to the car park. Whilst the cagoule kept the upper part of my body relatively dry, the cold water splashed off the pavement and seeped into my shoes. The thud of raindrops against the plastic material of the hood drowned out all other noises. A nagging feeling tugged at the edge of my subconscious, but I put it down to the circumstances in which I found myself, and not the slip of memory concerning the laptop bag.

Five minutes later, I sank into the driver's seat. The dampness soaked into the fabric, but my mind was on other things. I started the engine and set the fan to its highest speed to clear the layer of condensation forming on the interior glass. The wipers swished backwards and forwards in a hypnotic rhythm as they worked to shift the torrent from the windscreen.

I retrieved the handkerchief from my pocket and dried my face. Every movement caused more water to trickle off the slick surface of my raincoat and seep into the upholstery. Tossing the damp square of blue cloth onto the passenger seat, I lowered the zip of the coat far enough to reach into my shirt pocket and grab my phone.

I unlocked the screen and scrolled down the list of contacts until I came to the one for my brother-in-law. The ringing tone sounded in my ear as I gazed absent-mindedly out of the side window.

Jamie answered after three rings. "Twice on the same day, Percy?"

"Yeah, sorry about that, mate. Listen, I need your advice on something."

"Let me guess. Is it to do with that website?"

"Yes."

"Well, I'm certainly no expert on the dark web. What can I help you with?"

I hesitated for a moment before replying. "Would it be okay if I came around so we can discuss it face to face?"

My gaze tracked to the dashboard clock. Eight thirty-two. I hadn't considered the time when I asked the question.

"No problem. I'll just have to ask my harem of beautiful women to leave."

It hadn't occurred to me he might have company. He and my sister were separated, but that didn't mean he wasn't seeing somebody else. "If you're busy, I can always come tomorrow."

Jamie laughed. "I was only joking. I'm all on my own tonight—and every other night for that matter. It'll be good to share a beer or two."

"Thanks. I'll see you in about fifteen minutes."

I ended the call and returned the phone to my shirt pocket. By now, the windscreen fan had cleared a circle of glass a foot across. I cranked up the setting on the climate control system to twenty-six degrees. Within seconds, the warm air blasting out of the vents had turned the interior of the vehicle into a tropical greenhouse, but it had the desired effect, and I could see well enough to drive. I released the handbrake and navigated my way onto the main road.

I had driven a little over a hundred yards when I finally realised what had been nagging at my subconscious. Cursing, I performed a three-point turn and returned to my recently vacated space in the car park. I groaned at the prospect of braving the elements again, but I couldn't leave the laptop at the café. By the time I arrived back at the entrance, the water was sloshing around in my shoes.

The bell dinged as I entered, and a wave of warmth rolled over me. I lowered the hood of my cagoule, leaving a wet trail behind me. Excusing myself to the two girls sitting nearest the door, I reached over to grab a napkin and dabbed at my face. My gaze focused on the spot where I had left the case, but a young couple now occupied the table, holding hands and deep in conversation. There was no sign of the laptop.

My attention transferred to the serving area where Molly leaned forwards, concentrating on something just below the level of the counter. She looked up as I approached. A guilty expression flashed across her face.

"Oh, hi, Alex. I was trying to see whether there was an email address or a telephone number so I could call you."

As I peered down, she slipped my computer back into the black bag. "Um ... thanks," I said, unsure what else to say.

She handed the case over with a nervous smile. "I was thinking about dropping it off on my way home at the end of my shift, but I realised I don't know where you live."

I thanked her again and closed the zip fully. At the time, I didn't give it a second thought. It was only much later that I would consider her behaviour suspicious.

I raised the hood of my plastic coat and headed once more into the teeming rain. When I reached the car, the interior still retained some warmth. I tossed the laptop on the passenger seat and started the engine.

Richard T. Burke

The journey passed without event. As I drove, I ran over in my head what I hoped to gain by involving my brother-in-law. If I was honest, the main reason was to get a second opinion about what I should do next. I was almost certain my failure to connect to the site was unrelated to anything I had done differently from the first time. Jamie should be able to confirm whether that was the case. There was no real question in my mind I would call the police. In hindsight, I just wanted somebody else to tell me it was the correct thing to do.

I indicated right, swinging past the *For-Sale* sign as I steered onto the short drive. The house had been on the market for two months. From what I had learned from my sister, there had been few viewers. I was far from an expert on property prices, but it seemed to me that it was vastly over-priced.

In some ways, I think they were both reluctant to sell. Once they divided the proceeds, there would be no going back and no hope of reconciliation. My suspicion was that deep down, neither of them wanted to separate, but they didn't know how to bridge their differences. Both my mother and I had urged my sister to set up a session with a marriage guidance counsellor. Demonstrating the stubborn streak that runs through our family, she had told us in no uncertain terms to keep our opinions to ourselves.

Despite the bickering that took place in private, Cathy and Jamie were doing their best to keep it amicable for the sake of the girls. I had seen my sister reduced to tears when the younger of the two asked whether her mummy and daddy were going to get back together. Until they sold the property, they remained separated but not divorced. My nieces stayed with their father every other weekend and spent the rest of the time at their grandmother's house with their mother. Neither partner seemed keen to break the status quo.

I grabbed the laptop bag from the passenger seat and made the short dash to the front porch. My finger had barely touched the doorbell when the door swung open to reveal Jamie's stocky frame.

"Percy," he said standing back. "You look like a drowned rat. Come in and get out of the rain."

Jamie Saunders was in his mid-thirties. He didn't exercise enough and enjoyed his food too much, factors which combined to give him the slight paunch that protruded from beneath the blue and white striped rugby shirt he wore over faded jeans. His brown hair was thinning above his forehead; it wouldn't be more than a year or two before he developed a full bald patch.

Grey crescents rimmed his eyes, but the mischievous sparkle persisted.

"Why don't you go into the lounge, and you can tell me all about your adventures in the dark web. I'll get us a couple of beers."

I shrugged off my damp coat and hung it over the bannister. As I passed through the doorway, I couldn't help but notice the untidy state of the room. An assortment of empty mugs rested on the low, wooden coffee table alongside a dirty plate. An opened newspaper occupied one half of the sofa. A stack of computer magazines lay in a haphazard heap on the beige carpet. The scent of stale cigarette smoke lingered in the air. I soon tracked the source to a crumpled butt in a saucer resting on the seat of the armchair: another bad habit my brother-in-law had picked up. My sister would never have tolerated smoking in the house had she been in residence.

I cleared a space for myself and sank into the cushions. Something jabbed into my back. I retrieved the television remote control from behind me and placed it alongside the plate.

"Sorry about the mess," Jamie said, carrying a pint glass of beer in each hand. "Cathy always made such a fuss about keeping the place tidy. It must be the rebel in me. I make sure I clean up before the girls visit though."

"I didn't know you smoked," I said, accepting the offered drink.

He perched himself on the edge of the other sofa. "Yeah, just another thing for Cathy to complain about. You won't tell her, will you?"

"No," I replied.

"So, you caught a lad in your class passing a note to some other boy, and it contained a link to the dark web."

I stared into my pint for a second then raised my eyes. "Actually, that's not quite true."

Jamie frowned. "I guessed as much. What really happened?"

"I decided to go for a walk around lunchtime today. The route goes up through those fields behind the village. The footpath comes out on Mill Lane."

Jamie went quiet. The frown deepened. He placed his glass on the table. When he spoke again, his voice was deadly serious. "Isn't that the place where the murders took place this afternoon?"

I sipped from my pint. "Exactly."

"Christ, you aren't involved with that, are you?"

"I'm not sure. While I was walking, I found this note. The website address we discussed earlier was written on it."

Jamie shook his head. "You came across a piece of paper containing details of a page on the dark web, and you brought it home to give it a try?"

"I didn't know what it was."

"Where did you find it?"

"It was lying on the ground about a hundred yards from where the murders happened."

Jamie reached out for his beer, took a large swig and drained half the glass. As he put down his drink, I noticed a slight tremble in his hand. My gaze moved past his fingers and settled on three empty tumblers on the lower shelf of the coffee table. Perhaps he had picked up more than one bad habit in my sister's absence. He looked me straight in the eye. "And you think it has something to do with the killings?"

"After our conversation, I visited an Internet café and downloaded the Tor browser. Then I typed in the address on the note."

"And?"

"It took me to a login screen. I put in the username and password, and it displayed a website with two options: current jobs and your jobs. The current jobs page was empty, but the other one contained a single entry."

"Seriously, what were you thinking?"

"I wasn't," I replied.

"What did it say?"

"It had the first part of a postcode, a fee and a completion date. The status was set to awaiting confirmation."

Jamie's fingers twitched nervously where they rested on his legs. "You aren't saying ...?"

My eyes locked onto my brother-in-law. "I think it might have been a contract to kill those people."

He folded his arms. "Really?"

"The amount was around seven thousand pounds, the postcode matches the murder location, and I found the note close to the house where they discovered the bodies. The killer may have dropped it."

"Did you take a screenshot?"

"No, it didn't occur to me. If I'd been at home, I would have printed the page, but I was at the Internet café on my laptop." I pointed to the case at my feet.

"Have you still got the link?"

"Yeah, it's here." I pulled the paper from my pocket and handed it over.

"Neat handwriting. When you discovered there had been a murder, did you try it again?"

"I tried both on my home PC and on the laptop. Neither of them would connect to the site. I even revisited the Internet café, but that didn't work either. That's why I called you. Is there anything I could be doing wrong?"

Jamie stood. "Let's have a go on my computer. I've got a Linux setup with Tor already installed."

I followed my brother-in-law out of the room. "You don't think they can trace the connection back to me, do you?"

He paused at the doorway and looked over his shoulder. "It's unlikely. If you let me have a look at your machine, I'll have a quick poke around and make sure there's nothing there that shouldn't be. Fetch another two beers, and I'll get started. They're in the fridge in the utility room."

I handed him the laptop case.

"What's the password?" he asked.

"Elena with a capital E, nineteen ninety-five," I replied. I didn't need to explain the significance. He already knew most of our family history from my sister.

While he headed along the hallway, I entered the kitchen. As I pushed through the white, wooden door, the squalor that greeted me exceeded what I had witnessed in the lounge. Dirty plates filled the sink, spilling out onto the draining board. Empty ready meal packages lay strewn across the work surfaces. Rubbish prevented the lid of the over-full, silver, cylindrical bin from closing, no doubt adding to the sickly-sweet smell of decomposition assaulting my nostrils.

I wrinkled my nose as I passed through another doorway. I flicked on the light switch to reveal a small room containing a washing machine, tumble dryer and double-height fridge-freezer. When I opened the upper fridge door, the contents confirmed some of my suspicions; the interior contained between fifteen and twenty cans of beer and half a dozen bottles of coke. I assumed the soft drinks were for the girls.

Remembering I was driving, I grabbed one of each and retraced my steps, holding my breath as I did so. I discovered Jamie sitting in his study. Desks butted up to three of the four walls in a U shape. I identified at least three different computers. Technical manuals and computer magazines lay strewn across every available surface.

He glanced up at my arrival. "Thanks. I left my glass in the other room. Could you get it for me please?"

The laptop was open. Unusually, the screen already displayed the desktop icons. Then I remembered that Molly had powered up the machine. She must have closed the lid without performing the shutdown sequence.

I deposited the bottle and the can of coke on the nearest desk and headed back to the lounge. When I returned a few seconds later, Jamie's fingers were flying across the keyboard of his computer.

"I've started a malware search on your machine," he said, nodding towards the laptop. "It may take a while." A USB stick protruded from the side. "While that's going on, let's give this site a try," he muttered. The by now familiar Tor browser occupied the large monitor in front of him.

With great care, he transposed the letters into the address bar and tapped the enter key. The wait cursor began its circular dance. Ten seconds later, the *Unable to Connect* message appeared on the screen.

In the same way I had done less than an hour earlier, he checked he had entered the data correctly. Satisfied that he had made no errors, he hit the back button and typed *Test* in the search box. A long list of results filled the display.

Jamie turned to face me. "It looks as if they've taken down the site."

We both sat for a moment lost in thought.

Finally, I broke the silence. "Is there any way to retrieve the page I saw?"

"No. It's not like Google or whatever where you can browse your search history."

"Do you think I should tell the police?" I asked.

"I'm not sure it would do much good, but it's up to you. You do realise that technically you were breaking the law?"

"What do you mean?"

Jamie turned away from the screen and studied my face. "The Computer Misuse Act has been around for a while. It's what they use to prosecute hackers, although most hacks result from lazy or incompetent administrators not keeping their security up to date. I always strongly advise my clients to apply patches as soon as they come out.

"From what little I know, the police aren't normally that bothered unless somebody uses the information for financial gain. That said, I wouldn't admit to logging into a site with another person's credentials."

"So, if it was you, you'd keep it to yourself?"

"As I said, that's your decision, but I'd certainly advise you not to mention the dark web part. We've demonstrated the page is down, so I'm not sure what they could do even if you told them. Did you see anything while you were out walking that might help the police?"

"No, but it doesn't feel right to keep it to myself. Won't they want to eliminate me from their enquiries?"

Jamie shrugged. "I suppose."

Opening my wallet, I retrieved the scrap of paper on which I had written the number for the hotline earlier that day. "I've made up my mind. There's no time like the present. I'm going to phone them right now."

I pulled the mobile from my shirt pocket and typed in the PIN to unlock the screen. Halfway through entering the digits, I noticed the lack of a signal. It was a while since I had last visited the house, and I had forgotten about the poor network coverage.

"Damn. I'm not getting any bars."

"Reception is rubbish here, particularly with Vodafone. Do you want to use the landline?" Jamie asked.

I hesitated for a second. I could always make the call when I got home, but now I had come to a decision, I wanted to get it over with as soon as possible.

"Okay," I replied. "If you don't mind."

"There's a phone in the lounge. I just have a few things to sort out for work. I'll catch up with you in a minute."

Jamie remained seated, tapping away at the keyboard while I headed along the hall.

The handset sat on top of a cabinet containing a music centre. I stabbed out the digits, pacing backwards and forwards over the carpet as I did so. After a single ringing tone, an automated female voice answered.

"Thank you for calling the police incident hotline. We are currently experiencing an unusually high level of calls, and all our lines are busy at the moment. Please be aware your call is important to us. Press one to leave a message, and an operator will return your call as soon as possible. Alternatively, hold the line to speak to a member of our staff."

I hated leaving messages. I always seemed to stumble over my words when speaking to a machine. After five seconds, an orchestral arrangement of Lionel Richie's *All Night Long* started to play. As the song reached the chorus, the music stopped, and the computerised voice interrupted. "We apologise for the delay in answering. Your call is important to us. You are number twenty-seven in the queue. Press one to leave a message, and an operator will return your call. Alternatively, hold the line to speak to a member of our staff."

After a short pause, the orchestra resumed from where it had left off. Thirty seconds of musical torment passed before another interruption. My position in the queue remained the same. The irony of the song title was not lost on me.

Jamie came into the room holding the laptop case.

I removed the handset from my ear. "There are twenty-something callers before me."

"Can't you leave a message?"

"I think I might do that."

The next time the music stopped, I had risen to the dizzy heights of twenty-six. Aware that I was encroaching on my brother-in-law's hospitality, I lowered the phone from my face and tapped the screen.

"Thank you for contacting the police incident hotline. Please leave your full name, a contact telephone number, and a brief summary of the information you wish to provide. An operator will call you back when one becomes available."

I stammered my name and home telephone number. For a moment, my mind turned blank. I hadn't thought through what I would say. "I was out walking this afternoon near the site of the murder—um ... Mill Lane that is. The time must have been around one o'clock. I ... ah ... don't remember seeing anything suspicious. I'm not at my own house at the moment. It'll take me about half an hour to get back. Um ... 'bye."

I stabbed the disconnect button.

"Very eloquent," Jamie said, a wry grin on his face. "And no mention of the note."

"No, I think you were right. I'll keep that bit to myself."

"I guess that means you won't be staying for another drink."

"Thanks for your help, but I need to go."

"No problem. I'm happy to be of assistance. Let me know what happens."

"Of course." I grabbed my coat from the bannister and held out my hand. Instead of accepting my grip, Jamie dragged me into an awkward, one-armed hug.

"Look after yourself," he said, patting me on the back.

"You too," I replied. "Take care."

He stepped away and handed over the laptop. "It's clean by the way. The search didn't pick up anything nasty."

I left Jamie's house to discover the rain had miraculously stopped. The journey passed quickly with the damp conditions keeping other drivers off the roads. The beer and coke sat heavily in my stomach as my mind churned over the situation. I arrived home without coming to a conclusion. The dashboard clock read 9:35.

As I slowed and indicated right for my house, the headlights picked out a figure approaching along the verge. A lead stretched from the person's hand towards the hedge where a tiny bedraggled creature squatted as it did its business. The hood obscured the woman's face, but it wasn't difficult to identify her: Mrs Owens and her delightful rat dog. She lowered her head and squinted at me through the windscreen. The fact that somebody had committed a serious crime in the vicinity would have provided her with all the encouragement she needed to patrol the neighbourhood with renewed vigour.

She confirmed my suspicions by following the car as I reversed onto the drive. I turned off the engine and hauled myself out of the driver's seat. She marched forward, dragging her pet behind her. A gust of wind brought down a flurry of water droplets on our heads from the tree in the neighbour's garden.

"Did you hear about the murders?" she asked even before I closed the car door.

"Yes, I watched the news this evening."

"What a terrible business. I don't suppose you saw anything suspicious."

"No, but if I had done, I'd be sure to tell the police." I didn't want to encourage her by revealing I had been walking near the crime scene that afternoon.

"My friend has been to the house. She said all the rooms were huge and very expensively furnished."

"Oh."

"I'm going to recommend that we set up regular patrols at the next neighbourhood watch meeting, at least until they've caught the person responsible. I've brought the next one forward to tomorrow at midday at my place."

The prospect of attending one of her gatherings filled me with dread. "I'm sorry, but I've got something on."

"But I thought—"

I backed toward my front door. "It's a bit wet out here, so I'm going inside."

"Okay, well if you change your mind, you know where I live."

"'Bye, then." Before she could add anything else, I slipped the key in the lock and let myself in. I hurried through to the small study where I pressed the power button on the computer's front panel. While I waited for the machine to boot, I went into the lounge and grabbed the phone handset. The absence of a flashing red light on the base unit told me nobody had left a message.

As soon as I logged in, I started up a browser window. The first term I entered in the search box was *Computer Misuse Act*. It was as Jamie described. Parliament originally introduced the legislation in 1990 and made it illegal to gain unauthorised access to a computer. What if the site I had visited was entirely innocent? If I told the police about viewing the page, would I be leaving myself open to prosecution?

The logical part of my brain said not, but the stakes were high. If I gained a criminal record, I would lose my job. That was a price I wasn't willing to pay. I justified my decision by telling myself that the small amount of information I had seen on the web page would make no difference to the investigation. All I would accomplish by mentioning it when questioned was to put my livelihood at risk.

Having confirmed my resolution to keep quiet about the note, I turned my attention to learning more about the murders. The BBC news website contained much the same information as the television. It seemed the police were still without a suspect, and they were appealing to anybody who might have seen something suspicious to come forward. The only additional material was an interview with a neighbour. The woman revealed that the victims were a couple who kept themselves to themselves. She claimed they spent a lot of time travelling abroad.

Other sites offered little more. Most contained photographs of the leafy lane where the crime had taken place. The local newspaper website carried a piece by a former police inspector who maintained the murders possessed all the hallmarks of organised crime. The article failed to identify the reasoning behind the statement.

I glanced at the time in the bottom right corner of the display: 21:57. Perhaps there would be more information on the ten o'clock news. Leaving the computer switched on, I made my way into the lounge and turned on the television. I returned the telephone handset to its cradle then flopped onto the sofa. The credits for a sitcom scrolled up the screen, followed by a trailer for a new thriller series.

After a moment's silence, the familiar theme music played. A sombre, male newscaster summarised the headlines. The murders ranked only third after a political scandal and a terrorist attack in Egypt. A breaking story about a politician failing to declare his financial interest in a company receiving government grants occupied the first ten minutes of the programme.

It wasn't until a quarter of an hour later that the killings became the focus. The report was even briefer than the one I had watched earlier. After a sentence or two from the newsreader in the studio, the picture shifted to the location of the crime.

The reporter faced the camera. The brightly lit fascia of the mansion contrasted with the blackness of the night sky behind him. He presented the basic details of the case but added nothing I didn't already know. In the corner of the shot, a figure wearing white coveralls emerged from the front door. A brief pre-recorded interview with the Chief Superintendent followed. The section culminated in another appeal for witnesses to contact the police information line.

Maybe the local news would contain more details. I turned down the sound as the topic shifted to the 0-0 scoreline between England and France in a meaningless, friendly football match.

The sudden ringing of the telephone made me jump. I pressed the answer button and held the handset to my ear. "Hello."

"This is Sergeant Dawkins from the police incident hotline. May I speak with a Mr Alex Parrott?"

"That's me."

"And can you confirm you contacted us earlier with information about the crime committed today in Mill Lane?"

"Yes, I did."

"What did you want to tell me?"

I described the route of my walk past the scene of the murder but omitted the note from my description. The policeman asked me whether I had seen anything suspicious in the vicinity, and I answered in the negative. He requested that I come into the local police station to make a formal statement. I agreed to drop by the next morning. The man ended the call by thanking me for my assistance.

My head was spinning in a whirlwind of indecision as I replaced the handset. Had I been right to omit details of the note? I could always mention it the following day during the face-to-face interview. But wouldn't they wonder why I hadn't referred to it tonight? I let out a groan of frustration. My actions had placed me in an impossible situation. Why had I picked up the damned thing in the first place?

I hardly slept that night. My brain refused to turn off, spinning round and round, trying to find the solution to an unsolvable problem. Central to everything was the note and the website it pointed to. Perhaps the police could use the site address to track the murderer. By keeping the information to myself, I might be denying them a vital clue that would allow a killer to go free.

I knew it was selfish to think about myself when two people were dead, but I continued to worry about the anonymity of the dark web. Was it possible for the site owners to trace my location? I reassured myself that even if it was feasible, the only time I had successfully connected to the page was from the café. Would they be able to track my attempts after they took down the site? I assumed not, but I had no idea how the system worked. In my head, I made a further list of questions to ask Jamie the following morning.

If it was possible to link the successful login attempt to a location, would they be capable of tracing it back to me? I wracked my brains, trying to think how I had paid. With a surge of relief, I remembered handing over a five-pound note, so they wouldn't be able to trace me through my payment details. That only left anything the computer might reveal. Jamie had checked the machine for malware and found nothing. He also reassured me it was highly unlikely they could obtain my identity by monitoring my access to the site.

After tossing and turning for a couple of hours, I gave up trying to sleep. I turned on the lamp and reached over to grab the paperback from the bedside cabinet. It was an action thriller and the sort of book that didn't stretch the intellect: exactly what I needed to distract me from my troubles. I finished the page and realised that despite reading all the words, I hadn't taken in any of the meaning. In frustration, I tossed it on the floor and threw back the covers.

I shuffled along the hall and into the lounge. There, I flicked on the television and channel hopped until I found an old episode of Star Trek. If Kirk and Spock couldn't distract me, then nothing else would. I put my feet up and watched the programme with one half of my mind while the other half spun over the events of the previous day.

A tap on the glass jolted me from my contemplative state. For a moment, I seriously considered leaping off the sofa and using it for cover. The sound repeated, and the rational part of my brain took over; it was highly improbable that anybody wishing me harm would alert me first. I crept to the window, my pulse rate soaring, and pulled back the curtain in one sudden movement. The tapping noise grew louder, but the source soon became apparent; a shrub adjoining the house was badly in need of a trim. The strong breeze was causing the branches to scrape against the pane.

When the hammering of my heart had slowed a little, I rearranged the cushions and lay across the sofa. I lowered the volume and closed my eyes. After what seemed an age, I finally drifted off. When I awoke, it was five o'clock in the morning, and the light was seeping around the edge of the curtains.

I didn't know it then, but my fears were well founded. The people behind the website were already on my trail.

Richard T. Burke

Twenty-five years ago: Wednesday, 8th February, 1995

*S*omething woke me. The glow from the streetlight on the main road crept around the edges of the curtains, casting orange bands against the walls. Rather than being disturbed by the bright patches, I found them a reassuring relief against the darkness. My gaze tracked the familiar lines from halfway up the wall onto the ceiling.

I lay with my eyes open, my ears straining to pick up any unusual sounds. The distant buzz of a motorbike carried through the night. Over the course of the next few seconds, the engine note changed pitch as the driver accelerated rapidly, then gradually faded away. I turned on my side and was drifting off when a thud from the hallway dragged me back to full wakefulness.

My hand reached to the ceiling-mounted pull-cord above the bed. I blinked as light flooded the bedroom. Pushing myself upright, I stared at the white, wooden door, listening hard for a repetition of the noise. A glance at the red digits of the alarm clock revealed the time to be a little after two-thirty. After several early morning visitations, my parents had given me strict instructions to stay in my room if I woke before seven o'clock.

Throwing back the covers, I swung my legs to the side of the bed. My foot landed on something cool. I looked down at The Magic Faraway Tree. *My mother had left the book on the carpet after reading to us.*

I padded across the floor and stood with my ear pressed to the painted wood. The only sound I could hear was the thudding of my heart. A shiver ran through me although I couldn't tell if the cause was the chill of the early morning or the strong sense that something was wrong.

I remained in the same spot for over a minute, listening for a repeat of the noise. There was no recurrence, so I gave up and turned towards my bed. That was when the unmistakable click and swish of the front door opening reached my ears. I rushed back, opened my bedroom door and stared along the corridor. A nightlight cast a circle of illumination from its position on the floor, revealing the open doorway to Elena's room.

Unsure what to do, I raced to my window and threw aside the curtains. A figure dressed in black hurried across the short drive. He carried a white shape slung over his shoulder. Upon reaching the closed gate, he fumbled with the latch for a moment, then bent down and deposited the object on the frost-encrusted grass.

He stepped forward to fiddle with the mechanism. With the shock of realisation, I identified what he had been carrying: my younger sister. Dressed in a white nightie, she lay unmoving on the frigid ground. My fists hammered against the glass, and I screamed at the top of my voice. The man twisted his head and stared up at me. Then he crouched, picked up Elena's inert body, and jogged through the gateway to the road.

Seconds later, the flare of taillights lit the night. I watched in horror as a dark-coloured car—the orange streetlights made it impossible to determine the exact hue—raced along the street away from the house.

Day Two:
Tuesday, 28th July, 2020

Richard T. Burke

The television was still turned on, showing a sitcom from the eighties. The black bands down the sides of the picture, the bouffant hairstyles and the canned laughter provided a good indication of the era. I switched over to the twenty-four-hour BBC news channel without changing my position on the sofa. I watched for over thirty minutes until the headlines repeated.

The politician who had been at the centre of the political scandal the previous day was under intense pressure to resign. The death toll in Egypt had risen to over forty, but the newsreader made no mention at all of the murders a few miles away.

It wasn't yet six o'clock when I shoved myself off the cushions and padded along the corridor to the study. There, I spent another fruitless hour searching the online news feeds. It seemed little had changed in the police investigation. They were still appealing for witnesses and apparently had no suspects. One story suggested the male victim may have had links to organised crime, but the article was careful to avoid an outright accusation.

Part of me considered making another attempt to access the website on the piece of paper. I convinced myself it would be a bad idea; if the page was operational once again, I would feel obliged to inform the authorities, and that might put my career in jeopardy. No, it was far better to steer well clear of the dark web and all its secrets.

My stomach lurched as I contemplated the statement I had promised to give that day. I had no idea what time the police station unlocked its doors or even whether it closed overnight. A quick Internet search confirmed that on weekdays, the front desk opened at eight in the morning and remained open until eight at night.

Lack of sleep and worry combined to limit my appetite. All I could manage for breakfast was a single slice of buttered toast. I showered until the hot water turned cold then dressed casually in jeans and a T-shirt. When I slipped the watch over my wrist, it was a little before seven thirty. I did a quick mental calculation and worked out that if I set off now, it would be after eight o'clock by the time I parked the car.

I emerged through the front door to discover a clear morning. An occasional puddle provided the only remaining evidence of the previous night's torrential rain. The air had that warm, slightly earthy scent that always reminded me of British summers. As I navigated through the gate posts, I glanced to the right. Fifty yards away, Mrs Owens waited while her tiny dog sniffed at the roadside bushes. She squinted in my direction, removed a notebook from her pocket and made an entry. Shaking my head in disbelief, I turned left, watching her in the rear-view mirror.

I battled my way through the rush hour traffic and found myself a place in the pay and display car park. By the time I bought a ticket at the machine, it was twelve minutes past eight. The short walk to the police station added another ten minutes. I pushed through the outside door into an area with three reception desks, only one of which was occupied.

A variety of posters adorned the walls, ranging from an exhortation for females to be alert when walking alone to an advertisement for men to call a helpline if they needed help to control their anger. Other than the white-shirted policeman, the room was deserted.

The man glanced at me briefly then continued to study the computer screen in front of him. I approached the desk and waited for him to acknowledge my presence. A rectangular sign alongside a pushbutton read, 'Press for attention'. For a fleeting moment, I considered pressing the button but thought better of it. Finally, he raised his eyes and asked how he could help.

"I spoke to a police officer yesterday on the helpline about the murders on Mill Lane. I'm here to make a statement."

The policeman's interest perked up. "Oh, right. If you'd like to take a seat, I'll get somebody to have a word. Can I have your name?"

"Alex Parrott."

The man stared at me suspiciously, studying my face as if he didn't quite believe me. Finally, he gestured towards some chairs. "Wait there, Mr Parrott. Someone will be out to see you in a minute."

I crossed the room and lowered myself into a wooden chair covered with lumpy, yellow padding. The police officer waited until I was far enough away not to eavesdrop on his conversation then spoke into a telephone handset with a hushed voice. His eyes flicked towards me several times during the discussion. He ended the call and returned his attention to the computer screen.

A few minutes later, a door to the side of the reception desk opened. A uniformed policewoman surveyed the waiting area. "Would you like to come with me, Mr Parrott?"

She stepped back to allow me to pass then led the way along the bare corridor to a steel door labelled 'Interview Room 1'. As I followed her, I picked up the scent of a soapy smelling deodorant. She gestured toward a chair. "Please take a seat."

She smiled as she sat on the opposite side of the metal table. "Thanks for coming in, Mr Parrott. My name is Sergeant Susie Mayhew. I believe you called the helpline yesterday evening. Please tell me what happened. Just so you're aware, I'll be recording this conversation."

She reached forward and pushed a button on the electronic device occupying the middle of the shiny, metallic surface. Now I had the chance to study her, I could see she was in her early thirties. Her hair was dark and cut short, framing an attractive, open face. I found my gaze wandering to her left hand. No ring.

I went through the events of the previous afternoon, gradually relaxing as she asked me to clarify a few points.

When I had completed my story, she leaned forward, resting her elbows on the table. "I'd like you to confirm you didn't encounter anybody during your walk."

"That's right."

"And you saw nothing suspicious?"

If I was going to mention the note, now was the time. "Um ... no, I don't think so."

She seemed disappointed. "Well, if you remember anything else, you can contact me here." She pushed a business card across the table.

I picked it up and, after studying it for a second, shoved it in my back pocket. "I will do."

"One last thing; were you carrying a phone during your walk?"

"Yes."

"May I take your number, please?"

"Of course." I dictated the digits. "Are you going to call me?"

Her cheeks dimpled as she smiled. "Probably not."

"So why do you need my number?"

"The software inside a mobile is always trying to connect to the strongest signal. The telecoms providers maintain a log of the devices in range of each cell tower at all times. It might help us track the perpetrator's location if he was carrying a phone and left it turned on."

"How do you know it was a man?"

An amused expression worked its way across her face. "Statistically, over ninety per cent of homicides are committed by men, so it's a fairly safe bet."

"Does that make me a suspect?"

She laughed. "Not at the present time."
Unfortunately for me, that was all about to change.

Richard T. Burke

I left the police station far happier than when I had arrived. The surge of relief at having given my statement combined with the lack of sleep made me feel lightheaded. I smiled to myself as I reran in my head the conversation with Susie Mayhew. There were probably rules about police officers fraternising with witnesses. When they had caught their man and the court case was over, I might pay her a social call. I suspected I wouldn't have the bottle to follow it through, but there was no harm in fantasising.

As I settled into the car, my thoughts turned to the plans for my holiday. When I arrived back home, I would go online and book my windsurfing package deal. Before that, however, it was time I paid my mother and sister a visit. From my present location, it would take me less than a quarter of an hour to reach the house where I grew up.

According to the dashboard clock, it was just after nine o'clock. My mother was always complaining I didn't call around enough, so that's what I planned to do. The girls had started their school holidays that week and my sister's job as a teaching assistant meant she too would be at home. It might have been a bit early for most people, but Cathy wasn't one to lie in bed on a day off—even if her two daughters would allow it.

As I turned into the leafy avenue, my feeling of wellbeing waned a little. The house held many memories, not all of them good. Whenever I saw the stone frontage, it took me back to the events of that night, twenty-five years ago, when my baby sister was taken. For a year or two, our family became a hot news topic as the police searched for the kidnapper.

I wasn't sure how my mother could bear to live where it all happened. If it was my property, I would have moved out long since. She justified her continued habitation there on the basis that if my missing sister ever escaped from the person holding her, this was the first place to which she would return. Although my mother wouldn't admit it, we both knew Elena was dead. She had told me many times that, as a parent, you can never give up on your child, no matter how unlikely the probability they are still alive.

I pushed the negative thoughts to the back of my mind and rolled onto the gravel drive, parking behind Cathy's people carrier. I had barely opened the car door when the squeals of delight and the sound of running feet reached my ears.

"Uncle Alex. Did you bring us a present?"

The elder of my two nieces, Sophia, flung her arms around my midriff in a tight hug. Zoe, the younger of the siblings, followed three paces behind. I swept her into the air and planted a big kiss on her cheek. Giggling, she promptly wiped it off with the back of her hand.

She was the same age as my baby sister when she had been abducted all those years ago. The similarity in appearance was startling. The blond hair, blue eyes and gap-toothed smile were exactly how I remembered Elena. Every time I looked at her, it generated painful memories.

"How are my two favourite nieces?" I asked, forcing a cheery note into my voice.

"We're your only nieces," Sophia replied in the confident tone of an eight-year-old.

"You're still my favourites, though."

"Put me down," Zoe demanded, wriggling in my arms. "Did you bring us something?"

It was my fault. Every time I came around, I gave them a small gift. Now they expected it. I rummaged in my pocket and pulled out two one-pound coins. "Here you go, girls. Don't spend it all at once."

"Thanks," they chorused together as they skipped through the front door. I heard an excited voice announce, "Uncle Alex is here," as I followed them in. "He's given us a pound each. I'm putting mine in my piggy bank."

"Come and play with me on the computer, Uncle Alex," Sophia called from her room.

"I'll be with you in a minute," I replied. "Let me have a chat with your mum and nanna first."

My sister emerged from the kitchen and enveloped me in a hug. "You're spoiling them."

"Yeah," I said, "but I can't help it."

A stooped figure shuffled through the doorway behind her. Releasing Cathy, I embraced my mother. Every time I saw her, she seemed a little frailer than before. It had been clear for a while that something was wrong, but despite our protestations, she had refused to see a doctor until a month ago. "How are you?" I asked although I didn't expect an honest answer.

"Oh, I'm fine," she replied.

We both knew that to be a lie. The specialist had diagnosed the lung cancer a fortnight earlier, and she was due to start a round of chemotherapy the following week. A ten-year smoking habit starting in her early twenties was the probable cause. She had stopped immediately as soon as she discovered she was pregnant with Cathy, but the damage had already been done.

"I'll make you a cup of tea."

"No, you sit down, Mum," Cathy said. "Let me sort it out. The kettle has just boiled."

I followed my mother into the lounge. She lowered herself slowly into an armchair, wincing as she did so. She questioned me about my job then switched to her favourite theme.

"What else have you been up to?" she asked. "Any girlfriends?"

I rolled my eyes. "None at the moment."

"I probably don't have that long left. You'd better get a move on if I'm going to have any more grandchildren."

The subject of grandchildren was a regular topic of conversation. Only since the diagnosis had she added the morbid aspect. Cathy spared me any more of the inquisition by entering the room carrying a tray on which rested three steaming cups of tea.

We chatted about the girls' activities and the latest gossip from the neighbours before the subject turned to the murders. Reluctantly, I recounted how I had been in the vicinity around the time the killings took place. I omitted any mention of the note.

"Did you see anything?" my sister asked, a worried expression clouding her face.

"Nothing. It was all very unexciting. I only heard about it afterwards on the news."

Cathy frowned. "That's probably just as well. Who knows what might have happened had you bumped into the murderer?"

My mother patted my hand and tried to lighten the mood. "Are you a suspect?"

"That's exactly what I asked the policewoman when I gave my statement earlier this morning," I replied, laughing, "but apparently, not."

"What's it like living in the crime capital of the world?"

I shook my head in puzzlement.

"Well, two murders in a population of about two hundred is one per cent. There can't be too many places where the murder rate is that high."

"I think we'll be alright. We've got our own patrol force headed up by rat dog lady."

Cathy let out a snort of laughter. "I'm sure you'll be safe with that ferocious animal to guard the neighbourhood."

A pause developed in the conversation.

"How are things with you?" I asked to break the silence.

"Fine apart from you know who."

"There's no prospect of reconciliation, then?" I didn't want to reveal that I had spoken to my brother-in-law less than twelve hours earlier.

"The bastard wouldn't even pick up the phone when I called him this morning."

"Maybe he was in the shower," I suggested.

"What? For an hour and a half? I think he's just ignoring me."

I said nothing, but a flutter of worry wormed its way into my stomach.

Richard T. Burke

I placed the key in the front door of my house, feeling slightly less upbeat than I had upon leaving the police station. The decline in my mother's condition had shocked me; she seemed far frailer than one might expect of somebody in their sixty-fifth year. Despite the specialists' optimistic prognosis, for the first time, I seriously considered the possibility she wouldn't recover.

After Elena disappeared, she became the glue that held the family together. My father lacked her strength and went into a decline after the abduction. It took a while, but I have little doubt that the events of that night and the gradual withering of hope afterwards triggered the fatal heart attack three years later.

Losing both a sister and a father before the age of thirteen hit me hard. I'm not one for self-analysis, but I can't help thinking the loss of two immediate family members during my formative years played a big part in my inability to build meaningful relationships. Whenever I became close to somebody, negative questions would coalesce in the dark corners of my mind. How would I cope if I lost them? Would I crumble like my father? Invariably, the doubts caused tensions in the friendship, leading to its ultimate demise.

I would gladly have traded everything I possessed to get my sister and father back, but one small consolation was my father's life insurance policy. It left us relatively well-off and provided me with the capital to purchase a house when my trust fund matured at the age of twenty-one.

I was so lost in my thoughts I failed to notice Mrs Owens hurrying up behind me. I only noticed her presence when the dog emitted a high-pitched yap.

"Hello, Alex," she said, her face flushed with excitement. It seemed we were now on first-name terms although I didn't know hers.

I tried to force a positive tone into my voice. "Hi, Mrs Owens. How are you?"

She ignored my question. "Two men were here."

I shrugged. "Two men? Who were they?"

Once again, she failed to answer. "They rang your doorbell then went around the back. They stayed there for at least ten minutes. I've no idea what they were doing."

I registered the first twinge of concern. "Did you call the police?"

"That's the thing. I wrote down their registration number and waited by the gate. I made sure I got a good look at them when they returned."

"What happened?"

"They were chatting to each other. They didn't carry anything out, so I assumed they weren't burglars. I asked them who they were. The taller of the two said they were policemen, but neither of them wore a uniform."

"Did you ask for identification?"

"The shorter one showed me a card, but he flashed it so quickly I didn't get a chance to examine it properly. It did say police at the top though."

I frowned in puzzlement. "You're telling me a pair of policemen came to visit. I wasn't in, and they left. I don't see the problem."

Mrs Owens shook her head as if I was being particularly stupid. "Yes, but why did they want to talk to *you*? And what were they doing for ten minutes around the back of your house?"

I didn't intend to tell her about making a statement at the police station. If I did, I'd never get rid of her, and the news would spread through the village in a flash. "It's a mystery, Mrs Owens. I'm sure they'll return if they need to speak to me. Now, I've got some jobs I have to do. Thanks for keeping me up to date."

The woman seemed taken aback. "Oh ... right. I'll let you know if I see anything else suspicious."

"'Bye," I said, slipping through the front door and closing it behind me.

I picked up the two letters on the doormat, both apparently junk mail, and carried them through to the kitchen. Dumping them on the work surface, I pondered what Mrs Owens had told me. Had the police thought of another question after reading my statement? Had they learned about the note? And why did they spend ten minutes in the back garden?

For a moment, I toyed with the idea of using the business card in my wallet to call Susie Mayhew, the policewoman who had interviewed me three hours earlier. A smile crept onto my face at the prospect of talking to her again. But what would I say? She had my contact details if she needed to ask any more questions. I decided to leave it for now.

My mind turned back to the murders. Had they made any progress in the investigation? Perhaps there would be an update on the news websites. As I headed along the hallway towards the study, my nose detected the faintest presence of a strange smell. It was so incongruous that at first, I couldn't place it. I frowned, trying to identify the source. Then it came to me: cigarettes.

The scent was so faint. Was I imagining it? I remembered the butt in the ashtray at Jamie's house the previous evening, but what I was picking up now differed subtly from that of stale smoke. I wracked my brains. Suddenly, I identified what made it so distinctive; it was the same musty odour that lingered on the clothes of the regular smokers amongst my pupils.

My thoughts spun back to what Mrs Owens had said. The two men had been behind my house for ten minutes. Had they come inside?

I carried on down the hall to the guest bedroom. The top part of the window was open, but the gap was far too small for anybody to fit through. I sniffed several times, failing to pick up the same scent. Perhaps I was imagining it.

On impulse, I hurried back to the front door and out into the garden. I followed the route that Mrs Owens had described to the rear of the house. Standing outside the window to the guest room, I cast my gaze around the frame: no sign of tampering. I was about to give up when something caught my eye on the gravel by the brickwork. I bent down and poked the half-smoked cigarette butt with my foot. As a non-smoker, I couldn't explain how it had arrived there.

The evidence was stacking up. It seemed at least one of the men had entered my property. One person could corroborate my theory. I jogged back to the front gate and stared both ways along the road: no sign of Mrs Owens. Desperate for an answer, I turned left and sprinted towards her house. The dog was already inside, and she was taking off her boots as I raced up. She whirled around in alarm at my approach.

"You gave me a fright, Mr Parrott." It seemed the period of detente was over, and we were back to surnames.

I wasn't in the mood for niceties. "The two men who you saw earlier—did either of them smoke?"

"Why do you ask?"

When I didn't answer, she scratched her ear for a moment, deep in thought. Her face brightened. "Now you mention it, one of them had a cigarette in his hand. I remember thinking it would be unfair on the other man if he smoked in the car."

"Can you describe them?"

"Let me think. The shorter of the two was roughly your age, early to mid-forties, and carrying a few extra pounds ... the same sort of physique as you, I suppose." She flashed a wry smile. Clearly, she hadn't forgotten the dog incident and was making the most of the opportunity to get her own back. "The taller man was a lot thinner, almost gaunt I'd say."

"You said you recorded the registration number. Do you still have it?"

"Oh, yes. I write everything down. You can never tell when it might be useful as evidence. That's one of the things I'm going to recommend that everybody does at the neighbourhood watch meeting. It starts in forty minutes. You will be there, won't you?"

I made a non-committal grunt. She flicked through the notebook until she found the correct page. "Do you have something to write on?"

"Can I borrow your pen, please?"

She handed it over, the suspicious look indicating she doubted whether I would return it. As she read out the characters, I wrote them on the palm of my hand. When she had finished, I repeated them back to her.

She nodded in agreement. "Yes, that's right. May I ask why you need it?"

"I just want to check up on something," I replied, returning the pen.

"I'll see you in a few minutes then."

"Maybe," I mumbled as I retreated and headed across the road to my own house.

Richard T. Burke

W hat the hell was going on? Had the police searched my house? If so, what were they looking for, and why hadn't they left any notification? I had noticed nothing missing. The only evidence they had been inside my property was the faintest odour of cigarettes and Mrs Owens' observations. Before doing anything else, I needed to understand my rights.

I returned to the study and started up the computer. Once it had booted, I opened a browser window and typed *UK search warrant absent* into the address bar.

The first hit was an item with the title, *Powers the police have to search premises and search warrants*. As my eye ran down the page, I picked out several key facts. In most cases, officers required a warrant signed by a magistrate before searching a property. The article listed a number of exceptions, including the prevention of a breach of the peace, to save a life, and to arrest someone in connection with certain serious offences. As far as I could tell, none of those circumstances applied.

Reading the piece more carefully, I discovered that provided the police held a warrant, they had the right to force entry in the absence of the occupier. If I was correct in my suspicions, it seemed to be the only logical answer. But what crime did they suspect me of committing, and what evidence did they possess to convince a magistrate to issue a search warrant? And did it relate in any way to the murders?

I selected another web page from the list of results, but it only confirmed what I had already learned. For several minutes, I sat with my head in my hands, debating what to do next. Maybe I was worrying unnecessarily; it was possible the two men had remained outside, and the smoke wafted in through the open window. Was my sense of smell accurate enough to distinguish the difference between stale smoke and the odour of a smoker's clothes?

I still had Susie Mayhew's card. Perhaps she could provide me with some answers. I removed it from my wallet and tapped the digits into my mobile.

She answered after only one ring. "This is Sergeant Mayhew. May I ask who's calling?"

"It's Alex Parrott. We spoke earlier this morning at the station if you remember."

The faint sound of male voices emerged from the background noise although I couldn't distinguish individual words. She was obviously in an open plan office.

"Of course I do, Mr Parrott. Have you remembered something else you can tell us?" I may have been misinterpreting the tone of her voice, but she seemed genuinely pleased to hear from me.

I hesitated for a second. "Actually, I'm not calling about the murder case— or at least I'm not sure it's related."

"Okay. What's this about, then?"

"I visited my mother and sister after talking to you, so I didn't get home until just after eleven o'clock. As I was opening my front door, one of my neighbours told me that while I'd been away, two men came into my garden and round the back of the house. They stayed there for ten minutes, or so she said."

"Okay." A note of scepticism tinged her voice. "I'm not sure what you're telling me. Have you been burgled? Because if that's the case, you need to call the main station number, and they'll put you in touch with somebody who can investigate."

"No, it's not that. Or at least I don't think it is. Apparently, the men informed my neighbour they were from the police. One of them showed her a badge or something."

"You mean a warrant card?"

"Yeah, that's right."

"Do you have a name?"

"I'm afraid not. The neighbour told me she didn't have time to read any of the details. She did write down the registration number of their car though. Anyway, as I said, they were round the back and out of sight for about ten minutes. When I entered the house, I picked up the faint smell of cigarettes. I've never smoked, so I suspect at least one of them must have been inside my property."

"Let me get this straight." Her tone was business-like now. "Two men visited your home while you were away. They told your neighbour they were from the police, and you think they may have entered without proper authorisation."

"That's correct."

"I don't understand how this connects to the murder case."

I felt my face redden. "Um ... I'm not sure it does. I was just wondering ..."

A sigh came from the other end. She lowered her voice. "Look, Mr Parrott, I shouldn't be doing this, but I'll help you out this once. I can check the system to see whether any search warrants are open on your property. I'm fairly certain I won't find anything because if there was something, it would've popped up when I entered your details earlier." The tap of keys rose above the sound of background voices. She asked me to confirm my address.

The silence stretched down the line. After what seemed like an age, she spoke again. This time, her speech contained a definite frosty edge. "I'm sorry, but I can't help you. I suggest you call the main switchboard. Goodbye."

The muted click signalled she had hung up. I checked the screen and returned the mobile to my pocket, shaking my head in confusion. What had just happened? Did her response mean there really was a search warrant on my property?

The hammering of fists on the front door soon answered my question.

Leaving the computer running, I made my way to the front porch. The loud knocking reverberated through the house once again. "This is the police. Open the door, or we will use force."

I twisted the latch and pulled the handle towards me. Three men stood on my doorstep. Two of them were empty-handed, but the third held a sheet of paper.

"We have a search warrant for this property," he said, thrusting the form in my face. The heading read, *Warrant to enter and search premises.* Below that came my address and a scrawled signature. "Please step aside, sir."

The policeman stared at me from beneath a flat police cap. His uniform comprised a zip-up, sleeveless jacket over a black shirt. He wore a radio clipped to the left side of the jacket. The other two were dressed in plain clothes, both wearing long-sleeved shirts over denim jeans. Even though I had never met either of them before, I immediately recognised them as the men Mrs Owens had described. The taller of the pair had a thin face topped by an unruly mess of dark hair, greying at the temples.

The shorter man was in his mid-forties, and as my neighbour had reported, more than a few pounds overweight. Up close, his bulbous nose and ruddy complexion portrayed the look of a drinker. As I stood back, he dropped the cigarette he was smoking on the paved bricks of my drive and ground the butt with his heel.

The two plain-clothes officers edged around me and headed along the hall.

"What were you doing here before?" I said, addressing the smoker.

He flashed me a smug grin as he barged past, ignoring the question.

As I made to follow, the man in uniform placed a hand on my shoulder. "Please remain here, sir." The final word carried a slight sneer.

I turned back to him. "What's this all about?" I asked although I had a sick feeling that I already knew at least part of the answer.

"We're searching your premises in relation to an ongoing police investigation."

"You don't say." Despite my shock, I couldn't keep the note of sarcasm from my voice. "What exactly are they looking for?"

The man's eyes bored into me, but he said nothing.

I decided to change tack. "Those two were hanging around my house earlier today. My neighbour told me. What were they doing there?"

"I'm sorry, sir. I can't tell you that."

"Can't or won't?"

The policeman folded his arms and gave me the stare once again.

Frustrated at the lack of response, I continued my attempts to obtain answers. "One of them was inside the house less than an hour ago. What the hell was he doing here?" I didn't know that for sure, and I had no evidence other than Mrs Owens' description of the men, but it was too much of a coincidence.

The officer shook his head. "If you have any complaints, you can take them up with the Independent Office for Police Conduct, but quite frankly, I think you're going to have far bigger concerns to worry about."

"So, you do know what this is about?"

The policeman frowned. "Look, sir. You'll find out soon enough if they press charges. I'm just here to help with the search, so if you don't mind, let's keep it quiet and wait for them to finish."

An awkward silence developed between us. Movement from several yards behind the waiting police officer caught my attention. Mrs Owens stood at the entrance to my property, staring in through the open gate. The dog was nowhere to be seen. Our eyes met for a second.

A loud crash came from somewhere inside the house, and I dragged my gaze away. "What are they up to? Trashing the place?"

"Let them do their job. We'll be out of here in a few minutes."

Right on cue, the taller of the two plain-clothes officers struggled along the hallway carrying a large black object in a clear plastic bag. As he came closer, I recognised the contents as the base unit of my computer.

"What are you doing with that?" I asked.

"We're seizing this item as evidence," the man replied. It was the first time I had heard him speak. His voice carried the hint of a northern accent.

"That thing cost a lot of money. When are you going to return it?"

The uniformed officer answered the question on his behalf. "It'll be held until there's a court case, or they decide to drop charges. Either way, I wouldn't count on getting it back any time soon."

The breath caught in my throat at the mention of charges. Until that point, I hadn't considered the implications, but now the reality of my situation came crashing down on me. If they chose to prosecute, the school would undoubtedly suspend me with immediate effect. With that my livelihood would disappear. My savings might tide me over for a few months, but they wouldn't last forever. The worst part was that I still had no idea of the crime for which I was being investigated.

"You haven't told me what this is all about."

"Somebody's been downloading stuff they shouldn't," the smoker replied.

My mind immediately switched to the dark web. "I know what I did is technically against the law, but it's not as if I stole the login details. They were on a note I found. I only logged in once."

The taller man flashed a tight-lipped smile. "If you downloaded it all in one session, it must have taken a while."

I shook my head in confusion. "What are you talking about? I didn't download anything. I only opened the page."

The smoker chuckled, the laugh morphing into a coughing fit. He withdrew a handkerchief from his pocket and cleared his throat into the blue material.

"I really need to lay off the fags," he said when he had regained his breath. "Let me guess; somebody hacked your machine and downloaded all those files while you were somewhere else. We've heard it all before."

A rushing sound filled my ears. It seemed they weren't talking about the site on the dark web after all. Then it occurred to me; I had never logged in to the page on my home computer. The only time I had ever connected successfully was using my laptop from the Internet café. My thoughts spun to Jamie's warning about making sure I downloaded Tor from the official website. Perhaps I installed an infected version, and somebody had been hijacking my connection to download something illegal.

"What ... what material do you mean?" I asked, trying to hide the stammer in my voice.

"Give me your car keys," the taller man said, ignoring the question.

"Why do you want them?"

"We need to search your vehicle too."

I reached into my pocket and handed them over.

The policeman's gaze focused on the memory stick. It was a free gift and possessed limited capacity by modern standards, but it was a quick way of transferring files from one machine to another when I was at school. "We'll take this as evidence too," he said, unclipping the rectangular block from the ring. He removed a clear plastic bag from his pocket, dropped the gadget inside and handed it to the uniformed officer.

The two men split up, one going to each side of the car. The smoker started at the front passenger door. He opened the glove box and pulled everything out. After finishing there, he turned his attention to the rear, checking the door pockets and beneath the seat. His partner repeated the process on the driver side. They completed their tasks at the same time and moved around to the back of the vehicle.

The taller man lifted the hatchback. At any moment, I expected them to haul out the laptop bag. Then I remembered bringing it into the house the previous night. I had left it in the gap between the two sofas. Their bodies blocked my view as they bent over and inspected the contents.

"Nothing here," the smoker announced.

Why hadn't they found the laptop during their earlier search? It wasn't in plain sight, but neither was it well hidden. And how had the illicit material ended up on my hard disk? The policemen had suggested that the incriminating data, whatever that might be, was on my desktop computer. My first thought was that it had something to do with the dark web. But I hadn't even installed the Tor browser on that machine.

The uniformed officer broke me out of my thoughts. "That's it. Sign here to acknowledge that we've taken these two items." He thrust a form at me.

I gave the sheet of paper a quick scan and met his gaze. "What if I don't?"

He sighed. "I'll sign it on your behalf, and I'll be even more pissed off than I am right now."

I scribbled my signature and entered the date in the box. "Am I under arrest?"

"Not at the moment, but I wouldn't try to leave the country."

The plain-clothes officers were already walking back to their car. The taller of the two carried the base unit. Smoke rose from the recently lit cigarette in the other man's hand as he passed through the open gate.

"Pricks," the uniformed officer muttered under his breath as he handed over my car keys. Then he too turned away.

I started with the car. All the doors hung open, and the contents of the glove box lay arrayed across the front passenger seat. I returned everything to its place and moved onto the boot. They had lifted the cover to reveal the spare wheel. I tidied up, then breathing in deeply to steady my nerves, headed inside.

Sofa cushions littered the floor in the lounge, but they had disturbed little else. The laptop bag remained where I remembered leaving it, on the carpet between the two sofas. A quick check confirmed the case still contained the machine. The dining room was unaffected. In the kitchen, the breadbin and most of the cupboards were open. An overturned box of breakfast cereal spilt its contents onto the work surface and from there onto the grey, stone tiles. I grabbed a dustpan and brush to sweep up the mess.

I headed along the hallway to the study. This was where I expected the most disruption, and it came as no surprise to find the room trashed. Books lay strewn across the carpet where they had been pulled from the shelves. The monitor sat askew. The keyboard and mouse trailed leads to where a dust-free area of the desktop indicated the previous location of the base unit.

Flashing lights drew my eye to the printer, which lay on its side to the right of the desk amidst the spilt contents of the paper tray. That must have been what caused the crash I heard earlier. It took several minutes to tidy the mess. At least there didn't seem to be any lasting damage although I wouldn't know for sure until I reconnected the system box.

I made my way upstairs to the bathroom. Apart from the open cabinet door, nothing seemed to have been disturbed. The spare room told a different story. All the drawers yawned open, and the mattress rested on its side beside the base. The main bedroom was in a similar state, but here every drawer lay on the floor, the contents regurgitated into haphazard heaps across the beige carpet.

Twenty minutes later, I had restored most of the disturbed items to a tidy state. What should I do next? At the moment, all I could be certain of was that the police suspected me of accessing something illegal on my computer. I tried to recall the conversation with the policemen. At the time, I had been convinced their main area of interest lay in the dark website, but the taller of the two plain-clothes officers had accused me of downloading a large number of files.

Richard T. Burke

As far as I knew, my download history didn't include any illegal material. Yes, I had accessed the occasional porn site. After all, I was a single heterosexual man in the prime of life with no partner to help fulfil my sexual urges. But I had never watched anything hardcore that veered towards the unlawful.

If I hadn't downloaded the incriminating files—whatever they contained—then who had? And what was their motive? As my mind ran through the possibilities, my thoughts kept returning to the dark web. The coincidence was too great to assume my accessing of the site and the police visit were unrelated. But if that was the case, how had the illegal data ended up on my desktop machine?

An idea hit me. I used a cloud-based storage solution on both of my machines. The software stored files on a remote server and synchronised it between connected computers. That meant the incriminating evidence might have been downloaded on the laptop and transferred automatically to the desktop PC. The night before I had spent several hours in front of the computer screen, ample time to synchronise the data from one machine to the other.

It still didn't explain how or why the files had been copied to my computer in the first place. Had I been using an infected version of the Tor browser? Jamie had checked out the laptop the previous night and given me the all clear. My thoughts turned to the Internet café. After forgetting to take the computer with me, it had been out of my sight for ten or fifteen minutes. I had returned to discover Molly looking at the screen. Was she the person responsible for downloading the material? I found that difficult to believe. What motive could she possibly have?

I desperately wanted to check out the laptop's hard drive to confirm the validity of my theory. However, my recent experiences had left me with a strong sense of paranoia. The police already possessed a search warrant, so it wasn't too much of a stretch to assume they would realise there was another machine and return for a second examination of my house. If that happened, I would lose any opportunity to discover what they were accusing me of downloading.

I also had some hard questions for Molly. The best solution was to visit The Café Corner in person. The police might follow me there, but I doubted it. It was one thing to record my Internet usage, but it would take a serious level of manpower to track my movements. The fact they hadn't arrested me yet implied the case against me lacked evidence—at least for now. With my mind made up, I headed to the car.

As I slammed the driver's door shut, Mrs Owens came through the gateway to my property without the dog. She had clearly been loitering outside, waiting for signs of movement. I was in no mood to talk to the nosey cow. I started the engine and kept my eyes forward as I edged the vehicle past her. Glancing in the rearview mirror, I noted with a warm glow of satisfaction the surprised expression on her face.

Fifteen minutes later, I navigated into a parking space at the pay and display car park in the centre of Basingstoke. I was no expert in detecting surveillance, but the roads were so quiet I felt certain I would have spotted any tail. Continuing my journey on foot, I stopped several times along the route to look into shop windows, but nobody seemed to be following me.

With a final glance each way along the pedestrianised street, I pushed through the door of The Café Corner. As on the previous afternoon, the place was almost empty. There was no sign of Molly. I approached the counter and waited for the girl preparing a coffee to finish. She had pink hair and a small gold stud through one nostril. Her arms were painfully thin, and the striped uniform hung off her as if it was on a coat hanger. I put her age at no more than seventeen or eighteen years old.

"I'll be with you in a minute," she called before carrying the white mug to an elderly man sitting by himself in the corner. She returned seconds later and smiled at me. "What can I get you?"

"Actually, I wanted to have a chat with Molly. Is she here?"

"Oh, you must be her old teacher. She mentioned you'd been in yesterday. She's on her break at the moment. I'll go and find her."

Before I could say anything, she disappeared through the door behind the serving area marked *Staff Only*. After a few seconds, she returned. "Molly will be out in a moment." She flashed another brief smile and set about wiping down the espresso machine.

A short while later, Molly emerged from the back room. She grinned at me. "Hi, Alex. I think you've already won the competition for most visits in a week." Her behaviour did not seem typical of somebody with a guilty conscience.

"What did you do on my laptop yesterday?" I asked.

A slight frown creased her brow. "I wasn't one hundred per cent sure who it belonged to, so I powered it up. As soon as I saw the login box, I knew it was yours. Like I told you last night, I tried to find an email address or phone number inside the case so I could contact you. Why? Is something wrong?"

I ignored her question. "And you didn't log in or anything?"

Her head jerked backwards in surprise. "How would I do that? I don't have your password."

"So, nobody else used it?"

The frown deepened. "Well, obviously I asked if any of our customers wanted to borrow your computer to do some browsing. No, of course I didn't let anybody else use it. Why do you think they would want to use your old laptop when almost everybody in the country has a mobile phone?"

"I'm sorry. I wasn't implying ... Is there any chance somebody logged on or connected something to it while you weren't looking?"

Molly folded her arms. "You left it by the table. I noticed it almost immediately, so I picked it up and put it behind the counter. Then I switched it on to confirm it was yours, and a few minutes later you came back. Nobody else had time to use it. What's all this about?"

"Don't worry. It's nothing."

"Is it something to do with that dark web stuff?"

The girl cleaning the machine turned around and stared at me for a moment. It was obvious she had been listening in to our conversation.

I lowered my voice as I leaned in closer to Molly. "I'm not sure what's going on. It was just a theory."

"If I were you. I'd stay well clear of anything like that. My boyfriend says there are some seriously dodgy people on there."

"I can believe it. Thanks for looking after the laptop for me. As a matter of interest, what does your boyfriend do for a living? How come he knows so much about the dark web?"

"He tells me he uses it to buy stuff, but to be honest, I don't really understand what he does. I've seen him using that special browser thing a few times. He doesn't like to talk about it." Her voice took on a lighter tone. "Anyway, while you're here, can I get you a drink?"

I ordered another Americano. I handed over a five-pound note and once again told her to keep the change. As she prepared my coffee, I returned to the table by the wall where I had sat the previous afternoon. I retrieved the laptop from its case, plugged in the charger and pressed the power button. After several whirring and clicking sounds, the login prompt eventually popped up.

I tapped in my password and waited for the desktop to appear. After another minute of mechanical grating noises, I clicked on the Windows Explorer icon. I didn't really know what to look for. For several minutes, I investigated directory contents including the online synchronised folder but discovered nothing out of place. Whatever the policemen had found on my desktop machine, it seemed my laptop was not the source.

As Molly approached the table, I closed the lid.

"Is everything alright?" she asked, placing the mug beside me.

"I'm not really sure."

She hesitated for a moment, waiting to see if I would elaborate. When I didn't, she shrugged and made her way back to the serving area.

I sipped at the drink, trying to decide what to do. The obvious next step was to ask Jamie for his advice, but I was reluctant to involve him further. In any case, he was probably still at work.

I desperately needed to talk to somebody. I didn't want to discuss my problems with my mother or sister; my mother was in no fit state to handle the stress of the situation, and I didn't trust Cathy not to mention my dilemma to her. I couldn't think of anybody else close enough to me with whom to share my troubles. For a moment, I considered unburdening myself to Molly, but I barely knew the girl. No, the only viable option was my brother-in-law.

I drained the mug of coffee, packed away the laptop and headed for the door.

W hen I arrived back at the car, I placed the laptop bag in the boot. By now, the time was just after half past two. Jamie would still be at work for another three hours, perhaps even longer. I retrieved my mobile phone and selected my brother-in-law from the list of contacts. We probably wouldn't be able to meet immediately, but at least I could set something up for later.

The ringing tone rang eight times then transferred to voicemail. I decided against leaving a message, unsure of what I would say. I leaned back in the seat, drumming my fingers on the steering wheel. After two minutes, I tried again with the same result.

On this occasion, I spoke after the recording of Jamie's voice. "Hi, it's Alex. Look ... um ... the police paid me a visit this morning. I think it might be related to what we discussed yesterday. Please call me back. It's really urgent."

The seconds ticked by. I was about to try a third time when another idea occurred to me. Switching from the phone screen to a browser window, I searched for the number of Jamie's company. The first result displayed a green telephone beneath the link. I tapped the icon. Somebody answered within one ring.

"Saunders Web Design," a female voice said. "How may I help you?"

"Hello. My name is Alex Parrott. I'm Jamie Saunders' brother-in-law. I wonder if it would be possible to speak to him, please."

"Just a minute, Mr Parrott. I'll put you through."

An electronic version of Greensleeves played. A few seconds later, the music stopped.

"I'm sorry, Mr Parrott. Mr Saunders is working from home today. Can I take a message?"

"Don't worry," I replied. "I've got his number."

I pressed the end call button and switched back to the contacts list. This time, I scrolled to my sister's name. I still hadn't updated her contact details since she had moved out.

After six rings, Jamie's recorded voice came down the line. "I'm not in. Leave a message."

I pounded the steering wheel in frustration and ended the call. Why wasn't he answering the phone? I came to a quick decision. The house was nearby. It would take less than a quarter of an hour to get there at this time of day.

I turned on the engine and navigated out of the car park. Perhaps I was being paranoid, but I checked my rearview mirror every few seconds to see if anybody was following me. Once again, the roads were quiet enough to convince me I would have spotted any tail. Thirteen minutes later, I pulled up beside the *For-Sale* sign.

Jamie's car, a black Jaguar, sat on the driveway. At least he was home. I hurried to the door and pressed the bell. The ding-dong chime echoed from within. I stared through the frosted glass, waiting impatiently for signs of movement. When nothing stirred, I pushed the button again.

I rapped on the dark wood with my knuckles, but still nobody responded. He had told me before that when he was working on a difficult problem, he liked to isolate himself from the outside world by listening to music. In all likelihood, he was wearing a set of headphones and hadn't heard the doorbell. I approached the lounge window and cupped my hands to block out the light. A beer can perched on the edge of the armchair in the same place I had left it the previous night. A dirty plate rested atop a pile of papers on the coffee table. There was no sign of my brother-in-law.

I let myself into the back garden through the wooden gate. Moving around the side of the house, I peered through the kitchen window. The sink overflowed with unwashed plates, but there were no other signs of life. The dining room was a similar story.

I walked across the rear of the property to the narrow path running beside the brickwork. The first window belonged to the study, Jamie's most likely location. As I drew nearer, I could see the curtains were drawn. Had they been closed the previous night? I wracked my brain trying to remember. Eventually, I concluded they probably had been.

I hammered the palm of my hand against the glass. "Jamie, it's Alex. If you're in there, open the door."

I tried again. Surely he would have heard me knocking by now even if he was wearing headphones. Where the hell was he?

Grabbing the phone from my pocket, I selected Jamie's name from the contacts and once again dialled his mobile. The faint sound of a musical ringtone permeated through the pane from inside. After six rings, the call reverted to voicemail.

All manner of dark thoughts ran through my head. Had he suffered a heart attack? His sedentary lifestyle and lack of exercise made it a distinct possibility. At that moment, he could be lying on the floor, clutching his chest and unable to summon assistance.

"Jamie, I'm outside your house. Why aren't you answering your phone? Is anything wrong? I'm starting to get worried."

I stabbed the red icon to hang up. What should I do next? I sensed movement to my left and whirled to confront the elderly man studying me from the other end of the narrow pathway. The scruffy grey cardigan and muddy trousers brought to mind the image of a tramp.

"What are you doing here?" he asked, his face a mask of suspicion.

"My brother-in-law's car is outside, but he's not answering either the doorbell or his phone."

The man seemed to relax. "That's right; I know you. You're Cathy's brother. I live next door." He pointed toward the adjacent property. "I've been watching you. When you walked around the back, I wondered if you were up to no good. You can't be too careful these days."

"Have you seen Jamie today?" I asked, eager to keep the conversation on track.

The man's eyes narrowed in thought. "No, I'm not sure I have. Some people came to visit earlier. Now I think about it, they went inside, so he must have been here to let them in."

"What time was this?"

"I don't know ... maybe nine, nine-thirty."

"Did you see them leave?"

"I was working in the garden." That explained the scruffy clothing. "They weren't here long."

"Did you—?" The ringtone of my phone interrupted before I could complete the sentence. I glanced at the screen to identify the caller. The word *Jamie* stared back at me in large black letters. I pushed the answer button.

"Jamie, I was getting worried. Why aren't you answering the door?"

My brother-in-law spoke in a hushed voice. "I can't talk. They know you accessed the dark website. I'm not sure what they'll do next, but if I was you, I'd find somewhere to hide. You need to stay away from me ... and your sister. Don't ring me again. I've got to go."

A click came down the line. When I removed the mobile from my ear and stared at the display, the message indicated the call had ended after a duration of eighteen seconds. I remained stationary, trying to make sense of what had just happened.

"I take it everything's okay?" the neighbour asked, his bushy, grey eyebrows lowering in a frown. When I didn't reply, he repeated the question.

"I ... I'm not sure. Yes, I think so."

"Right, well if that's the case, I'll return to my gardening. Nice meeting you."

I followed him to the front of the house, my mind whirling in a jumble of confusion. When I reached my car, I turned back toward the lounge window. The shifting shadows revealed movement inside. The silhouette of a figure moved forwards, extended an arm and tugged first one then the other curtain closed.

Richard T. Burke

I sat in the driver's seat, my mind swirling with conflicting thoughts and ideas. What the hell was going on? It seemed Jamie had some association with the people behind the dark website. He had warned me to find somewhere to hide. What words did he use? *They haven't decided what to do yet* or something to that effect. The fact they were aware I had accessed the page from the Internet café implied some sort of link between them and the murders. And if my brother-in-law was telling me to disappear, that meant he believed I too might become a target.

So, why hadn't he called the police? Maybe he had, and that was the reason for the search warrant on my house. Alternatively, perhaps his mysterious visitors had threatened him. The more I thought about it, the more convinced I became the second alternative was the correct answer. It would explain why he had instructed me to stay away from both him and my sister.

But who were these people, and how did Jamie know them? The only person who could tell me that was Jamie himself, and he had refused to talk to me. If I was going to hide, I needed to understand from whom I was hiding. Working on the supposition they were the same men who had visited him earlier that day, the neighbour might be able to provide a description. The old man had witnessed them arriving.

I shoved the car door open and strode along the road to the neighbouring house on the left. As I entered the well-kept garden, the elderly owner glanced up from the flower bed where he held a plastic bottle, spraying soapy water onto the leaves of a rose bush.

"Oh, hello," he said, squinting myopically at me. "I've got an infestation of these damned greenflies. Washing up liquid; that's the solution."

"Hi. We talked next door a few minutes ago."

A scowl developed on the man's face. "I know that. Just because I'm getting on a bit, it doesn't mean I'm senile."

"I apologise. I wasn't trying to—"

He straightened up, holding his back as he did so. "Never mind all that. One day you'll be old too. Now, what do you want, young man?"

I hesitated for a moment. "You said some people visited Jamie this morning. Can you describe them?"

"You just had a chat with your brother-in-law. Why didn't you ask him?"

I decided that truth was the best option. "He's still not talking to me. It might have something to do with his visitors."

"Is this about the separation? I'm not sure I want to take sides."

"No, it's nothing to do with that. I suspect they may have ... well ... threatened him."

The old man fixed me with his watery grey eyes. I met his gaze.

"There were two of them," he said. "I was busy, so I didn't get a good look."

"Can you remember anything about them?"

"No, I don't think so. My eyesight isn't what it used to be."

"Were they big? Small?"

"About average height, I'd say."

"I assume they came by car. Did you recognise the make?"

The man tugged at an earlobe. "It was a dark colour, but I couldn't tell you who made it. All cars look the same to me these days. I'm sorry I can't be more helpful."

"Never mind," I said. "Thanks for your time."

As I turned away to leave, the neighbour spoke again. "Actually, I do remember something, although I'm not sure how much use it'll be to you. One of them was smoking. The smoke drifted across. I haven't had a cigarette in over forty years, but I could still murder one every now and then."

I thanked him once again and made my way back to my car. My thoughts switched to the two policemen who had searched my house. Was it a coincidence that one of the men who had paid a visit to my brother-in-law was also a smoker? Mathematics wasn't my strong suit, but I guessed the odds of finding somebody who smoked in a random sample of two would be fairly high.

The only person who could provide an explanation was Jamie. All I needed to do was convince him to tell me more. I sank into the driver's seat and pulled out my phone. First, I called his mobile. I didn't hear even a single ringtone before it switched to the automated reply.

I left a terse response. "It's Alex. I'm not going anywhere until you talk to me."

Next, I tried the landline. On this occasion, it rang out six times before the pre-recorded message played out. I responded in the same way.

It seemed the technological route was getting me nowhere. It was time for a more direct approach. I marched up to the house. The whole frame shook as I hammered my fist against the stained wood.

"I know you can hear me, Jamie. If you don't open the door by the count of three, I'm going to smash the window and come in to find you. One ... two ..."

The final number was forming on my lips when I picked up the sound of the interior porch latch unlocking. The blurred outline of a figure appeared through the frosted glass.

Jamie's anxious voice came from the other side. "For Christ's sake, Alex, are you trying to get us all killed? They're watching me. If I put a foot wrong, they said they'd go after Cathy and the girls. You have to leave now."

"Who are they? What do they want?"

"It's a long story. You can't be seen here. It may already be too late. These are very dangerous people."

"You still haven't answered my questions."

"The less I tell you, the better. I'll try to help, but you must leave immediately. If you won't do this for me, at least do it for your sister and nieces. And whatever happens, don't approach the police. You'd be signing all our death warrants."

"Are you saying the police are involved?"

"I'm not sure. They said they would find out if I contacted them."

"Some policemen paid me a visit this morning. They took away my computer. Do you know anything about that?"

"Look, Alex, I can't help." His voice quivered with desperation. "Just leave. I promise I'll be in touch. And please don't ring me."

"But it's not safe to go home?"

"That's the first place they'll search for you. If you want my honest advice, you need to hide somewhere, at least for the time being."

The sound of a ringing phone emerged through the letterbox.

"Shit," he muttered. "That'll probably be them. I've got to take this call."

Jamie's blurred outline retreated. The clunk of the inner porch door closing followed a second later.

It seemed I had received all the information I was going to get.

Twenty-five years ago: Wednesday, 8th February, 1995

*S*creaming at the top of my voice, I sprinted towards my parents' room. I burst through the door and turned on the light. My father jerked upright, tossing the sheets to one side.

"Alex, what the hell's going on?"

"Somebody has taken Elena."

At that, my mother sat up too.

"You're just having a bad dream," my father said. "You need to go back to bed."

"No, I'm not dreaming," I yelled, my voice squeaking in panic. "I saw him take her to his car and drive away."

"I'll check it out, Alan," my mother replied. She ran a hand over her cheek and shuffled sideways. A stray strand of hair fell across her forehead, and she tucked it behind her ear. "What time is it?"

My father glanced at his watch. "Two-forty. It's the middle of the bloody night."

My mother slid her feet into a pair of fluffy slippers and followed me into the hallway. I clicked on the light switch in Elena's room, knowing in advance she wouldn't be there. The bed was empty.

"Elena," my mother screamed, rushing to the far side to make sure my sister hadn't fallen onto the carpet.

My father appeared in the open doorway.

"She's not here," my mother yelped.

"Maybe she went to the toilet," my father said.

I shook my head violently. "I already told you. A man took her. He drove off with her. She wasn't moving."

My father ran the short distance to the bathroom. He returned after a few moments, his face blanched of all colour. "She's not there either."

My mother clasped him by the arm. "We have to call the police, Alan," she said, every word laced with panic.

He sprinted back to the bedroom. Seconds later, his voice drifted through the open door. "Police... My daughter's been abducted ... My son looked out *of his window and spotted somebody carrying her away ... Six-years-old ... Elena, Elena Parrott ... Eight, Rookery Lane ... That's right. Please hurry."*

"Did you see who it was?" my mother asked, grabbing my hands in her own. She squeezed so tightly, my knuckles cracked.

"I only saw him for a second."

"What about the car? What was he driving? Could you make out what colour it was?"

Tears rolled down my cheek. "I only got a quick look. It was so dark I wasn't able to tell the colour. What will happen to her?"

Cathy appeared in the doorway, rubbing the sleep from her eyes. "What's all the noise about, Mum?"

"A man has taken Elena. Your dad just called the police."

My sister's gaze alternated between the two of us. She was in her first year of secondary school and desperately trying to prove she was an adult, but in an instant the façade fell away, revealing the frightened child beneath. "I don't understand. Why would somebody do that?"

My mother shook her head. "I have no idea. We should all get dressed so we're ready when the police arrive." Suddenly, her resistance crumbled. She buried her face in her hands. Deep sobs wracked her body. My father placed an arm around her shoulder and guided her back to the bedroom.

I returned to my own room and hurriedly put on my school uniform. It was the early hours of Wednesday morning. At that stage, it didn't occur to me that I wouldn't be attending lessons later in the day. As I slipped my feet into the black lace-up shoes, a fuzzy feeling enveloped my head. The ceiling light suddenly seemed much brighter than usual. A sharp pain developed behind my eyes, throbbing in time with my pulse.

It was obvious the police would need details of Elena's abductor. I squinted against the brightness and tried to recall the man's features. Casting my mind back, I pictured the scene I had witnessed: Elena lying on the frozen grass, her abductor staring up at me. I recalled the dark outline of his body, even the condensation emerging from his mouth in the frigid night air, but his face was a total blank.

Panic overtook me. How could I give a description of the man if I had no memory of what he looked like? The search for my sister's kidnapper depended on me being able to describe his appearance. Tears blurred my vision. My breath came in a rapid series of small gasps. I rushed to the window and stared down at the garden. The hedge separating the property from the road cast long shadows from the streetlight.

The man had been standing by the gate. He twisted around when I banged on the glass. At the time, there couldn't have been more than twenty yards between us. Why didn't I remember anything about his face?

I spun away and raced through the doorway to the staircase. Turning the corner at the bottom of the stairs, I immediately noticed the open front door. A blast of freezing air ruffled my hair. I sprinted along the hall and discovered my parents standing in the cover of the porch.

"He was just here," I screamed, running to the spot on the lawn where I had seen my sister's motionless body. I learned afterwards that my trampling of the ice-coated grass destroyed any forensic evidence the police might have been able to gather.

My mother broke away from my father. She grabbed me by the shoulders and shook me. "Why didn't you stop him?"

"I ... I ..." The words wouldn't have come out even if I'd known how to answer the question.

My father reappeared beside her. "Leave the boy alone, Mary. He woke us up. There's nothing more he could have done."

"My baby," she wailed. She buried her face in her hands, deep sobs of anguish rocking her shoulders.

"I need to do something," my father announced. "I'm going out in the car to look for her." He opened the wooden gate then jogged back towards the red Volkswagen Golf parked at the side of the house. My mother's gaze followed him as he accelerated onto the road. Seconds later, Cathy joined us, shivering in the sub-zero temperature. Her hand shot out and grasped my own.

Suddenly, my mother seemed to remember her parental responsibilities. "It's too cold out here for you two. Go and wait in the house."

Cathy opened her mouth to say something then thought better of it. She pulled me inside to the relative warmth of the hallway. "Don't worry. They'll find her."

I shook my head in silence. She studied me for a second then drew me into a hug. Despite our two-year age difference, we were the same height. After a while, we broke apart and sank to the floor with our backs resting against the wall. We stayed in that position until the distant wail of sirens announced the imminent arrival of the police.

I put the car in gear, unsure yet of my destination. Jamie had suggested I shouldn't go home. He also told me to stay away from my sister, Cathy. What other options did I have? My initial thought was to book a cheap hotel. I had no real idea how much it would cost per night. The first course of action was to do some research.

I could have used my mobile, but I needed time to plan my actions. The laptop remained in the boot. One obvious location for connecting to the Internet immediately sprang to mind. The prospect of seeing a friendly face provided an additional incentive.

I reversed onto the road and headed back towards town, my gaze shifting frequently to the rearview mirror. The start of rush hour was still a good ninety minutes away, but traffic was heavier than it had been earlier in the day when travelling in the opposite direction. If somebody was following me, I didn't spot them.

The pay and display car park was almost full, but I found a space on my second circuit. I paid for a two-hour stay and placed the ticket behind the windscreen. The wind had increased in strength, and the dark grey clouds scudding in from the west hinted at further heavy rain. Glad of the lightweight raincoat, I hunched my shoulders as I made my way along the pedestrianised streets to The Café Corner.

A blast of cold air followed me inside, sending the stack of paper napkins on the nearest table swirling in a mini cyclone. I retrieved the ones within reach and placed the salt and pepper shakers on top to hold them down. The place was approximately a third full, but nobody occupied my favourite spot by the wall. I deposited the laptop bag on the tabletop and headed to the counter.

Molly studied me as I approached, a half-smile curving her lips. At least she didn't seem to be holding my accusation of the previous night against me. "Hello, Alex. This must be the fourth or fifth time in the last couple of days. Maybe you should think about buying a season ticket."

"There's still a problem with the Internet at home, and I have work to do."

"Work that involves using that special browser?"

When I didn't answer, Molly stared at me for a second. The smile slipped, and her face turned serious. "I'm sorry, it's none of my business what you do online. What'll it be, the same as usual?"

"Yes, an Americano please."

"That'll be three ninety-nine."

I handed over a five-pound note. She thanked me and told me she would bring it over.

As I navigated around the tables to my chosen corner, my phone produced a short ping. The icon at the bottom of the display signalled an unread text. I didn't recognise the sender's number.

Drawing in a deep breath, I tapped in my PIN and opened the message. The words made no sense, but I immediately recognised the format.

jaasgdqu.onion/login

user2587 / sjY76fR3d

I exhaled slowly through my mouth. Why was Jamie sending me another link to the dark web? What was he mixed up in? I stared at the letters for several seconds. This was how I had landed in this mess in the first place—at least that was my current assumption. Now it seemed he was asking me to repeat the exercise.

"You look like you've seen a ghost."

I jerked my head up as Molly placed the mug of coffee on the table.

"Thanks," I muttered.

"Just give me a shout if you need anything else."

I looked down at the screen again, but it had turned off. My mind spun through the possibilities. Realistically, Jamie had left me no choice. Given the seriousness of my situation, I couldn't afford to ignore the message.

I pulled the laptop out of the case and plugged in the charger. While the machine clanked into life, I unlocked the mobile's display once again. For a moment I thought about calling my brother-in-law, but he had explicitly warned me against contacting him.

Eventually, the icons on the computer's desktop popped into existence. I double clicked the small picture of the Earth. A green progress bar moved from left to right. When it reached the end, a large purple banner proclaimed, "Welcome to Tor Browser."

I placed the phone on the table and transcribed the website address, username and password into a text file. After checking for mistakes, I copied the address to the clipboard and pasted it into the browser window. When I hit the return key, an untitled white dialogue box appeared. As on the previous occasion, the form requested the account details. After transferring the information from the document, I moved the cursor over the OK button and tapped the touchpad.

My heart thudded against my chest as I waited for the webpage to load. After a short delay, the display updated. The page seemed identical to the one from the previous day. As before, a toolbar occupied the upper area of the screen. This time, however, it offered four options: *All Jobs, Your Current Jobs, Your Completed Jobs* and *Create a Job*.

The blue underlined text informed me I was looking at the first of those. A single entry in the table contained fields running down the page; *Click for job details, Postcode: RG27, Initial fee: £7000, Bids: 3, Lowest bid: £5400, Completion deadline: Friday 31ˢᵗ July 2020, Time remaining: 00:00:27.*

The mobile pinged, signalling the arrival of another text message, but my eyes remained glued to the laptop's display. As I watched, the timer continued to count down. Determined not to make the same mistake as on the previous occasion, I pressed the *Print Screen* button to capture a screenshot. Next, I opened the word processing application and pasted the clipboard contents into the document.

By the time I returned to the webpage, fifteen seconds remained. The number of bids had risen to six, and the lowest bid was now five thousand two hundred pounds. If this was what I suspected, I was witnessing a contract being placed to end somebody's life. A sickening feeling hit me in the stomach like a physical blow. The postcode provided the clue. It wasn't complete, but the first four characters matched those of my own property.

I rolled my finger across the trackpad, selected the *Click for Job Details* link and tapped the left button. A shiver ran through my body as my eyes ranged over the text.

Termination required with immediate effect. The subject is an unsuspecting single male aged 34 with no training in assassination evasion techniques. Address and additional information will be provided to the successful bidder. Full payment on notification through news channels.

I stabbed a finger onto the *Print Screen* key and once again pasted the clipboard contents to the document. When I switched back to the Tor program, the job details had disappeared, and the page had reverted to the *All Jobs* screen. The onscreen table was now empty.

For several seconds, I stared at the laptop display. I had little doubt as to the identity of the unsuspecting subject referred to in the contract description. The age and the postcode matched my own. Why else would Jamie have sent me the login details?

I placed my head in my hands and let out a low moan. The sound must have been louder than I imagined because a handful of my fellow customers glanced in my direction. I remained in the same position for two or three minutes, my brain refusing to operate as waves of dizziness washed over me. A single thought kept spinning through my mind; a professional killer was being paid to murder me.

Eventually, my breathing slowed, and I regained a modicum of self-control. I switched back to the word processor and saved the file before rereading the text. The description was vague enough to apply to a large number of people. But no matter how much I tried to convince myself it didn't refer to me, the coincidences stacked up far too high. But what should I do?

A growing determination overcame my initial panic as I forced myself to think logically. The first task was to check whether I could glean any more information from the website. Returning to the Tor browser, the *All Jobs* page remained empty. I clicked the *Your Current Jobs* option; that was a similar story. *Your Completed Jobs* also came up blank.

As I focused on the words, a question occurred to me; did the titles refer to contracts placed or contracts accepted? The last alternative, *Create a Job*, implied I had the ability to place a contract. However, when I switched to the page, a message stated that the account held insufficient funds. A button labelled *Add Funds* presumably provided the means to rectify the situation.

The time for caution was long past, so I clicked the button. A form popped up. A blank box marked *Amount* occupied the top. To the right were the words, *Minimum payment £5000.* Below that lay another button containing the text, *Pay by Bitcoin.*

I had heard about Bitcoin in the news, but my knowledge extended to little more than the basics. I knew it was a digital currency and that the exchange rate to hard currencies fluctuated with demand. Rapidly increasing values had brought a flood of speculators, who saw their investment rise by several hundred per cent. I had overheard some of my fellow teachers in the staff room at school discussing whether to purchase a few, but I had no idea where to even start.

"Is something wrong with your drink?"

I looked up sharply to see Molly standing a short distance away.

"It doesn't look like you've touched it," she added.

"No, it's fine thanks. I've ... um ... been a bit engrossed and totally forgot about it."

"I can heat it up for you in the microwave."

"Okay," I replied. "Yeah, why not?"

She smiled and picked up the mug. I watched as she returned to the serving area. I switched my focus back to the webpage. Once again, I recorded a screenshot and added it to the document.

There was little else to learn from the site, so I closed down the Tor Browser and the word processing program. My thoughts reverted to my situation. I couldn't go home. Jamie had told me that was the first place they would look for me. The idea of staying in a hotel still ranked highly on my list of possibilities. I could hide away until the deadline passed, and the solitude would provide me with plenty of time to come up with a better plan.

Turning back to the laptop, I started a conventional browser. I navigated to a search page and typed *cheap hotels near Basingstoke* into the box. Travelodge came up at the top of the results. I had used the chain before and knew they provided no-frills accommodation at various locations across the country. Several clicks later, I had selected a single room for four nights at a place six miles away. The grand total summed to a little over two hundred and fifty pounds.

I clicked on the *Book Now* button. The site offered me the option to check in as a guest but still required a name and email address. I tapped in my details and scrolled to the payment section at the bottom of the page. Removing a card from my wallet, I entered the account information, moved the mouse pointer over the *Make Payment* text and tapped the touchpad. The wait cursor spun around for several seconds, then a message box popped up informing me my bank had declined the transaction.

I frowned at the screen. The last time I had checked, my account was in credit by at least seven thousand pounds. I had planned to use this money to pay for my expensive holiday. I re-entered the information, checking each digit carefully as I typed. Once again, I clicked the payment button. Moments later, the same error message appeared.

How could this get any worse? Had the police blocked my account? As children, my parents frequently lectured us about the lure of easy finance and the perils of falling into debt. As a consequence, I had never owned a credit card. Now I regretted following their advice. With no method to pay, the hotel was no longer a viable solution.

Despite my brother-in-law's warning, approaching the police seemed like the only remaining option. If I told them the whole story, surely they would protect my sister and her family. With the hard proof I possessed, they would have to take me seriously. The search warrant for my house still worried me, but I had committed no crime. When they examined the evidence, it would all become clear.

As it turned out, I couldn't have been more wrong.

I shut down the laptop and packed it away in the carry case. Now I had come to a decision, a huge weight had lifted from my shoulders. I still needed to plan how to contact the police. My instinctive reaction was to call 999.

The other option was to telephone the female sergeant, Susie Mayhew. She had taken my original witness statement, and I had kept her card in my wallet. There was little doubt in my mind that the dark web page provided the links between the threats to my life, the double murder and the search of my house. But would she talk to me? The last time we had spoken on the phone, she practically hung up on me. She might not even be on duty.

The more I thought about it, the more convinced I became that I should call the emergency services. I could let them know my current location and wait for their arrival. Surely no hitman would make an attempt on my life in front of witnesses.

As my hand reached for the phone, Molly returned with my coffee. "There we go. All warmed up again."

I thanked her and waited until she was out of earshot before picking up the mobile. As I extended my finger to unlock the screen, the jangle of the bell above the door signalled a new arrival. I raised my eyes to watch as a blast of cold air sent the napkins on the tabletop nearest the entrance flying again despite my earlier precautions.

The newcomer made no move to pick them up. He stood in the open doorway, surveying the interior, seemingly oblivious to the irritated stares of the seated customers. A second smaller man, carrying a small backpack, muttered "Excuse me" as he edged around the first. Another gust toppled the menu holder on the adjacent table. Eventually, the man stepped inside.

He was in his late twenties with close-cropped brown hair. As he strolled towards the counter, he unzipped the grey, leather jacket he wore over a black T-shirt and blue jeans. A gold stud through his left earlobe flashed in the light reflected from the polished chrome surface. He carried the air of somebody who knew how to look after himself. It was clear from his physique that he spent a lot of time at the gym. Every eye in the place studied him as he spotted Molly and spoke to her in a low voice. She leaned forward and whispered something in his ear. His face cracked into a grin as he reached out a hand and caressed her forearm.

Richard T. Burke

The room seemed to utter a collective sigh of relief and the volume of conversation rose once again as the man crossed the tiled floor and pulled out a chair at the table two down from mine. He sensed me inspecting him and met my stare. I looked away. *This had to be the boyfriend Molly had mentioned.*

In a sudden burst of insight, my brain settled on a new theory. My mind flashed back to what she had told me about him spending a lot of time on the dark web. The link was inescapable. Suddenly it all made perfect sense. He must have gained access to my laptop when I had accidentally left it behind the previous night. No wonder she had been curious about my activity on the Tor browser. How much did she know about his activities? Had she called him to tell him I was here again?

My head spun in a panic. In an instant, all thought of waiting for the police to arrive disappeared. As my gaze darted about the room searching for a way out, a flash of pink at the next table caught my eye. At first, my conscious mind failed to pick up the incongruity of the scene, but something dragged my attention back. The man who had entered the café behind Molly's boyfriend held a mobile in his hand—a bright pink mobile with yellow stars dotted across the rear.

What sent me spinning from panic to outright hysteria was that I recognised the case. Three years ago, I had given the exact same cover to my sister for her birthday. She had complained she was always leaving her phone behind when she went out. The garish colour was an attempt to ensure she wouldn't fail to notice it. To make it more distinctive, my nieces had decorated the back with stick-on yellow stars. Now the same brightly coloured mobile was in the possession of a man in his early forties with a pinched face and thinning grey hair. The two men were obviously working together.

Without conscious thought, I shoved the table away from me. I reached out to grab the laptop bag and lunged for the gap between the tables. My sudden movement stopped all conversation in the room outright. The smaller man leapt to his feet so quickly his chair toppled over backwards. He stood, blocking my route to the exit. Molly's boyfriend remained seated, a frown creasing his forehead. As I barged past him, a voice called after me, "Wait!"

I ignored the command and rushed towards the counter. Molly was holding a milk jug over a mug of coffee. She stopped in mid-pour, her face locked in a state of surprise. A sense of outrage flooded my veins.

"It was you who set me up," I snarled, spittle flying from my lips.

"I ... I don't—"

Her mouth opened in shock. I didn't wait for her to finish the sentence. I pushed the bag ahead of me and hurdled the chrome plated surface, sending the cup and milk container spinning to the floor. Scalding hot liquid soaked through the leg of my trousers, but I ignored the pain and barrelled through the door marked *Staff Only*. Sensing rapid movement behind me, I risked a backwards glance to see Molly's boyfriend running towards the gap at the end of the counter.

A wall of heat hit me as I emerged into the kitchen area. My eyes rapidly scanned for an exit. A pair of stainless-steel, deep fat fryers occupied the centre of the room. To the right, a man in a white top with a blue bandana tied around his head looked into a large microwave oven, inspecting the contents. A few feet away, a similarly attired woman stood at a sink, running water over something I couldn't see. They both jerked their heads in my direction at the sudden intrusion.

My gaze settled on the green and white emergency exit sign on the far side of the fryers. Other than the doorway through which I had entered, it provided the only possible route outside. I skirted the vats of boiling oil and prayed the way out was unlocked. I extended my hand and shoved the handle away from me. My heart sank as it refused to give. Cursing my stupidity, I realised it opened inwards.

I stumbled out into the cool afternoon air. A gust of wind caught the door but I desperately hung onto it. Slamming it shut behind me, I found myself in an alley leading down the side of the café. If I turned left, I would end up back on the pedestrianised road by the main entrance. I had no idea where the constricted pathway went in the other direction. I hesitated for a moment, unsure which way to turn.

The appearance of the smaller man, silhouetted against the narrow wedge of sky, took the decision out of my hands. I headed to the right, the red brickwork rising on either side of me.

A shout came from behind. "Hey! Stop!"

I sprinted at top speed, the breath hoarse in my lungs. I knew I wouldn't be able to keep this pace up for long. My only hope was that the man pursuing me was less fit than me.

I was forced to slow as the alleyway split at a T-junction. A rapid backwards glance confirmed only a single pursuer. He was twenty yards behind me, the rucksack slung across his back. What did he have in there? Did the bag contain a weapon? If it did, I needed to put enough distance between us to ensure he had no opportunity to use it. My spirits rose as I noted his face was already flushed from the chase.

Richard T. Burke

Darting to the left, I lengthened my stride. My pursuer's footsteps echoed off the sides of the building. I had no inkling where I was going. My only plan was to get far enough ahead to lose him. In front of me, the passageway opened out into a car park. I sprinted across the road, narrowly avoiding a car reversing into a space. The driver alerted me with a blast of the horn, but I skipped around the tailgate without stopping.

The parked cars gave me an idea. If I could find the way back to my vehicle with a sufficient head start, I would be able to drive off and leave him behind. First, I needed to get my bearings. I emerged onto the main road and raced along the pavement. Rush hour had started, and traffic was already building. Maybe I could flag down a motorist and ask for help. I glanced backwards. The distance between us extended to thirty yards: not yet far enough to risk stopping.

My arm was tiring from carrying the laptop bag. For a moment, I thought about ditching it. The computer wasn't worth much, but it contained my only evidence of the dark web page. Slowing slightly, I swapped it to my other hand and resumed my original pace.

My gaze raked the skyline, trying to identify any familiar landmarks. As I turned my head to the left, I spotted the tower at the entrance to the shopping centre. Suddenly, I recognised my location; this was the road out of town leading to one of the major industrial estates. My car lay in the opposite direction. A stream of swear words spilt out of my mouth.

I needed a new plan. At the next junction, I veered left towards the warehouses and parking areas beneath the stores surrounding the plaza. I knew security guards patrolled the centre. If I could find a way inside the glass-domed atrium, I could ask one for help.

My pace increased as I followed the street in its descent down the shallow incline. Where it levelled out, I turned once more to estimate the gap to the man chasing me. He stood approximately eighty yards up the road, head down, his hands resting on his knees. He raised his eyes and stared at me although the distance was too great to gauge his expression.

A satisfied grin worked its way onto my face. He wouldn't catch me today. In a display of overconfidence, I even threw him a wave.

I turned away from him and broke into a jog. That was when the sudden searing pain in my calf signalled a muscle tear.

I pulled up immediately, clutching the injury. Somebody had inserted a red-hot metal rod in the back of my lower leg. I gently probed the area, wincing at the stabs of pain where I touched the torn muscle. When I looked up, it seemed the man had noticed my sudden standstill. At first, he walked. His pace quickened as I straightened up and tried to move.

I found I couldn't place my full weight on the damaged limb. The best I could manage was an exaggerated limp. At this rate, he would catch up with me before I had covered more than a hundred yards. In mounting desperation, I continued along the road, searching for somewhere to hide.

Wide shuttered barriers lined both sides of the street. Most had an intercom system outside and a sign asking visitors to press the button for attention. I knew that even if somebody answered immediately, given the time I would need to explain my situation, there would be no opportunity to get inside before my pursuer caught up with me.

I was about to take my chances anyway when the rattle of moving shutters reached my ears. The grey panels diagonally opposite me rose at an excruciatingly slow pace. I hobbled across the road, casting anxious glances at the man closing the distance behind me. By now he was sixty yards away and accelerating as he arrived at the foot of the incline.

The rumble of a diesel engine merged with the clanking of the mechanism. By the time I had limped to the opening, the gap at the bottom had widened enough that I could make out the number plate of a white delivery van. Crouching, I scuttled beneath the rising barrier, groaning in pain as I did so.

I made my way along the passenger side of the vehicle, leaning against the bodywork for support. I emerged into an underground warehouse. Harsh, fluorescent lighting illuminated the grey, concrete interior. Scuffed, metallic shelving holding an assortment of brown, cardboard boxes lined the walls. White arrows painted on the ground signalled the route of the narrow roadway.

The sound of the van door opening echoed in the cavernous space. A voice called out from behind me. "Oi! What's your game?"

I ignored the driver and limped towards the low archway from which the road markings originated. My eyes scanned my surroundings, looking for somewhere to hide. I didn't spot anywhere suitable. I hurried through the opening as fast as my injury would allow. The second half of the warehouse matched the first except for the concrete steps against the rear wall leading to a green wooden door.

I risked a backwards glance. A man in blue coveralls strode in my direction. "Hey, this is private property. Where the hell do you think you're going?"

I hobbled towards the door, figuring it would lead to the shopping centre. I was still twenty yards short when a rough hand landed on my shoulder and spun me around.

The driver's angry face jutted forwards. "Are you bloody deaf? I just said you can't come in here."

"I'm sorry. Someone's chasing me. He's trying to kill me."

The man's eyes widened in alarm. "What are you talking about? I didn't see anybody else."

I pointed towards the green door. "Does that lead out of here?"

He glanced back before replying. "Yeah, it comes out in a staff only area of the store but—"

"We both need to go. Now."

"I can't leave the van blocking the entrance with the engine running. If this is a windup ..."

The sound of approaching footsteps echoed through from the other section.

"Come on," I hissed, resuming my limp towards the door.

The man backed up, his eyes focused on the archway. He rummaged in the pocket of his overalls and withdrew a large set of keys. As he fumbled for the right one, my pursuer jogged into the warehouse.

A grin appeared on his face. "Not so cocky now, I see." He reached behind him. When his hand came back into view, it gripped the handle of a knife. The bright overhead light glinted off the five-inch blade.

The delivery driver whimpered in panic as he tried to locate the correct key. He settled on one and fumbled with the lock, throwing anxious backward glances.

The armed man brushed a trickle of sweat from his forehead and strolled forwards. "You," he said, pointing at me, "stay right there." He continued to close the gap to the driver. "If you want to live, give me your phone and the key to that door."

The keys jangled as the driver stretched out an arm. "It's the one with the red t-t-tag. My phone's in the van."

I watched on helplessly as the man who had chased me for the last fifteen minutes twisted the key and pulled the handle towards him. He gestured to the open doorway. The van driver raised his hands and inched sideways, his back pressed against the wall.

"Come on, I haven't got all day," my pursuer growled. The driver needed no second invitation. He stumbled through the opening and raced up the staircase. The knifeman twisted the key, leaving it protruding from the lock.

Despite his instructions, I limped backward towards the exit.

He frowned as he stepped closer. "I thought I told you to stay there."

"Why are you doing this?" I asked with a trembling voice although I knew the answer had something to do with the five-thousand-pound contract. I'm not proud to admit it, but my bladder released at that moment. A patch of warmth spread down my inner thigh.

An expression of disgust occupied the man's face as he glanced towards the expanding stain. "Christ almighty, have you pissed yourself?"

"Please let me go," I babbled as I raised the laptop bag to protect myself.

The grimace morphed into a malicious grin. "What do you think I'm doing here?"

"Somebody ordered you to kill me."

The man suppressed a snort of laughter. "If I wanted you dead, we wouldn't be having this conversation; you'd be lying on the ground in a pool of blood by now."

A wave of confusion swept over me. "I—I don't understand."

The man folded the knife and returned it to his back pocket. "I haven't been paid to bump you off. The contract is to keep you alive, although I have to say that after chasing you halfway across town, I was rapidly coming to the conclusion it was more trouble than it was worth."

My mouth dropped open in shock. "So, you ... don't want to kill me?"

The man rolled his eyes. "You're not particularly quick on the uptake, are you? This is going to be a long few days."

"Let me get this straight. Somebody paid you to protect me. Is that right?"

"Bingo."

"Who's paying you?"

"Look, this whole thing is supposed to be anonymous. The person who contracted me said you would be expecting me."

"Nobody told me anything." A sudden thought occurred to me. I pulled the mobile out of my pocket and unlocked it. The icon at the bottom of the screen signalled a single unread text message. I tapped the display and scanned the brief note from the same unknown number.

Arranged for somebody to keep you safe. I gave him an old phone.

The man studied me with folded arms. "I take it my employer contacted you after all. It's a shame you didn't bother to read your messages before dragging me all this way. Anyway, much as I enjoy this whole getting-to-know-you business, we have to get out of here. I suspect our friend will be back soon." He held out a hand. "And I need you to give me that."

"The mobile?"

He nodded.

I handed the device over to him. "What are you going to do with it?"

He prised off the case, slid open the rear cover and removed the battery. Placing it in the breast pocket of his shirt, he returned the other parts to me. "If I can track your phone, so can anybody else. Let's get a move on."

"I can't really ..." I gestured toward my injured leg.

The man shook his head. "You shouldn't have tried to run away, should you? Put your arm over my shoulder."

I did as instructed, and we hobbled side by side to the white van. The engine was still running, and the smell of exhaust fumes greeted us as he guided me to the passenger door. He helped me in, jogged around the front and climbed into the driver's seat.

"Where are we going?" I asked.

"We need to lie low for a few days. We'll stay in a cheap hotel."

"And the plan is to drive there in this?"

He twisted sideways and threw me a disdainful glance. Placing the van in gear, he swung the wheel to the left and accelerated up the service road.

"What are you planning?" I said as we took the first turn at the roundabout.

"Look, if I have to explain everything to you before we do it, it's going to get very annoying very quickly. If you want to stay alive, there's only one rule you need to remember; do exactly what I tell you when I tell you: no questions, no discussion."

I leaned back against the headrest and closed my eyes. The stench of stale urine rose in waves from my crotch.

Five minutes later, my new protector guided the van into the last remaining space in a busy car park and turned off the engine.

The man reached into the back seat and grabbed his rucksack. He pulled out a dark-blue hoodie and tossed it to me.

"Put that on," he commanded.

Seconds later he handed me a pair of sunglasses. "Pull the hood up and wear these too."

"What shall I do with this?" I asked, lifting the lightweight jumper I had removed.

"You can't leave it in here, so you need to take it with you."

"Is there room in your bag?"

The man gave me a hard stare. "What am I, your mother?"

I rolled my pullover tightly and stuffed it into the corner of the case. He studied the bulging material suspiciously. "What else is in there?"

"Only my laptop. By the way, what should I call you?"

He narrowed his eyes for a moment before replying. "You can call me Nick."

"Let me guess. That's not your real name, right? I'm Alex."

Nick grunted. He withdrew a second hoodie and slipped it over his head.

"What's the deal with the tops?" I asked.

"There are cameras everywhere. I don't want to make it too easy for anybody to track us. I'll lead the way. You follow at least ten yards behind. When you see me go into another car park, I want you to keep walking past the entrance. I'll pick you up in a few seconds. Got that?"

I nodded. "Remember I can't move too quickly at the moment."

Nick opened the driver door, leaving the keys in the ignition. I followed suit and studied him as he strode towards the main road. The pain in my leg had reduced to a persistent ache, but even so, I struggled to keep up. Gradually, the distance between us increased until he had extended the lead to thirty yards. Hobbling as fast as I could, I was relieved to see him turn into another car park. As I continued along the pavement, I watched him approach a red Ford Focus and get in.

For a fleeting moment, I contemplated whether to leave him behind. If I crossed the road now, I could disappear into the shopping centre. Without the phone to track me, he would struggle to locate me again. But what would I do after that?

Jamie clearly thought somebody was trying to kill me and had paid this man to protect me. Should I stick with him or take my chances with the police? I remembered Jamie's warning to stay away from the police, but was I any better trusting Nick? What would he do if I tried to escape a second time?

I didn't have enough information to make an informed decision. The last two days had taken their toll, and the prospect of fending for myself terrified me. I decided to stick with my new guardian for the time being, so I carried on walking.

The red Ford Focus drew up alongside. I opened the door and was about to get in when Nick held up his palm. "I don't want you getting piss all over my car. Sit on the jumper you put in your bag."

I stared at him for a few seconds without moving. My trousers were mostly dry by now. I was sorely tempted to ignore his instruction, but eventually I complied. I spread the pullover across the seat and lowered myself down, wincing at the pain from my torn muscle.

Nick pulled away from the kerb before I had time to fasten the seatbelt. I clicked the buckle home and raised my hand to lower the hoodie.

"No, leave it on," he said, keeping his eyes on the road, "and carry on wearing the sunglasses too. There are loads of traffic cameras along here, and we don't want to make it easy for them to track our movements."

"Aren't you being a bit paranoid?" I asked, turning sideways in the seat to look at him.

"Paranoia is what will keep you alive for the next few days," he replied. "Have you already forgotten what I said about no questions and no discussion?"

"Am I allowed to ask where we're going?"

"You'll find out soon enough." He reached out and clicked on the radio. The strains of a popular Duran Duran track from the eighties blared out of the speakers.

"Do you have to have it on so loud?" I asked.

In response, Nick leaned forward and turned up the dial another notch. When I extended my hand, he slapped it away. I folded my arms and sank back in the seat. The song eventually ended, and the over-enthusiastic presenter promised more music from the same era after the commercial break. As the advertisements started to play, Nick twisted the knob and reduced the volume to a more comfortable level.

We drove without speaking for another ten miles. At no point during the journey did Nick exceed the speed limit. As we approached a junction to the left, he flicked on the indicator and slowed. The green logo of a Holiday Inn sign appeared over the tops of the trees.

"This will do for now," Nick announced. "I want you to stay in the car while I book us into a room."

"There's something wrong with my card. I tried to make a payment on a website a few minutes ago, but they declined me."

Nick flashed me a disdainful look. "I don't expect you to pay. If you engaged your brain for more than a microsecond, you'd realise that credit card payments are a pretty good way of locating somebody, especially if they're charged to a hotel."

He steered into a space close to the reception. Removing the key from the ignition, he lowered his hoodie and opened the door. Before closing it, he leaned back inside. "Remember, stay here."

I watched as he strolled towards the entrance and disappeared from view. The silence was a welcome relief after twenty minutes of music I would never have chosen to listen to.

It was five fifteen by the time Nick emerged. He strode towards me, the shades hiding his eyes. He opened the door, levered himself inside and started the engine.

"Are we not staying here?" I asked.

"I'm moving it to the end of the row," he replied, apparently forgetting his directive for me to ask no questions. "If anybody comes asking, we don't want them to remember the car—although that's why I chose this model and colour. I'll also swap the number plates over when it gets dark."

When he had reversed into the space furthest from the entrance, he twisted in the seat to talk to me. "When we go in, keep the hood up and the sunglasses on. If possible, try to face away from the camera, but don't make a big thing of it. It's mounted above the reception desk."

"Okay."

"Try to act natural. The receptionist thinks we're a gay couple."

"Right. Why would she think that?"

Nick sighed and shook his head. "Two men sharing a room? And she's a he."

"It's been a long day," I muttered.

"Let's go."

I got out of the car, grabbing the jumper from the seat and stuffing it in the laptop bag. The period of inactivity had caused the torn muscle to tighten. I limped behind Nick as he made his way to the entrance. I trailed after him through the rotating door, past the reception area and towards the *All Rooms* sign. As we passed the desk, I kept my head angled away from the white dome of the camera.

"Enjoy your stay, Mr Dixon," the male receptionist called as I followed Nick through the open doorway. My protector didn't reply. He turned right and strode to the end of the corridor. There, he withdrew a keycard from his pocket and swiped it through the lock.

Nick shoved the door open and marched straight to the window. He parted the hanging blinds and stared out at the car park. The red Focus occupied the parking space right outside.

"Good," he said, tossing his rucksack on the nearest bed. "The ground floor makes it easy to get out if we have to leave in a hurry. There's also a fire escape at the end of the corridor."

"How many nights did you book us in for?"

"Two, but the receptionist told me I could always extend if necessary."

"And how long do you need to keep me alive to earn your money?"

"The contract runs until midnight on Thursday."

"What happens after that?" I asked, flopping onto the mattress.

"I record proof of life and leave. Before you ask any more questions, I have some of my own. By the way, I'm sorry if I was a bit short with you earlier."

I frowned in puzzlement. It was as if Nick's character had changed at the flick of a switch. Suddenly, he was apologising for his previous behaviour.

"In this business, it's essential to stay focused," he continued. "When we're out there, I need you to react instantly to what I tell you. If you stop to question my instructions, you will probably die. You have to trust I'm competent at what I do. I was also pissed off that I had to chase you across town." His face cracked in a grin.

I stared back at him humourlessly. "You said you had some questions."

"Yeah. Do you know who's trying to kill you?"

"No—well actually, I'm not sure. You entered the café just after another man. He's the boyfriend of the girl serving behind the counter. She's a former pupil of mine. It's possible he might be the killer."

Nick laughed. "The beefy guy? An assassin? I don't think so, not unless he's a total amateur. The secret of being successful in my line of work is to go unnoticed. If you stick out in any way, people will remember you or see you coming. Anyway, why is he after you? Did you bonk his girlfriend?"

"No, I was her teacher."

"What's that got to do with it? She looked old enough to me."

"I didn't have sex with her, okay? I suspect it's all tied back to the dark web."

Nick's eyes narrowed. "You better explain. I need to hear everything, no matter how unimportant it may seem."

I started with finding the note on the day of the murder and took him through my statement to the police and the appearance of the three policemen at my house. He allowed me to talk, only stopping me to ask an occasional question. I described the visit to my brother-in-law and his reluctance to speak to me. I ended with the text message containing the new login details, the blocking of my bank card, and the simultaneous arrival of Molly's boyfriend and Nick at the café.

Nick scratched his cheek. "It sounds like you've got yourself involved with the wrong people. I take it you don't know what the police were looking for on your computer."

"Not a clue. Jamie—he's my brother-in-law—told me to stay away from them."

"Good advice in my experience," Nick said with a grin.

"I assume Jamie hired you," I asked.

"That's the most likely scenario from what I've heard. The whole point of the dark web thing is anonymity, though, so I can't be sure who I'm really working for."

"How will you get paid?"

"I use an encrypted messaging app to send and receive messages. Payment is in Bitcoin."

A sudden thought occurred to me. "What exactly did the job description say?"

Nick fixed me with a stare. When he spoke, his voice was subdued. "It was originally for a killing."

"You're saying you accepted it expecting you were going to have to kill someone?"

"When the person who placed the contract contacted me to provide the details, he offered me a fifty per cent bonus to turn it into a protection assignment. He also added five hundred quid in expenses. That's what is paying for this room."

"Let me get this straight. You perform executions for a living?"

Nick folded his arms. "Don't judge me. I joined the armed forces at age eighteen and gave twenty years of my life in the service of my country, travelling to the arse end of nowhere and killing people on behalf of the government. The only difference is now I get paid properly for doing the same thing. When I left the army, I drifted in and out of a few jobs. The exact details aren't important.

"My skills aren't exactly transferable to civilian work, so I'm basically unemployable. Yeah, I could earn minimum wage stacking shelves or working as a bouncer, but what sort of existence is that? By taking on this job, I'll take home more in a few days than most people make in two or three months. In any case, most of the targets who wind up dead are criminals themselves, so they're no great loss to society.

"For example, one of my contacts told me that guy who was murdered on Monday was into drugs and prostitution in a big way. Whoever knocked him off was doing us all a favour."

"It wasn't you, was it?" I asked.

The grin returned to Nick's face. "Well, if it was me, I wouldn't tell you, now would I? So, there's no real point asking."

Another question occurred to me. "What time today did you accept the contract?"

Nick raised his eyes in thought. "It must have been one-thirty, two o'clock."

"The timing is wrong. The job I saw on the site when I was in the café couldn't have been the one Jamie placed."

"No, I accepted mine at least two hours earlier."

"Which means there are two separate jobs. Somebody else is trying to kill me."

Nick shrugged. "It looks that way. But don't worry; you've got me to protect you."

"Until Thursday midnight," I added.

"Yes, until Thursday," he agreed.

The conversation lapsed into silence.

I broke it by asking another question. "If you aren't sure that Jamie placed the contract, how did you get my sister's phone?"

"The pink thing with stars? He put it in a plastic bag, hid it and sent me a message telling me where to find it. I have no use for it anymore. You may as well take it back."

Nick rummaged in his rucksack, pulled out Cathy's mobile and removed the rear cover. "I'll hang onto the battery for the moment if that's alright. It's not that I don't trust you, but it would be best if there was no temptation."

"Can't the authorities track a phone even if it isn't turned on?"

Nick laughed. "You've seen too many spy films. How can it send a signal if there's no power?"

"I've no idea how mobile phones work."

"Believe me; it won't be a problem."

"Right."

"Anyway, I'm going to take a shower. Don't leave the room and don't open the door to anybody."

Nick pulled the hoodie over his head and stripped off the T-shirt beneath. As he turned towards the bathroom, I couldn't help but notice the puckered scar on his left shoulder blade and the blue tattoos ringing his biceps.

Nick emerged from the bathroom fifteen minutes later with a towel wrapped around his waist.

"It's all yours," he said as he stretched out on top of the bed.

I limped through the doorway, turning the lock behind me. A curtain of humid air, tinged with a fruity scent, hit me as I entered. The small, white-tiled room contained a toilet, a washbasin and a shower. A thick layer of condensation coated the mirror above the sink. A stack of towels occupied a metal rack to the right of the porcelain bowl. Two white towelling dressing gowns hung from a hook on the back of the door.

I stripped out of my clothes and leaned into the cubicle to turn on the water. When it had reached a comfortable temperature, I stepped inside and cranked the dial towards the hot end. The jets scalded my skin as I shuffled from side to side, trying to wash away the memories of the day. I remained under the flow until clouds of steam filled the small room.

Shutting off the tap, I grabbed a towel and approached the sink. I wiped the mirror with the palm of my hand and leaned forward to inspect my reflection. The face staring back at me belonged to a stranger. How could I have changed from an ordinary person who taught teenagers English to somebody who needed a bodyguard to protect him from a hitman in the space of fewer than two days?

The condensation quickly misted the surface. I glanced at the heap of discarded clothes. The thought of putting them on again in their currents state didn't appeal. I cracked the door and peered through the gap. Nick lay in the position I had left him with his hands behind his head.

"Are we eating out tonight?" I asked.

Nick snapped his gaze in my direction. "We need to keep you out of sight. There's a takeaway around the corner, so I'll get something from there in a bit."

"I was going to wash my clothes after ... Anyway, they should be dry by morning if I leave them on the radiator."

Nick's lips twisted in a malicious grin. "Good idea. I don't want to spend three days cooped up in here with you stinking of piss."

I closed the door, turned on the hot tap and filled the sink. Pushing my jeans and boxer shorts under the water, I added the contents of one of the mini shower gel bottles and worked it into the fabric. It took a long time to rinse all the soap out, but eventually, I wrung the clothes dry and draped them over the radiator. Tomorrow, a floral scent would follow me around, but it was far better than the alternative.

I grabbed a white dressing gown from the back of the door and returned to the bedroom. When I entered, Nick was fully clothed and bent over tying a shoelace.

He looked up at me. "I'm going out to get something to eat. Is a burger okay? I'll shop for other supplies tomorrow."

I wasn't a great fan of fast food but didn't care enough to object. "Yeah, fine."

Nick straightened up. "The same rules apply as before. Don't open the door to anybody. Keep the curtains closed. Don't wander off anywhere. I'll be back in a few minutes."

The latch clicked as the door swung shut behind him. I picked up the television remote control from the writing desk and flopped onto the bed. I prodded the power button and flicked through the channels. The first two stations were showing advertisements. The BBC six o'clock news had just started on the third channel. As I switched over, a male newscaster finished announcing the headlines.

The main story focused on the politician who had failed to declare his membership on the board of a company, which had received government grants. The man had finally bowed to pressure from both his colleagues and the press and resigned his seat. I found it hard to believe only twenty-four hours had passed since this had been breaking news on the night I first learned about the killings. A lot had changed for me in that time. Two days ago, I had been looking forward to six weeks of vacation. Here I was now, stuck in a hotel room with a professional hitman for protection, hiding from somebody who wanted to kill me.

Half an hour passed with no mention of the murders. Nick had still not returned when the programme ended, and the theme tune for the regional news started. I glanced at my watch even though I knew the time. All thoughts of Nick's whereabouts vanished when I heard the headlines and saw my face plastered across the television screen.

"The hunt is on tonight for a local man suspected of involvement in child pornography. Police have issued an arrest warrant for Alex Parrott, aged thirty-four, a teacher of English at a secondary school in Fleet, Hampshire. They are seeking the help of the public in tracking down the suspect.

"Mr Parrott disappeared from his home shortly after officers searched the premises and removed computing devices for further analysis. A spokesman urged anybody who might know of Mr Parrott's whereabouts to come forward. While it is not believed he poses any specific danger, official advice is to call the emergency services rather than approaching him directly. There will be more on this story in our later bulletin at ten-thirty."

The blood drained from my face. A block of ice formed in my stomach. I stared at the screen in disbelief. A whooshing sound rushed in my ears. Scrabbling across the bed, I pulled the laptop from its case, plugged the power lead into the wall and turned it on. I waited impatiently for the machine to complete its start-up sequence.

While it booted, I grabbed the brown, leather-covered booklet from the dressing table and scanned the contents for the Wi-Fi passcode. After what seemed a lifetime, the password box popped up. With trembling fingers, I typed in my abducted sister's name and the date of her disappearance. After another interminable wait, the desktop appeared. I immediately clicked on the wireless network icon. *Holiday Inn Guest* occupied the top spot in the listed connections. I transposed the code and started a browser window.

I figured the quickest way to get more facts was to search for my own name. A long list of news websites headed the results. Topmost was the BBC page. I selected the link. My eye ran down the screen, scanning the text. There was little additional information above what I had already heard on the television. I tried several other pages but discovered nothing new.

I switched off the laptop and returned it to its case moments before the door to the room opened. The odour of fast food wafting from the bag clutched in Nick's hand turned my stomach. I scrambled off the bed and rushed into the bathroom, the pain from my damaged calf muscle wiped from my mind. Hunched over the toilet, I dry heaved several times before the bile rose in my throat, flooding my mouth with the acrid taste of vomit.

Nick followed me in and stared down at me, an expression of consternation on his face. "Is something wrong?"

I spat into the bowl, my arms still wrapped around the white porcelain. Slowly, I raised my eyes and met his gaze. Another heave forced me to bend over the plastic seat rim again.

When I was certain the spasm had passed, I reached for the toilet roll holder, tore off a few sheets and wiped my mouth. Nick watched on.

I shook my head without replying. With agonising slowness, I pushed myself upright. The damage to my calf muscle broke through the fog that had settled on my mind, causing me to gasp in pain.

I turned to Nick, resting my weight on the good leg. "The television. Local news." My brain seemed incapable of stringing together a coherent sentence.

A frown creased Nick's brow. "What are you saying? You saw something on the TV?"

I closed my eyes and placed a hand on my forehead. My skin felt clammy. How could I even begin to explain? Discovering that somebody wanted me dead was shocking enough, but I had pushed that thought to the back of my mind. In some ways, it hadn't seemed real. Up to that point, I had considered myself the victim. I had consoled myself by hoping to clear up everything with the police and resuming my life as normal afterwards.

The sight of my photograph on the television screen for everybody in the country to see pushed it to a whole new level. Now they were portraying me as the perpetrator. Any hopes I may have harboured about returning to my job when this was all over had just vaporised.

For a teacher, even the slightest hint of impropriety with a student would result in instant suspension. Having my face splashed across the media accused of paedophilia had effectively ended my career. Whether or not it was true, no parent would entrust me with their child's education after such an accusation.

"The local news," I said in a dull voice. "They showed my picture saying I was wanted for child pornography."

Nick suddenly went still. His gaze burned into me. "You're not a nonce, are you?"

"A nonce?"

"Yeah, you know, a kiddie fiddler, paedophile, whatever you want to call it."

I shook my head. "Of course not."

Nick studied me for a moment longer, then seemed to relax. "I can't stand those bastards. If you were one of them, I'd walk out of here and leave you to it however much someone offered me to protect you. In fact, I'd hand you over myself."

He paused, his brows lowered in deliberation. "They're trying to flush you out." Seeing my confusion, he continued as if explaining to a child. "If somebody is attempting to kill you, they can't do that if they don't know where you are. By getting your face on the news, they're hoping the public will help to locate you."

I nodded in understanding.

"Depending upon who it is that wants you dead, they may well have people in prison who can do their work for them. More likely though, if somebody reports your location, they pass it on and try to get to you first. After all, they won't want you spilling your guts."

"What do we do next?" I asked, my voice quivering with tension.

"We sit tight and make sure nobody sees you."

"And what happens at the end of the week?"

Nick narrowed his eyes for a second but didn't respond. He glanced down at the bag in his hand as if suddenly aware of its presence. "I'm starving. Let's get stuck into this."

My appetite had deserted me, but I followed him back into the bedroom. The television flickered on the far wall. The news programme had finished, and the pictures showed a daily current affairs show.

Nick plonked himself on the edge of the bed and rummaged in the takeaway bag before withdrawing a package wrapped in greaseproof paper. He handed it over, stuck his hand inside again and retrieved a carton of French fries. Despite my lack of hunger, my stomach growled at the pervasive odour of warm food.

Nick took a large bite from his own beef burger. I forced myself to follow suit, sinking my teeth into the soggy bun as the grease stained my fingers.

I ate in silence, my brain rattling through my predicament, trying to find a solution that didn't exist.

At that stage, I had no idea my situation was about to become even worse.

Richard T. Burke

Time passed slowly. The remains of my half-eaten burger lay in its wrapping at the bottom of the waste bin where I had tossed it after forcing myself to eat. A knot lodged in my stomach although I couldn't tell whether it originated from the food or nervous tension. The heavy smell of cooking fat still permeated the room, rising in waves from the discarded packaging.

With nothing else to do, Nick and I watched a documentary on global warming. Despite my attempts to follow the programme, I found my attention wandering as I mulled over the events of the day.

When the ten o'clock news started, Nick turned up the volume. There was no mention of either the murders or the police hunt for me on the national programme. When it came to the regional news, the information was largely the same as earlier, but this time the story included a short video segment. A reporter stood on the road where I lived.

"Yes, Jenny, I'm standing outside the home of secondary school teacher, Alex Parrott. Police are eager to question him about data of an unspecified nature discovered on the hard disk of his computer. We understand the material includes images of naked children. Parents at the college where Mr Parrott teaches are said to be deeply concerned. Questions have been raised about how he passed background checks.

"Mr Parrott hasn't been seen since earlier today and is believed to have gone into hiding. The police are urging members of the public to come forward if they have any information as to his whereabouts. Although not considered dangerous, a spokesman advising that Mr Parrott should not be approached directly."

The camera returned to a middle-aged woman sitting behind a desk in the studio. "Thanks, Jack. You can read more about this story on the BBC website. In other news—"

Nick clicked the remote control, muting the sound but leaving the picture turned on. He twisted sideways on his bed and stared at me for a second before speaking. "From what you've told me, it seems likely the two men your neighbour saw outside your house broke in and planted the evidence on your computer."

"Why would they do that?" I asked, returning his stare. "I mean, other than ruining my career, what were they hoping to achieve?"

"My guess is, they were trying to discredit you. They must believe you know something they don't want the police to hear. By setting you up, they made it far less likely that anybody would listen to your story."

I sank back on the pillow. "But why take the risk of breaking in? If they were going to put the photographs on my computer, why not do it when they came with the search warrant?"

"You mentioned there were three policemen," Nick said. "I imagine they didn't know in advance if they would have the opportunity to be left alone with the machine. The other possibility is they were worried about having enough time to load all the data. How long did your neighbour say they were there for?"

"I think she told me ten or fifteen minutes," I replied.

"That's probably it, then. The third policeman might have become suspicious if they spent a quarter of an hour with your computer—always assuming he's not involved too."

The conversation halted, both of us pondering the implications. As the thoughts wormed through my head, a sudden question sprang to mind. "Can't they work out when a photograph was added to a hard drive?"

Nick shrugged. "I'm no expert, but you could well be right. It's possible to change the date of a file. Maybe that's why they took so long."

"But surely—"

Nick cut me off. "Look, I don't know enough about it. Rather than worrying about the computer, the first priority is to keep you alive. It would help if I knew what—or more to the point who—we were up against."

"What's the plan?" I asked.

"I need to have a think. Normally the boot is on the other foot, and I'm the one doing the tracking down."

"How would *you* go about finding me?"

"That depends. Most of the time, the target isn't aware that somebody is targeting them, so it's a lot easier. If I had access to CCTV cameras, I'd start there. My guess is they're hoping a member of the public will call in with your location. For that reason, it's essential nobody sees you."

"What about the cleaning staff?" I asked. "Won't they want to get into the room to clean the place?"

"We can put the don't disturb sign on the door, but I can't guarantee they'll pay any attention to it. Ideally, we could do with somewhere with no chance of being disturbed. Do you have any bright ideas?"

"Could we break into an empty house or something?"

Nick rolled his eyes. "We also need a location that isn't going to raise suspicions. If the neighbours were to see somebody inside a property that's supposed to be unoccupied, the police would be round faster than a ferret up a trouser leg."

"Okay, so what about a holiday rental?"

Nick rubbed his fingers across the stubble on his cheek. "Possibly, but that sounds like it might be expensive."

"I've saved some money for ... Shit, I forgot; my card got declined." I reddened at the stupidity of my suggestion. "And you already told me it's easy to track."

Nick swung his legs off the bed. "We'll be alright for tonight. Let me think it over. I'm going out to change the number plates."

"Why are you doing that?" I asked.

My protector stared at me as if the answer was obvious. "If by some chance, they picked us up on a traffic camera, they won't be able to track our movements if I swap over the plates."

"Where do you get the numbers from? Do you just choose them randomly?"

Nick shook his head. "No. The police would pick up on that straight away. I go to the second-hand car sales websites and look for ones with the same make and colour as mine. That's the main reason I drive a red Ford Focus; it's one of the most common models you can buy.

"Most of the pages either list the registration or have photos that include the plates. Then I contact my mate who puts together a copy. The fact that most of the vehicles are sitting on a garage forecourt makes it even less likely that anybody would ever spot two identical looking cars with the same number plate driving around at the same time. I've made them magnetic so I can change them over quickly."

Much as I wanted to wipe the smug expression off his face, this was the man whose expertise would keep me alive, so I chose to remain silent.

"I'll only be a minute or two," he said, pulling the door shut behind him.

I rested my head on the pillow and closed my eyes. A few seconds later, I picked up the muffled sound of a car boot opening. Sliding across the bed, I rose and slowly tugged back the edge of the blinds. Nick knelt at the front of the red Focus, apparently unaware of my surveillance.

As I watched, he used a screwdriver to lever off the existing plate and replaced it with one from a bundle at his feet. With a quick glance around, he moved to the rear of the vehicle. There, he crouched down and disappeared from my line of sight. Seconds later, he reappeared, leant inside the open boot, then straightened up and slammed it down. A chirrup accompanied the flash of the indicators as he pressed the lock button on the key.

Still oblivious to my scrutiny, Nick turned towards the main entrance. He hesitated for a moment as his hand reached to his back pocket. As he moved out of range of my vantage point, I picked out the bright glow of a mobile phone screen held to his ear.

Richard T. Burke

Twenty-five years ago: Wednesday, 8th February, 1995

*A*t the sound of the approaching siren, Cathy pushed herself upright and opened the under stairs cupboard. *"Here,"* she said, holding out my black woollen coat. *"Put this on."* She shrugged her narrow shoulders into her own and stepped outside once again.

My mother stood in the road, waving frantically as the blue flashing lights approached. A white police car steered onto the drive. The abrupt cessation of the siren made the subsequent silence seem all the deeper.

Two policemen emerged from the vehicle. One of them removed a notebook from his black jacket and began to ask my mother questions. Cathy and I hung back a few yards. My gaze focused on a white mark on the second man's trousers. He followed the direction of my stare and rubbed self-consciously at the stain. The adults spoke in low voices. After a few minutes, my mother turned and beckoned me forwards.

The policeman taking notes patted me on the head and addressed me with a cheery voice. "Hello, young chap." The streetlight gave his bald patch an orange hue.

"Tell them what you saw, Alex," my mother said.

"Um ... A noise woke me up. I looked outside, and this man was standing just there." I gestured toward the spot from which the kidnapper had stared up at me. "Elena—she's my sister—was lying on the ground. She wasn't moving."

The policeman studied the frontage of the house. "Which one is your room?"

I turned and pointed upwards. Mine was the only window with open curtains.

"Can you describe him?"

The moment I had been dreading had arrived. Once again, I desperately tried to bring to mind the abductor's face. No matter how hard I concentrated on recalling his features, the only aspect I could picture was his dark attire.

"I ... I ... I'm not sure."

"For Christ's sake," my mother yelled, "tell him what you saw."

That set me off crying again. I stared helplessly at the two policemen.

114

"Come on, son," the one with the stain said. "You can't have been more than ten or twenty yards away. Surely you can remember something about him."

I shook my head, mutely.

"What was he wearing?"

I drew in a deep breath. "Black."

"Are you saying he was dressed in black or his skin was black?"

"He wore black clothes."

The note taker wrote a few words in his book and smiled at me. "That's a start. What else? Was he young or old? Tall or short?"

I wiped my nose on my sleeve. My mother opened her mouth to speak, then caught the eye of my interrogator and remained silent.

"He was a grown up and about the same height as you."

"Your mother said you watched him drive off. Can you describe the car?"

Another shake of my head. "I didn't really see it. I think it might have been a dark colour."

The policeman tapped his pen against his teeth. He turned to my mother. "We haven't got much to go on. I'll get the sketch artist to work with him in the morning. Could you bring him down to the station at around nine o'clock?"

She stared at him. "Is that it? Is that all you're going to do?"

The man looked to the side, unable to hold her gaze. "We'll put out an alert for a dark-coloured car. The forensic officers will be here shortly. They'll want to go over your daughter's room, scan for prints and so on. I need to ask you some more questions. It's a bit cold out here. Can we continue inside?"

My mother nodded and turned away. She marched into the porch without looking behind to check whether anyone was following. Upon reaching the door to the lounge, she stood to the side and ushered the policemen towards the sofa.

As Cathy and I made to follow, she blocked the way. "You two should go back to bed." We both protested, but she was adamant. Eventually, after several exchanges, she screamed, "Just go upstairs as I've told you." Tears glinted in her eyes, and she lifted a shaky hand to brush them away. Neither my sister nor I had seen our mother behave in this manner before. Normally, she was the picture of calmness. If anybody in our family had a temper, it was my father.

My lip quivered as I tried desperately not to cry again. Cathy put an arm around me. "Come on. I'll tuck you in."

More often than not, we quarrelled at the slightest excuse, but at that moment in time, I'd never felt closer to my sister. I allowed her to guide me along the hallway. At the foot of the stairs, she had to release me; the staircase was too narrow to ascend side by side.

We trudged up to my room in single file. At the top, both of us stopped to stare at the open door of Elena's bedroom.

"Do you think they'll find her?" I whispered.

Cathy didn't reply immediately. Then she said, "Yes," but the hesitation belied her true thoughts.

"Why did that man take her? What's he going to do to her?"

My sister shook her head. "I don't know, but I'm sure the police will get her back."

As it turned out, she was wrong.

Day Three:
Wednesday, 29th July, 2020

Richard T. Burke

I didn't sleep much that night. The peril of my situation, the unfamiliar room and the presence of another person lying in the adjacent bed all contrived to disturb my rest. Several times, I jerked upright in the darkness, my heart pounding like a piledriver until my addled brain eventually caught up and made sense of my surroundings. The sounds of the plumbing clanking into life ensured I remained awake as soon as the first light edged around the curtains.

Nick slept in the adjacent bed, seemingly unaffected by either the change in environment or the noises of the hotel waking up. When I questioned him about it the following morning, he explained that his time in the army had taught him to take advantage of moments of inaction whenever the opportunity arose.

I hadn't mentioned the mobile phone because I was unsure how he would react to what might be construed as a case of me spying on him. That wasn't to say I didn't have questions about the person he had contacted and the subject of the call. I tried to reassure myself there was a rational explanation, but I couldn't help worrying something was going on he was keeping from me.

When Nick left to buy breakfast, I used the time to take a shower. As expected, my hand-washed underwear reeked of the flowery scented gel. My jeans felt like cardboard as I wedged my legs inside. A couple of damp patches persisted, but I figured they would dry quickly as I wore them.

I had just finished towelling my hair when Nick returned carrying a paper bag. "Two sausage, bacon and egg rolls coming up," he announced, reaching in and handing me a greasy package. "Eat up because we're moving on today."

I stopped in mid-bite. "What?"

Nick spoke through a mouthful of food. "We're leaving. Soon."

"I don't understand. I thought you reserved the room for two nights."

"That's right. But it doesn't mean we have to stay for the whole duration. When you mentioned holiday rentals yesterday, that got me thinking. I've booked a place for a few days through Airbnb. It's cheaper than here, and we aren't likely to be disturbed either. We'll go after we've eaten."

"Is that what you were doing on the phone last night?"

Nick lowered the hand holding his greasy meal. He fixed me with a hard stare. After a pause of a few seconds, he spoke. "That's right, but I didn't know you were spying on me."

"I ... I wasn't. When I looked out of the window, I saw the light from the screen."

His eyes narrowed. "It's not part of the job description to tell you everything I'm doing. Somebody is paying me a lot of money to keep you alive, so I suggest you let me fulfil the contract how I see fit."

"Of course," I said, sheepishly. "Whatever you say."

I finished the food in silence, trying not to think too much about the damage it was doing to my coronary arteries. Nick told me to wear the hoodie and the sunglasses then performed a quick sweep of the room.

He hefted the small rucksack onto his back and headed to the door. "Have you got everything?"

The only possessions I had brought with me other than the clothes I stood in were inside the laptop carry case. I raised the bag. "Everything's packed."

"Are you going to be able to walk okay?"

My calf still ached badly, sending shooting pains up my leg whenever I placed my weight on it. "I'll manage," I replied, "just don't ask me to run."

Nick strode along the corridor as I hobbled behind. When he reached the sign pointing to the reception area, he stopped and turned back to me. "Remember, the camera is above the desk. Keep your head facing away. You go first."

I was about to push my way through the swing doors when I spotted two people through the small square window. They had their backs to me and were deep in discussion with the receptionist. They looked vaguely familiar from behind, but initially, I didn't recognise them. One of them turned, removed a photograph from his jacket and showed it to the woman. The breath caught in my throat. Standing in the reception area were the two policemen who had searched my house.

I stepped back from the door, bumping into Nick. He threw me a puzzled look.

"It's the police," I hissed, "the ones who planted the stuff on my computer."

"Shit," he muttered, his head swivelling as he scanned our location. "How the hell did they find us?" The corridor was symmetrical, extending forty yards in both directions through a pair of fire doors halfway along the length. If the two policemen came through from reception now, whichever route we took, they would see us.

Richard T. Burke

"Quick, this way," he said, placing his shoulder beneath my right arm, the side of my injured calf. He dragged me in the opposite direction from our room. At any moment I expected a shout from behind. We barged through the swing doors.

Instead of continuing, he released his hold. "Keep going to the end and wait there."

I limped along the corridor, casting anxious backward glances every few paces. Nick crouched by the glass window with his back to me. Eventually, I made it to my objective. A green sign read, *Fire door. Push bar to open.*

Nick remained in position. One minute turned into two. After what seemed like an age, he rose to his full height and jogged towards me.

"They're heading to our room," he said when he reached me.

"How did they track us down?" I asked.

"I've no idea. Now, no more questions, I need to think."

His gaze ran around the periphery of the emergency exit. "As I expected, the door's got sensors," he muttered. "If we open it, the receptionist will know straight away."

"What are we going to do?"

Nick snapped his attention back to me. "I told you to shut up. Keep quiet and do as I say."

I raised my eyebrows but said nothing. It seemed he had reverted to parade-ground-sergeant-major mode. He paced backwards and forwards several times before apparently coming to a decision.

"Wait here." Turning away, he jogged along the corridor, retracing his steps. When he reached the swing doors, he peered through the window then eased his way through. I adjusted my position to see what he was doing, but as they swung closed, only a thin parcel of light remained. Seconds later, Nick reappeared. He beckoned for me to come closer.

When I eventually arrived, he shook his head. "Jesus, can't you move any faster?" Before I could reply, he continued. "They're still in there. I'm going to go through first and bring the car around to the main entrance. Have you got a watch?"

I raised my left wrist.

"Right, give it thirty seconds then follow me out. Don't approach the door until it's time. Like I said before, keep your head turned away from the camera. As soon as you're outside, move straight to the car and get in. Is that clear?"

I nodded. As Nick entered the reception area, I glanced at the analogue dial of my watch. The second hand seemed to creep around far too slowly. Had it stopped working correctly? I forced myself to breathe deeply. When the time was up, I pushed myself away from the wall and shoved my way through the swing doors.

"Good morning, sir," the female receptionist called. "Have a great day."

I hobbled towards the exit without replying, acutely aware of her eyes burning into me like a pair of lasers. As I emerged, the sudden brightness caused me to blink despite the sunglasses. I didn't have time to examine my surroundings before Nick's red Ford Focus drew up alongside me. He leaned over and shoved open the door for me.

I sank into the passenger seat with a sigh.

"Let's get out of here," Nick said, depressing the accelerator before I had even fastened my seatbelt.

I pulled the strap across and clicked it home as the car surged out onto the main road.

"Damn," he muttered under his breath. "That was close."

I turned around in my seat, trying to see if there was any sign of pursuit.

"Face the front," Nick snapped, his eyes flicking to the rearview mirror.

We drove in silence for several minutes. Finally, his grip on the steering wheel relaxed. "I'm fairly certain they aren't following us."

"How do you think they found us?"

Nick frowned. "That's a very good question."

"They didn't track your phone, did they?"

A small vein pulsed at his left temple, and his jaw muscles contracted rhythmically. When he spoke, his voice trembled with suppressed anger. "If there's any doubt in your mind that you'd have a better chance of survival without me, I'll drop you off somewhere this very minute and sod the money."

The ticking of the indicator suddenly sounded incredibly loud within the confines of the small car.

"Well?" he said, flashing a quick glance in my direction. "What's it to be?"

"You're the expert," I replied in a quiet tone, staring straight ahead.

"That's right. For your information, the phone I used last night hadn't been used before, and it won't be used again. It's what we *experts* ..."—he paused to let the word sink in—"... refer to as a burner."

"I'm sorry. I didn't mean to—"

He cut me off before I could complete the sentence. "I'm not a bloody amateur, alright? However they tracked us down, it wasn't through the mobile."

"How did they do it?" A sudden, awful thought sprang into my mind. "It's not possible to track a laptop, is it?"

Nick turned sideways in the seat. His eyes bored into me. "You're not telling me you connected to the Wi-Fi, are you?"

I swallowed hard. My silence provided the answer to his question.

"Jesus Christ. What's wrong with you? Are you trying to get yourself killed?"

"How can they do that?"

Nick ignored my question and turned on the radio. It was the same channel as the previous day. An old Madonna hit blared out of the speakers, preventing any further conversation. The song finished, and the presenter announced a commercial break before the news at the top of the hour.

Two minutes later, the advertisement for a local car dealership offered a never to be repeated offer followed by a rushed list of disclaimers. A short jingle preceded the headlines, read by a woman with a high-pitched, nasal voice. Each item received no more than twenty seconds.

The fourth story mentioned me by name. "In today's regional news, suspected paedophile, Alex Parrott, is still on the run. Police now believe the wanted school teacher is suffering from a minor injury sustained during his flight from law enforcement officers. A spokesman stated that a second, unnamed individual is thought to be assisting him. Chief Superintendent Andrew Jackson of the Hampshire Constabulary had this to say."

A man with a slight Welsh accent took over. "The suspect is in his early thirties and may be suffering from a damaged leg, causing him to limp. Witnesses have described seeing another person aiding Mr Parrott. If members of the public have any information on either of the two men's whereabouts, please contact the police as soon as possible."

The female newsreader resumed for the final item. "And finally, pop sensation, Adele, is—"

Nick reached forward and pressed the off button. "It's a safe assumption they know I'm helping you. They must have spoken to the van driver at the shopping centre."

"But I told him you were trying to kill me."

"It may have taken them a while, but it seems they worked it out eventually."

"Look, I apologise for using the laptop. It didn't occur to me they could track me through it."

Nick stared straight ahead. "Do me a favour and don't turn the bloody thing on again. For all we know, it could have been something else. Somebody might have seen us and called it in."

"It looks like we left the hotel at the right time. Why do you think only the two of them turned up?"

Nick drummed his fingers on the steering wheel. "Maybe they were there to finish the job themselves."

"What? You mean to kill me?"

He shook his head. "Thinking about it, that's unlikely. If you'd ended up dead, the receptionist would have mentioned their involvement. They can't afford to leave any loose ends."

A sudden idea occurred to me. "What if they wanted us to see them?"

Nick shrugged his shoulders. "I don't understand what you're saying."

"You just said they couldn't do anything to me at the hotel because there were witnesses. But what if their intention was to flush us out so they could deal with us somewhere else with nobody watching?"

Nick's gaze darted to the rearview mirror. "There's no sign of them at the moment."

"Let's hope it stays that way. They might have worked out where we've been, but they don't know where we're going next."

He sighed. "I'll have to change the number plates again. The bloody things aren't cheap."

"I'm sure you can afford it with the money you're making from this job."

"That may be the case, but it also means we'll need to take another precaution." A malicious grin worked its way onto his face.

"Why do I get the feeling I'm not going to like this?" I asked.

The grin widened. "Because you'll be lying in the boot where nobody can see you."

I tried to argue that I would not be visible if I lay across the rear seat, but Nick was adamant. He found an open gate leading into a field and parked the car so the hedge obscured it from the road. I stretched my legs while Nick swapped the number plates for the second time in twenty-four hours.

"Where are we going?" I asked.

"It's a surprise."

"Okay, well how long will it take us to get there?"

Nick relented. "It's only half an hour away. We'll be there before you even know it."

He wrapped the spare plates in a cloth and opened the boot, gesturing for me to climb in. I clambered over the bumper and lay on my back. He leaned forward with the bundle.

"Hang on," I said. "You're not planning on putting those in here with me, are you? They'll slide all over the place."

Nick studied me for a second, then shrugged and moved to the side of the vehicle. I heard him deposit the package somewhere inside the car. Returning to the rear, he grinned at me.

"Enjoy the ride."

I shook my head but said nothing. Seconds later, I was plunged into darkness as the hatch slammed with a thud. The rumble of the engine reverberated through the floor. A clunk from the gearbox signalled we were about to move off. The first few yards were the worst as the suspension failed to dampen the undulations from the rutted tyre tracks leading into the field.

After the initial series of jolts, the car accelerated, and the ride became a little smoother. Even so, the noise levels were far higher than in the passenger cabin. Every turn in the road led to me sliding across the rough, black carpet. Cursing under my breath, I braced my legs against one side of the confined space and angled my body so my head and shoulder butted up against the other. The pressure on my injured calf muscle sent a stab of pain shooting up my leg.

I twisted sideways to determine whether that would make the trip more comfortable, but there was no give in the floor panel where it pressed into me, so I soon resumed my original position. The faint sound of eighties music penetrated through the rear seats, mingling with the drone of the engine.

The journey passed slowly. I tried to picture the route we were following but gave up after a few miles. After what seemed like a lifetime, the long, straight stretches became fewer and farther between. I guessed we were coming into a town. Soon we were spending a greater proportion of our time stationary.

Nick's voice rose above the music. "Come on, you dozy idiot."

A car horn tooted although I couldn't tell whether it was ours or somebody else's.

The note of exasperation increased. "Oh, for crying out loud, are you waiting for a written invitation?"

Finally, we moved off again. A sudden burst of acceleration sent me sliding sideways. "Moron!" Nick yelled from the front.

After that, we made steady progress until the floor slowly tipped forwards, and the sound of traffic died away. We remained stationary for a moment, and a series of beeps reached my ears. It sounded like Nick was typing in a code. The tyres screeched on concrete as the car manoeuvred around several tight bends. Eventually, all movement stopped, and the engine turned off.

Despite the low light levels, I shielded my eyes against the sudden brightness as Nick lifted the boot. I sat up and clambered out.

"Did you enjoy the trip?" he asked.

Wincing as I put pressure on my leg, I shook my head. "Not particularly. I'd rather spend an afternoon at the dentist having root canal work done on my wisdom teeth."

"It reminds me of the old joke about why dogs are better than women."

When I said nothing, he continued anyway, an amused expression on his face. "Lock your wife and dog in the boot of a car. Keep them there for three hours then let them out and see which one is more pleased to see you."

I couldn't help smiling despite my bad mood. "Well, I'm neither your dog nor your wife, and I have no intention of doing that again any time soon. Where are we?"

"An underground garage in Reading. The flat I've rented comes with a parking space. Even if the police were on the lookout for my car, it's unlikely they'd ever find it down here."

"How big is this place we're staying in?"

"It's got two bedrooms with kitchen, lounge and dining room. The owners are away for a fortnight, so they've left the keys in a lock box in the lobby. I suggest you wait here while I pick them up."

"Can I sit in the front?" I asked sarcastically. "Or do I have to lie down in the boot again?"

"I'm feeling generous, so I'll let you remain where you are."

I sighed with pleasure as I sank into the soft fabric. Tilting the seat back, I closed my eyes and waited for Nick to return. Ten minutes later, he tapped on the window.

"Time to wake up. To get inside, there's a door with a keypad. The code is three six three one, got that? I don't want anybody to see us together, so you make your way in first. Call a lift and go up to the eighth floor. Here's the key. It's flat eight one one—the number's written on the fob. I'll follow you. And if you could possibly not limp, that would be good."

"I'll do my best."

Nick led me to a staircase and up two flights of stairs. "Remember, three six three one. Keep your hood up and the sunglasses on. I didn't spot any cameras, but there may be hidden ones."

I nodded and pushed my way through the door. The foyer was twice as long as it was wide with post box lockers lining one wall. A pair of tall, leafy potted plants sat on either side of a deserted desk. Ahead of me at the far end was another doorway with a keypad mounted beside it. I crossed the room, doing my best to walk with an even stride despite nobody being around to observe me. I tapped out the digits, and the lock opened with a click.

Two lifts lay diagonally to my left. I prodded the call button, and the doors on my right parted immediately. The control panel contained buttons labelled from G up to twelve. Moments after selecting the eighth floor, the metal panels swished shut, and the lift surged upwards. I emerged onto a dark-blue carpeted corridor and made my way to the sixth door on the right.

A narrow hallway with a bedroom on either side extended into a living area. The bedrooms were identical in size with barely enough space to walk around the double beds. I tossed my laptop bag on the bed in the room on the left. The lounge contained a pair of two-seater settees arranged in front of a large flat-screen television. A wooden writing desk butted up to the patterned wallpaper. A floor to ceiling patio window opened onto a small balcony containing three plastic chairs. Set in the adjacent wall, an archway led into a combined kitchen and dining room.

I was looking out onto the concrete square below when a tapping sound originated from the outside corridor. It took me a while to hobble along the hall. As my hand reached for the handle, I heard voices on the other side. Unsure what to do, I undid the latch and pulled it towards me, opening a crack between door and frame.

Nick was speaking to somebody out of my line of sight. "Well, it's very kind of you, but we'll be very busy over the next few days."

A female voice replied. "That's a shame. If you do get time, I'd be happy to cook you both a meal, maybe save your company from paying for you to eat out."

"It was nice meeting you. Perhaps I'll see you around."

"If there's anything you need, just ask. I'm in number eight one three. My name's Sarah by the way."

Nick didn't offer his name in return. "Thanks, but I think we'll be okay."

As he backed into the room, I glimpsed a short, dumpy looking woman with a mop of greying hair, wearing jeans and a dark-coloured top.

"Shit, shit, shit," he muttered, leaning back against the white painted wood of the door.

"What was that all about?"

"The owners told the bloody neighbour somebody was renting the flat while they were away. She must have heard me coming down the corridor and came out to talk to me. She wanted to know whether we were here on holiday. I said we were businessmen. She thought it would be a good idea to invite us over for a meal. I'm guessing you overheard the rest."

"What do we do now?" I asked.

"She didn't see you, did she?"

I shook my head. "Not as far I can tell."

"In that case, we should be alright as long as it's only your photo and not mine that appears on the news."

"Do you think we should ...?" I hesitated, my moral compass swinging in all directions as I considered what I was about to propose.

"Should we what?" Nick asked impatiently.

"Um ... I don't know, kidnap her or something."

Nick rolled his eyes. "You're suggesting we subdue her, tie her up then keep her captive for the next few days?"

His gaze bored into me. Unable to meet his stare, I looked away.

He ticked off the points on his fingers as he listed the failings of my poorly considered proposal. "Firstly, we have no idea whether or not she lives alone. Secondly, if she does live by herself but doesn't turn up to work, somebody might come looking for her. Thirdly, she may have family members who would notice she was missing. Do you want me to go on?"

"You're the expert as you keep telling me. It was only a suggestion."

"Well, it was a particularly bad one," Nick said, turning away and striding towards the balcony window. He stared out at the view below. "No, we should just sit tight."

I slouched with my feet on one of the sofas. Nick had left five minutes earlier to buy food. I had also asked him to purchase replacement underwear and a toothbrush. After a moment's hesitation, he had grudgingly agreed.

While I waited, I flicked through a file labelled *Useful Things to Know*, which I had picked up from the wooden desk. The first few pages dealt with the operation of various appliances including the heating system, the fridge and the cooker. Following that came a page about using the television. The last and biggest section contained details of nearby attractions and local restaurants.

I grabbed the television remote control and followed the instructions to turn on the screen. Daytime shows had never held much interest for me. As I flicked through the channels, I remembered why. All the programmes seemed to fall into one of three categories: property, cooking or quizzes. In frustration, I pressed the off button.

I missed having the ability to browse the Internet. With no access to either my laptop or mobile phone, I felt cut off from the world. I supposed people would be talking about me, the alleged paedophile schoolteacher. In some ways, I was glad I wouldn't be able to read what they were writing. That didn't stop me from wanting to keep up to speed with the investigation.

My thoughts turned to my family. What would they be going through? I was convinced my mother and sister would have no doubts about my innocence. Despite that, the news stories would make life hell for them. I knew from bitter experience the press would give no respite. They would be camped outside my mother's house like vultures around a corpse.

I had been only nine years old at the time of Elena's abduction, but I still remembered the never-ending knocks at the door and the persistent ringing of the telephone. My father disconnected the cable after a while. Desperate for pictures of the grieving family, one heartless photographer crept through the garden and held his camera to the window before my mother closed the curtains.

Our parents kept Cathy and me off school for a fortnight afterwards. When we eventually returned, we became the centre of attention. Much of it was well-intentioned, but everybody was curious to learn what had really happened. One classmate, who had taken an instant dislike to me, suggested my parents had killed my little sister and faked her disappearance. That was the only time in my life when I ended up in a fight.

I guessed my two nieces might experience a similar situation when they returned to school after the summer holidays. In their case, it would be worse. Cathy and I had been victims, whereas Sophia and Zoe were relatives of the alleged perpetrator. I could only imagine what they would go through.

A rattling noise from the corridor outside the flat broke me out of my reminiscences. I glanced at my watch. It was too early for Nick to be back; less than fifteen minutes had passed since he left. The sound of a key turning in the lock reached my ears. *Was it the owners returning prematurely from their trip?* If so, it was imperative I didn't let them see me. I pushed myself upright and hobbled towards the bathroom. I was no more than halfway there when the outer door swung inwards. I remained rooted to the spot.

To my relief, I identified Nick's outline silhouetted in the open doorway. He came inside and leaned back against the painted wood, his eyes locked on mine. I glanced at his hands. They were empty.

"Did you forget—?"

Nick cut me off. "I've got some bad news, Alex."

It was the first time he had called me by my first name. I shook my head in confusion. *How could things get any worse?* "What's happened? Have they identified you?"

"Look, I'm really sorry. I have to tell you this before you hear about it from some other source."

A swirl of competing thoughts raced through my head. Had he decided to sell me out to the police? Was he about to reveal he had accepted more money to perform the original assassination? But that made little sense; if that was the case, he would surely finish the job without trying to explain himself.

He walked towards me and took me by the elbow. "You need to sit down."

I shrugged off his grip. "Just tell me."

He searched my face and seemed to come to a conclusion. "There's no way to sugar coat this. Your mother's dead."

A wave of dizziness swept over me and I staggered backwards. Nick stuck out an arm to support me.

"The cancer?" I said, the words barely escaping my lips. It wasn't as if we were unprepared; the family had all been expecting it to happen sooner or later. I was aware the condition of sufferers could deteriorate rapidly and with little warning. It still came as a complete shock, rocking me to the core of my being. My one abiding thought was that she had died before I earned the chance to clear my name. Perhaps the recent media reports about my alleged crime had even been a contributory factor.

Nick shook his head, his voice barely more than a whisper. "I'm afraid it's worse than that. Somebody murdered her."

The words entered my brain, but at first, they didn't register. When I finally processed what he had said, it slammed through my chest like a shotgun blast. I sank to my knees and leaned forward until my forehead rested against the rough weave of the carpet. I brought my elbows up, covering my ears and locking my fingers behind my head. A deep well of anguish erupted in my throat and came out as a roar of pain.

"No!"

I inhaled and screamed again. "No! No! No!"

Nick's hand touched my back. "I'm sorry, Alex. I wish there was something I could do, but you've got to keep the noise down. The neighbours will wonder what's going on."

My shoulders rose and fell, choking sobs wracking my body. My mind splintered into a thousand fragments as all rational thought deserted me, every part of my consciousness mired in a deep pit of despair.

Eventually—time seemed to stand still, so I had no idea how long it took— I recovered sufficiently to regain a modicum of control. A sudden, terrible dread slammed into my brain.

I raised my head. Nick paced backwards and forwards a few feet away. He stopped as he spotted my movement.

"What about my sister and her two girls?"

Nick stared at me in confusion. "What about them? Why are you asking?"

"Cathy and my brother-in-law separated a while back. She and the kids live with my mother. They moved in about six months ago."

"The news I saw didn't mention anybody else."

"Tell me what you know."

"Don't you want to sit down first?"

I nodded. Nick helped me to my feet. Wrapping my arm around his shoulder, he led me to the sofa. I barely retained control of my limbs; every bone in my body seemed to have turned to rubber. He lowered me gently onto the cushions.

I leaned forward, my legs jiggling with unsuppressed tension. I hunched my shoulders and thrust my trembling hands under my armpits. Nick sank into the adjacent settee. He took a deep breath as he composed his thoughts.

Richard T. Burke

"I was heading through the shopping centre towards the supermarket when I passed an electrical goods shop. There was a television in the window, one of those huge flat-screen models. It was showing a twenty-four-hour news channel. If it wasn't for the subtitles, I would have missed it. It said something like *fugitive's mother found dead*. I went inside, but the sound was muted."

"How did you find out what happened, then?" I asked

Nick pulled a phone from the pocket of his hoodie. "While I was there, I bought another two mobile phones. They were the cheapest in the shop, but it still set me back over a hundred and twenty quid for the pair. I used one to log on to the Internet. I accessed the BBC news website. The article reported that she was murdered."

"How?"

A worried expression flickered in Nick's eyes. "Look, are you sure you want to hear this now?"

"How?" I repeated, louder this time.

"They said a man strangled her."

Nick's voice sounded muffled as if he was speaking down a long tunnel. The pressure seemed to build inside my skull. I buried my face in my hands and listened to the sound of my breathing as the air entered my lungs in ragged gasps. My pulse thundered in my ears. Several seconds of silence passed.

"Do they have a suspect?" I asked eventually, looking up.

Nick gave an almost imperceptible shake of the head.

Our eyes met as I locked my gaze onto his. "What's that supposed to mean?"

He turned away and swallowed hard. I had already guessed the answer before he spoke, but the confirmation still came as another blow.

"They're saying it was you."

"Me?" I experienced a strong sense of dissociation as if I was standing at a distance, watching somebody else speak through my mouth.

Nick nodded. "One of the neighbours reported hearing an argument. The police are speculating that you visited your mother asking for money, and she tried to persuade you to turn yourself in. A witness saw a figure running away afterwards. He identified the man as you."

"Who do you think really did it?"

He hesitated before replying. "If I were to hazard a guess, I'd say the same people who have been after you from the start are trying to get you out in the open."

"You're saying it's my fault?"

"No, of course not."

"But if I had handed myself in to the police at the beginning, my mother would still be alive."

"Maybe, but you'd almost certainly be dead."

"Well that makes me feel a whole lot better," I said. "You're implying I've traded my mother's life for my own."

"Not at all. You've been placed in an impossible situation, and there was no way you could possibly know in advance how far they would be prepared to go."

Once again, I lowered my head into my hands. My brain spun off into a multitude of different directions as I tried to make sense of everything. A sudden idea rose from the conflicting emotions. Over the next few seconds, my resolve hardened.

"I want to talk to her," I said. "I need to call my sister."

Nick studied me from the adjacent sofa. "That's not a good idea."

"I don't care. I need to know she's okay."

"You must realise the police will be monitoring her phone. If you call her, you'll be telling them exactly where you are."

I folded my arms. "If you won't help, I'll do it by myself. Give me back the mobile battery you took from me."

Nick hauled himself out of the chair and stood in front of me. "Look, I get that you're upset. Who wouldn't be? But throwing away everything we've worked for over the last few days, it's just ... I don't know ... a waste."

A dark rage flooded my veins. I levered myself upright and shoved him in the chest. "You say it's a waste, but what happens when the job finishes?" I pushed him again. "You leave me alone and collect the money, that's what. I'm stuck in the same mess I was in at the start, but now my mother is dead, murdered by the animals who are trying to kill me. I need confirmation my sister is unharmed. If you don't agree to help me, I'll walk out of the door right this minute, and your precious contract will be worth nothing."

Nick held up his hands in surrender. "Alright, I'll do it, but let me do some thinking first."

He turned his back on me and paced backwards and forwards. After a while, he unlocked the window and moved out onto the balcony. When I followed him outside, he was leaning on the brickwork, staring out vacantly at the concrete landscape below.

The raw pain of my loss still gnawed at my chest, but by now, I had calmed down a little. I adopted the same position as Nick. He didn't acknowledge my presence, lost in his own thoughts.

"Have you come up with anything?" I asked.

Nick turned his head to study me. "First of all, do you actually have to speak to her? What if you could find out whether she was okay without talking to her?"

A frown creased my forehead. "How would we do that? Anyway, I need to have a conversation with her."

"I thought you might say that. Do you have her number?"

"It's on my mobile but I'm not sure I can remember it. I do know the landline number though. That one's embedded in my memory after living there for over twenty years."

Nick scratched his head. "The house will be a crime scene, so it's fairly unlikely she's still there. We can't get the details off your phone without turning it on. If they've set up a trace, they'll know the moment we reconnect the battery."

"What do you propose we do?"

"That's a good question. One thing's for sure, we don't want to power it up here. As soon as the police detect its presence on a cellular network, they'll be able to track it to a rough location. They can use the signal strength from the cell towers to narrow the search area. That means we'll have to drive somewhere else. And you're aware you won't have long: one or two minutes at most. Is it worth it?"

Despite my normally laid-back nature, I was not about to be dissuaded. "I think it is, and that's all that matters. If you want your money, you're going to help me."

Nick sighed in exasperation. "Look, I said I would. I'm just trying to work out how to do it without getting caught. What we need is a diversion: something to send them looking in the wrong direction."

Several moments of silence passed. Suddenly, he stiffened. He slapped the metal bar running along the top of the wall with the palm of his hand. "I've got an idea."

"Go on then. Spit it out."

"Put your hoodie on. I'll tell you on the way."

"Where are we going?" I asked.

"You'll have to be patient," he said, the wicked grin returning. "And it'll entail more travelling like a dog."

I groaned. "Not the boot again?"

"Exactly," he replied as he stepped back into the lounge. "This time, I expect you to be pleased to see me when I let you out. Where's your phone?"

"In the laptop bag."

"Go and fetch it. We're leaving right now."

I limped to the bedroom, unzipped the black case and extracted the mobile. It felt light in my hand without the missing battery. When I re-entered the hallway, Nick was already waiting by the door to the corridor, the small rucksack slung across his back.

"You go first," he said. "Keep your head lowered. Can you remember how to get to where I parked the car?"

"Yeah, I think so."

"Wait for me when you arrive there."

I pulled the handle and slipped out. The swish of my feet on the blue carpet sounded incredibly loud in the hushed silence of the corridor as I hobbled towards the lifts. I stabbed the down button. The red digits above the right lift counted backwards from twelve. The left indicator displayed a G. Behind me, I heard the rattle of a key in a lock. My eyes stayed fixed on the decreasing numbers, praying that nobody would join me.

The doors glided apart, and I hurried inside. Immediately, I prodded the green G on the control panel. I took a step to the side and risked a glance along the corridor. As I watched, the woman from flat 813 dropped her keys into a large beige handbag and set off in my direction.

"Can you hold the lift please?" she called.

In a rising panic, I jabbed the button for the ground level repeatedly. After what seemed an age, the doors slid closed. I half expected them to reopen, but instead, the floor sank down as the metal chamber glided into motion. I emerged into the foyer. Limping towards the exit, I glanced back at the numbers above the lifts. The left display was set at two. As I watched, it changed to a one.

"Shit," I muttered, breaking into a half run that sent daggers of pain shooting through my injured calf. The sound of the lift sliding open followed me as I pushed through the swing door into the stairwell. I grabbed the handrail with one hand and rushed down the steps. Two flights from the bottom, I stumbled, my grip on the cold metal rail the only thing preventing me from tumbling the rest of the way. The sudden pressure twisted my wrist, adding a second painful item to my list of injuries.

I barged through into the parking area. My addled brain refused to cooperate as I tried to remember where Nick had parked the car. The muffled sound of heavy footsteps came from the closed door behind me. Mere seconds remained before the woman emerged. My frantic gaze darted about the underground space, searching for the red Ford Focus.

Time had run out. My only option was to hide and wait for her to leave. I hobbled around the back of the closest vehicle, a black estate, and ducked down just as the neighbour appeared in the open doorway. If the car was hers, I was sunk; there was no way she could fail to notice me if she approached the driver's door. I inched my head above the bottom of the window, trying to block out the pressure building in my bladder while I waited for her to make a move.

She stood panting for a moment before turning in the opposite direction. The chirrup of a vehicle anti-theft system came from somewhere outside my line of sight. I sighed in relief and sank back onto the rough concrete. The distant clunk of a car door opening echoed through the cavernous area followed moments later by the cranking of the starter motor. The sound increased in volume, and a wash of bright light swept over my hiding place.

Instead of carrying on past, the whine of an electric window reached my ears.

"Going out, are you?" the woman called above the rattle of the diesel engine. "Do you need a lift anywhere?"

For one terrible moment, I thought she was addressing me.

"I'm nipping into town to do some shopping." Nick's voice came from the other side of the bodywork. He must have had the misfortune to emerge through the doorway as she was passing. "I've got my own car, thanks."

"Where's your friend?"

"He's still in the flat."

"Oh. I could swear I saw a man I didn't recognise come down here. I guessed it was your colleague, but it seems it was somebody else. You can't be too careful, what with all the thieving and vandalism around these parts—not that there's much of that goes on in this building."

"Right. I've got to be going. I'll see you later."

"Okay. Have fun with your shopping."

The pitch of the engine increased again as a blue saloon rolled past me. I pressed myself against the driver's door, trying to make my outline as small as possible. Luckily, she didn't glance in my direction.

When I was sure she had gone, I uttered a sigh of relief and rose to my feet. Nick spotted me almost immediately.

"Christ, that was close," I said as he approached. "Why is it that nosey neighbours seem to have a thing for me?"

"Your suggestion of kidnapping her is sounding more sensible by the minute," he replied. "Let's get going."

Richard T. Burke

Twenty-five years ago: Wednesday, 8th February, 1995

*M*y father arrived home half an hour later. I was still awake, lying under the sheets in my school uniform. As soon as I heard the sound of the engine, I threw back the covers and rushed to the window. The police car sat in the same place on the drive, and by now, the forensic technicians' van was parked behind it, so he left the Golf on the road.

I didn't seriously expect him to return with my sister, but it was still a disappointment when he walked up to the house alone. The clunk of the front door rose from below, followed a short while later by the sound of voices. I crossed the room and edged out into the hallway. Creeping to the top of the stairs, I strained my ears to overhear the conversation.

I sensed somebody behind me and whirled around to discover Cathy emerging from her bedroom.

"Did Dad find anything?" she whispered.

"I don't think so," I said. "I'm trying to listen to what they're saying."

Both of us inched forwards. Downstairs the discussion came to a halt, and two men wearing white plastic coveralls and each carrying a small case, came into view. Cathy and I watched in silence as they trudged upstairs.

When they reached the top step, one of them pointed to the doorway of Elena's room and said, "Is that your sister's—"

"Have you found anything yet?" Cathy interrupted.

The two men exchanged a glance. The man who had asked the initial question shook his head. "I'm sorry, no. We're just here to collect evidence."

We stood back and stared at them as they made their way along the hall and through the open door.

"I'm going down to ask them what's happening," I announced.

Cathy followed me as I descended the stairs to the lounge. Low voices came from the other side. For a moment, I considered knocking. In the end, I barged inside.

My mother sat perched on the edge of the sofa. The two policemen stood together a few feet away. My father, who had been standing beside the men and facing me, whirled around, turning his back. He pulled something from his pocket. When he raised his hand, I identified the object as a handkerchief.

Up to that point, I had been confident they would find my sister. My father had always been the stronger of my parents; in my nine years of life, I had rarely seen him flustered, let alone crying. Observing him now as he dabbed at his face brought home the severity of the situation.

"I thought I told you two to go to bed," my mother said. "And why are you wearing your school uniform instead of your pyjamas?"

My father sniffled and turned back. The blotchiness of his cheeks confirmed my initial suspicions. "It's alright, Mary. Let them stay. Alex, Cathy, I need you to sit quietly while we talk to the policemen. Okay?"

I huddled beside my sister at one end of the sofa.

"Is there anyone you can think of who might have shown an unnatural interest in your daughter?" the officer with the stain asked. "Maybe a member of the family, a stranger hanging around the neighbourhood, or a workman?"

I couldn't remember what my sister's abductor looked like, but I did know I had never seen him before.

Richard T. Burke

T he journey started in the same way as the last one when Nick opened the hatchback for me to clamber inside.

"Is this really necessary?" I asked.

"It is if I say so. Just remember who's in charge here. Now get in like a good doggie."

The brief spell of sensitivity Nick had demonstrated when revealing the details of my mother's death seemed to have deserted him. I scowled but did as instructed. He still hadn't explained his plan, informing me he would reveal all when we reached our destination. When I asked how long the journey would take, he told me approximately half an hour.

The ride was as uncomfortable as the first time, but on this occasion, thoughts of my family provided a distraction. If Nick's theory was correct, I was the reason my mother had died. I was realistic enough to accept her days were limited, but somebody had stolen what remained of her life. In the darkness of the cramped space, I clenched my fists as I envisioned what I would do to the people responsible if I ever laid hands on them.

My reflections switched to my sister. There had been no mention of her in the news reports. Surely that must mean she was okay. My stomach churned at the possibility she too had come to harm. Even if she hadn't been hurt, what was she going through right now? And what about my nieces? How would they handle the murder of their grandmother?

My conversation time would be limited; Nick had told me I would have one or two minutes at most. That meant I needed to plan my words carefully. No doubt she would be aware of the accusations laid against me, but I was sure she wouldn't believe them. However, she had to be wondering why, if I was innocent, I hadn't turned myself in. I would have to explain that I was in mortal danger, and by inference, that she was too. Perhaps she had already come to the same conclusion, especially if Jamie had passed on the same message he gave me. It was clear he was involved in this mess, but for the life of me I couldn't figure out how.

There was a strong possibility the police would listen in to my call. I would have to be careful that whatever I said to my sister, I wouldn't be making the task of locating me any easier. One consequence of that decision was that I had to ensure I made no mention of Nick. There was little doubt in my mind that Nick was not my guardian's real name, but even the confirmation that somebody else was helping me would aid them in tracking me down.

A large jolt sent me airborne. I landed with a thud. Nick's voice filtered through from the front seat. I didn't pick up everything he said, but the meaning was clear and included several swear words. The ride became bumpier, and I found it hard to concentrate.

Eventually, the car stopped moving, and the engine turned off. I pressed the button on the side of my watch to illuminate the dial; a little over thirty minutes had passed since the start of the journey. I waited patiently for Nick to release me. A click originated from the back of the rear passenger seat. The barrier separating me from the rest of the car's interior folded down. I blinked at the sudden burst of daylight. Nick leaned into the vehicle through the open door.

"Sorry about the bumpy ride," he said. "There are damn potholes everywhere. Stay there until I give you the all clear."

He straightened up. Moments later, he ducked down again. "Right, you can get out now."

I rolled sideways and clambered over the coarse, black material. Holding the roof for support, I clambered out onto the kerb. Nick had parked at the end of a residential street of terraced and semi-detached houses close to a busy T-junction. Cars lined both sides of the road.

"Where are we?" I asked.

"We're on the outskirts of Reading," he replied.

"Are you going to tell me the plan now?"

Nick studied me for a second. "Are you sure you want to do this? The police will know we've been here."

"I need to talk to my sister."

"Alright. Let's get back in the car, and I'll explain how this will work."

Nick gestured to the front passenger door and climbed into the driver's seat. I limped around the side of the vehicle and lowered myself into the soft fabric beside him. He turned sideways and explained what he wanted me to do.

"Is that all clear?" he asked at the end.

I nodded.

"And no more than two minutes after you turn the phone on."

"You already said that," I replied.

"I'll be waiting here. Good luck."

Richard T. Burke

I raised my hoodie, pulled the handle towards me and lowered my feet to the ground. One hand held my mobile, the other clasped the battery. I nudged the door shut with my elbow and made my way to the end of the street. There, I headed left and hobbled along the pavement. Ahead of me, I recognised the sign Nick had described. As I drew nearer, the sound of building work increased. Every few seconds, an empty lorry emerged from the entrance to the site, leaving tracks of brown mud on the grey tarmac. Two trucks loaded with heavy machinery sat at the side of the road, their hazard lights blinking.

I approached the large billboard showing pictures of neat houses with tree-lined gardens. It was hard to equate the greenery of the image with the muddy landscape of the construction site. Glancing at my watch, I slid the battery into place and pressed the power button on my phone. At first, nothing happened, but a few seconds later, the body vibrated, and the manufacturer's logo scrolled across the display.

By the time the lock screen materialised, nearly half a minute had passed. With trembling fingers, I tapped in the passcode. Finally, it was possible to make the call. I pressed the dial button and selected the contact list. My sister's name appeared at the top of the recent contacts.

A flurry of pings announced the receipt of numerous email and text messages. They would have to wait. A prod of the finger and the trill of a ringtone sounded down the line. Another quick glance at my wrist: forty seconds gone already. I pressed the phone to my ear, trying to block out the background noise all around me.

Then my sister's voice: "Alex, is that you?"

I could barely speak, my throat choking up with emotion. Eventually, I forced the words out. "Cathy, thank God you're alright."

"Hang on a sec." The faint sound of children's television faded, followed by the thud of a door closing. "We're fine. Where are you?"

A hot feeling spread over my face. "I'm sorry, Cathy. I can't tell you. You know I had nothing to do with ..."

"It's okay. I knew you could never have done that to Mum."

"The other thing with the children—that's a lie too."

"I believe you. You're my brother. You're not capable of doing anything like that."

A tear trickled down my cheek. Despite what the press was saying, I could always rely on my sister. I brushed it away with the back of my hand. "How are you holding up?"

Silence for a few seconds. A choked sob. "It's been awful. The hardest thing has been telling the girls. They're aware their grandmother is in heaven, but they don't yet know how. So far, I've hidden what the reporters are saying from them, but they can't stay with their friends in case ... Anyway, it's not as if any of the parents have been asking for play dates recently."

"Where are you staying?" I asked.

"We're in a hotel for the moment. I'm not sure I can live in the house again after what's happened there. I'm only glad we were out at the time. God only knows what I'd do if somebody harmed the girls."

I opened my mouth to speak, but an incongruous sound made me hesitate. Was my imagination playing tricks on me? The longer I listened, the surer I became; another person was whispering in the background. I held my breath, trying to pick up the words above the clamour of the building site behind me. "Is somebody there with you?"

After a pause that extended down the line like a blast of icy air, my sister replied, her voice muted. "Yes, there's a police liaison officer here. They're worried in case ..."

I glanced at my wrist again. Two and a half minutes had passed since the start of the call. Cathy was still speaking.

"Look," I said interrupting her, "I've got to go. I love you."

My finger stabbed down on the disconnect button. My breathing was uneven, rasping through my throat in stuttering gasps. The blood rushed through my veins as if I had recently completed a marathon. Remembering Nick's words, I tried to focus on the job at hand. I limped forwards until I stood at the edge of the pavement where the service road entered the site.

The rumble of an engine signalled the approach of another empty lorry leaving the area. I waited until the vehicle drew alongside, then after a furtive inspection of my surroundings, tossed the phone into the cargo bed. It landed with a metallic clang.

I swivelled on the spot and headed back towards Nick's car. I had covered about ten yards when a voice came from behind me.

"Oi! What the hell do you think you're doing?"

I risked a backwards glance. A man was leaning out of the window of one of the parked trucks. I had failed to detect him during my hurried check.

"They're not fucking bins, you know."

I turned my back on him and lengthened my stride. The clunk of an opening door reached my ears. "Hey! I'm talking to you. Get over here."

In the short glimpse I took when I twisted my head, I could see the man had stepped down from the cab. Even beneath the baggy blue overalls, I could tell he was several pounds overweight. If he gave chase, it would be a close-run thing given the state of my injured calf.

"Wanker!" he called after me.

Pain shot up my leg as I staggered away from him. When I reached the street on which the car was parked, I flashed another glance behind me. The man stood beside a similarly attired colleague, pointing in my direction. As I watched, the second worker hurried back towards the cab of a lorry poking out from the site entrance.

I covered the last few feet to Nick's car and hauled the front passenger door open.

"Not so fast," he said, grinning. "It's another ride in the boot for you, my canine friend."

"There's no time," I gasped, slumping into the seat. "Somebody saw me. They'll be here in a second."

The grin slipped from Nick's face. He turned the key in the ignition, rammed the stick into gear and pulled away from the kerb with a screech of burning rubber. He raced between the lines of parked cars, only slowing to turn left at a junction. I twisted around to look out of the back window. The outline of a lorry blocked the entrance to the street.

"What the hell went wrong?" Nick asked.

"Everything," I replied.

We came to a stop a short way down a muddy lane leading into dense woodland. I sat in the passenger seat while Nick replaced the number plates for the third time. He had allowed me to remain where I was but informed me I would have to move before we returned to the flat.

The sound of distant sirens had reached us as we weaved through the side streets close to the building site, but I had no idea whether they related to my telephone call. During the ten-minute drive to our current location, his eyes flicked to the rearview mirror every few seconds, but there was no sign of pursuit.

Nick was philosophical about the drivers observing me as I tossed my mobile into the back of the truck. The original intention had been for the police to track the signal as it travelled to the supply depot where the next batch of building materials would be loaded, hopefully crushing the handset.

For all we knew, that part of the plan had proceeded as intended. It seemed likely the police would trace the phone back to its origin. They might eventually question the two men who had seen me, but it would all take time and by that stage, we would be miles away. Nick's only remaining concern was whether any witnesses had observed his car. Swapping the plates mitigated that possibility.

"That's another fifty quid down the drain," he said, tossing the cloth-wrapped bundle behind the passenger seat with a metallic clank. "I've only got one set left now." He moved around to the driver's door and glared in at me.

"I needed to know she was alright."

The scowl on his face softened a fraction. "Yeah, I get it, but from here on in, we stay hidden like good little mice."

"I assume we're going back to the flat," I said.

"That's the plan unless you fancy spending the next day and a half in the car. It's time to climb in the boot again."

I groaned. "It's pretty claustrophobic in there. Can't I lie across the back seat? Nobody will see me."

Nick studied me for a second then shrugged. "What the hell. Just make sure you stay out of sight. I must be going soft in my old age."

Richard T. Burke

I ended up lying on my side, my knees bent so I could fit in the available space. Whilst not exactly comfortable, my new position was a step up from the cramped darkness of the boot. The car lurched into movement across the rough ground. My calf ached as I braced myself against the door.

After a few seconds, an increase in the ambient light level and the rhythmic ticking of the indicator signalled our arrival at the main road. The ride became much smoother after that. Nick hummed an unrecognisable tune from the front seat. My mind turned to the conversation with my sister.

Somebody from the police had been in the room with her. Given the circumstances, that was hardly surprising. In some ways, it came as a relief to learn she was not alone. But why hadn't she mentioned their presence until I asked? What had they been whispering to her? Perhaps she had been instructed to keep me talking until they could trace my location.

"How was your sister?" Nick's question dragged me back to the present.

"Okay, I suppose. She had a police liaison officer with her."

His voice took on a sharper tone. "I take it you didn't give anything away."

"Of course not." I paused for a moment, a sudden burst of anger welling from deep below. Unable to hold myself back, I allowed the words to tumble from my mouth. "How do you live with yourself? Somebody like you killed my mother."

Nick's posture stiffened. He remained silent for several seconds. When he spoke, steel laced every syllable. "First, I'm not your mother's murderer. Second, I draw the line at women and children."

"But—"

"Let me finish. Third, most of the scum I kill deserve to die anyway. In most cases, I'm doing society a favour by ending their miserable lives. In any case, I don't have to justify myself to you."

"You're still a killer for hire."

"Who's being paid to keep you alive, so I suggest you show some gratitude. I could have trussed you up for the last few days and dumped you on the street at the end of the contract."

"Well, thank you very much," I said, my voice dripping with sarcasm. "I'm really glad you showed me such a great time."

From my position on the back seat, I saw Nick's jaw muscles clench. He inhaled deeply then held his breath for a few seconds, clearly fighting the urge to respond. Eventually, he shook his head and exhaled through narrowed lips. The journey continued in silence as the tension in the car gradually dissipated.

I wasn't about to apologise, but neither did I want the sour note between us to fester. I still needed Nick on my side.

"Do you have anybody?" I asked.

"Eh?"

"Is there somebody special in your life, like a wife or girlfriend, or perhaps even a boyfriend?"

Nick angled his gaze to the rearview mirror and snorted in amusement. I was too low down for him to see my reflection. "No, not really. My line of work isn't conducive to a long-term relationship. And just to be clear, I've never shared my bed with anyone other than a woman."

I smiled. "Don't you want to settle down?"

"Maybe one day, if I ever retire from this game. There is a person I'm close to, but I don't think either of us is ready to commit to anything."

"Who is she?"

Nick hesitated before responding. "A friend."

"Go on," I said.

"It's none of your business," he snapped, glancing once again at the mirror. He ran a hand through his hair. When he spoke again, his tone was softer. "She's the widow of one of the men in my unit. Her husband died out in Afghanistan. We look out for each other. She helps me out with some of the admin side. For example, she booked the flat we're staying in. She knows all about computers. I help her out with odd jobs around the house."

"Does she know what you do?"

"I've never discussed it with her, but she's not stupid, so she's more than likely got a good idea."

"And it doesn't bother her?"

"Like I said, we haven't talked about it. Anyway, I could ask you the same question about your love life."

"Currently on my own," I replied, "and with no special friend."

"That's probably not a bad thing in your current situation," Nick said.

"Yeah, you're right. I've had a few single parents throw themselves at me over the years."

Nick chuckled. "One of the hazards of the job, I suspect."

"Not for long," I said. "I don't think they'll let me work there again after all this."

"What will you do?"

"To be perfectly honest, I haven't even thought about it. There aren't too many career vacancies for English teachers who have been accused of murder."

We arrived back at the car park without further incident. Nick gave me the key and dropped me off by the staircase before driving around the corner to the allocated parking space. I hobbled up the stone steps with the hoodie drawn over my head. The foyer area was deserted as I tapped in the code to access the lifts.

The lift doors opened as soon as I pressed the up button. I emerged onto the eighth floor and hurried along the corridor as fast as my limp allowed, eager to gain the sanctuary of the flat before any of the neighbours popped out to make my acquaintance. I fumbled the key into the lock and sighed with relief as I crossed the threshold without being accosted.

Seconds later, a light tap signalled Nick's arrival. The distorted image through the fisheye lens of the peephole failed to disguise his impatience. I twisted the latch and stepped back to allow him to pass. He walked past me and flopped onto the sofa.

"Let's see what's on the news," he said, snatching the remote control. Sinking down into the adjacent settee, I glanced at my watch: 16:52. The screen displayed the closing stages of a game show. The grinning host stood beside a nervous-looking contestant, draping an arm across his shoulder.

"Bloody daytime television," Nick muttered. "That stuff rots the brain."

He pressed a button, and the image changed to the TV guide. He quickly navigated to the BBC News channel. The picture swapped to a slow-motion replay of a footballer lashing the ball into the goal from twenty yards out.

"Damned football," he added, muting the sound. "That's almost as bad. Twenty-two overpaid prima donnas kicking around a bag of wind."

Nick drummed his fingers on the armrest as the roundup of the week's action ran its course. The national weather forecast followed; judging by the preponderance of grey storm clouds across the country, it seemed more rain was on the way over the next few days.

Finally, the time ticked around to five o'clock. Nick prodded the button to unmute the sound. A sombre-faced male newscaster spoke into the camera.

"In our top story this evening, the manhunt for rogue schoolteacher, Alex Parrott, intensifies."

My scalp prickled, and my face flushed. I swallowed to clear the pressure building in my ears. My heart slammed against the wall of my chest.

"The thirty-four-year-old is accused of a string of murders, including the killing of his own mother. Over now to our home affairs correspondent, Brian Adlington, at the scene of the most recent crime."

A thin-faced man wearing a dark suit and red tie stood in front of a garden hedge, the blue flashing light of a police car from somewhere out of shot illuminating one side of his face in a hypnotising, pulsing pattern. Behind the reporter and slightly out of focus was the front of the house in which I had grown up.

The familiar image and the presence of the emergency vehicles set off a chain of memories I thought I had erased from my mind. Twenty-five years ago, the television pictures had been lower quality, but the setting was the same. Then, we had been on the inside looking out. I remembered my parents tuning into the news, hoping illogically that the reporters would reveal something positive the police hadn't already told us. Of course, that never happened.

"This is the house in which secondary school English teacher, Alex Parrott, grew up. It's also the house he is suspected of returning to yesterday evening to kill his mother, Mary Parrott. Officers are still questioning neighbours to establish an exact timeline, but it seems sometime around seven fifteen last night, Mr Parrott returned to the childhood home he left sixteen years ago. Minutes after that, it is alleged Mr Parrott strangled the sixty-five-year-old. The sister of the accused man discovered the body after arriving at the residence shortly after eight p.m. She has been living at the property with her two young daughters but had been visiting friends at the time of the attack.

"In a further development, the authorities are now linking Mr Parrott with the murders earlier this week of Victor and Tasha Romanov. On Monday, a cleaner discovered the couple, brutally murdered in their home less than three miles from Mr Parrott's house. Police have placed Mr Parrott at the scene but are still appealing for witnesses who may have seen or heard anything unusual to come forward.

"Officers are searching for a motive for the killings but believe the case could be tied to illegal activity including child pornography. Members of staff at the school where Mr Parrott worked as an English teacher, Saint Michael's Secondary in Fleet, were tonight unavailable for comment. Later, we'll be talking to some parents of children taught by Mr Parrott.

"Also in tonight's programme, politicians are calling for more stringent checks on teachers. We'll hear more about what could be done and the extra measures that are being proposed. We have an interview with the head of the Office for Standards in Education, Peter Dack."

Richard T. Burke

The walls of the room seemed to close in on me. All my attention focused on the rectangular screen as the reporter described the string of murders attributed to me. Person after person tried to explain how a secondary school English teacher with no previous criminal record had passed all the security checks and turned into the most wanted man in Britain.

I was so fixated on the programme that I didn't hear the knock at the door. It was only when Nick shoved himself out of the sofa that I emerged from my bubble of concentration. Our eyes met as he grabbed the remote control and lowered the volume. The tapping sound repeated.

I too hauled myself upright. "Do you think it's—?"

"No, it can't be the police," he interrupted. "They wouldn't knock. If they knew we were here, they'd smash their way in."

"Well, who is it then?"

Nick didn't answer. Instead, he held up his hand to silence me and crept along the hallway. When he reached the door, he peered through the peephole. With a slight shake of the head, he undid the latch and pulled the handle towards him. I glimpsed briefly a tangle of grey hair before he blocked my view. The murmur of a brief conversation carried along the hall, but the sound from the television prevented me from picking up any of the words.

After a few seconds, Nick closed the door and strode back to the lounge. "It's the neighbour from the next apartment. She says she's run out of sugar and wants to borrow some."

"What did you tell her?"

"I said I'd see if we had any."

"Didn't she just go out in the car?"

Nick narrowed his eyes. "Yes, I know."

"What's your plan?"

He inhaled deeply then shrugged. "Wait here." He continued past me into the kitchen and returned moments later carrying a cup. On the return journey along the hallway, he detoured via his bedroom. As he emerged, he slipped something into his back pocket.

He strode towards the door and opened it a crack. The woman's face appeared briefly in the gap as she looked over his shoulder. Once again, a short discussion took place. I was about to turn away and return to my position on the sofa when there was a sudden flurry of movement.

Nick flashed out a hand and grabbed the woman by the collar of her pale-green shirt. He hauled her towards him, stepping to one side as she stumbled past him through the doorway and into the flat. A quick glance each way along the outside corridor and he slammed the door closed behind him. His hand reached back and emerged holding a knife. He held the blade to her throat and moved his face to within six inches of hers.

"If you make a sound, you're dead," he growled. "Do you understand?"

The woman whimpered in fright and dropped the cup. As it hit the floor, it split in two with a dull crack, spilling white crystals in an arc across the carpet.

"I asked if you understood," he repeated.

She squeaked a single syllable response and nodded her head a fraction.

"Good. Now walk slowly into the lounge."

He turned to me. "Get the duct tape from my bag."

I stood aside as the woman edged past me. Her eyes met mine. The telltale flash of recognition spread across her face. She blinked rapidly as she tried to hold back the tears.

"Sit down on the sofa," Nick commanded, prodding her with the knife blade.

"You're not going to hurt me, are you?" she asked in a timid voice.

"Not if you follow my instructions and answer my questions."

I limped into Nick's bedroom. The small rucksack lay on the bed, the zip at the top already open. I opened it wider and peered inside. A mass of crumpled clothes concealed the items beneath. I pushed them aside, reached in and rummaged at the bottom. My fingers closed around a cold metallic object. I pulled it out and found myself staring at a matt black pistol.

"Shit," I muttered, hurriedly releasing the contoured grip and dropping the weapon on the mattress. *What else was in this bag?*

I continued the search, my hands sensing a length of coiled rope before settling on the hollow cylinder. Withdrawing the roll of tape, I left the gun on the bed as I returned to the lounge. The woman sat in the centre of the sofa, her eyes flicking between Nick and the now muted television.

"Are you going to kill me?" she asked, tears rolling down her cheek.

"Get a chair from the kitchen," Nick said to me, ignoring her question.

I hobbled through the doorway and grabbed the nearest of the two wooden backed chairs.

"Put it there," he said, indicating a spot in front of the sliding door to the balcony. He watched as I dragged it over the carpet. He turned back to the terrified neighbour.

"Sit," he commanded, pointing with the knife.

The woman edged forward and pushed herself off the cushion. Nick followed a pace behind as she shuffled across the room.

Richard T. Burke

As soon as she was seated, he spoke over his shoulder to me. "Tie her arms and legs to the chair. Two layers should be enough."

I located the end of the reel and tore off a length of the grey material. Kneeling to one side, I started with her left arm. The woman whimpered as I strapped both wrists to the wooden frame then moved on to her ankles.

When I had finished, Nick stood over her and waved the knife in front of her face. She mewled in terror. A dark stain spread from her crotch accompanied by the acrid stench of urine.

"Answer my questions and I'll let you go afterwards."

The woman nodded vigorously. "Yes, yes." A thin stream of mucus dribbled from her right nostril.

"Let's start by asking your name."

"Sarah. Sarah Wells. I introduced myself when you arrived."

"Very good, Sarah. Now, do you know who we are?"

"I don't recognise you, but he's that teacher, the one who killed all those people."

"I didn't kill—"

Nick held up a hand. "Leave this to me, Alex." He lowered his head and stared hard into the woman's eyes. "Did you tell anybody else?"

Her gaze flicked between the pair of us. "Um ..."

Nick raised the knife. "Who was it?"

"I wasn't sure if you were ... I drove over to see a friend of mine this afternoon and we discussed my suspicions."

"Did you call the police?"

The woman paled. She nodded.

"When was this?" Nick asked. "What did you tell them?"

"She told me I should do it, so I called about half an hour ago. They took my details and wanted to know how certain I was. I said I couldn't be sure. That's why I came around. I thought if I could see him again ..."

"Shit. We need to leave. They could be here any minute."

"What are you going to do to me?"

Nick studied her with narrowed eyes but said nothing.

"Please don't kill me. I swear I won't say you were here."

"I have no intention of killing you, but we can't have you shouting for help, so I'll have to tape your mouth. The police will free you when they arrive. And just so you know, he didn't do it."

The woman glanced at me. "I promise I'll tell them that."

"Good. I'll also need your car keys."

"They're in my pocket."

Nick moved to her side, bent down and slipped his hand inside the denim material, frowning distastefully at the damp patch. He tugged free a bunch of keys. Stepping back, he gestured towards her face. "Alex, can you do the honours?"

I tore another strip of tape off the reel and taped it across her mouth.

Nick inspected my handiwork and nodded his approval. "I'll find the car. Pack your stuff and follow me down. I'll meet you by the staircase."

Richard T. Burke

I limped into the bedroom and grabbed the laptop bag from the bed. The sound of the apartment front door closing travelled along the hallway. I returned to the lounge and scanned the room, checking I had left nothing else behind. The woman stared at me with pleading eyes.

I studied her for a moment, desperately needing to justify my behaviour. "Look, I'm sorry about all this. It's true what my colleague said; I didn't commit any of the murders they're accusing me of. Somebody is trying to frame me."

She nodded furiously, small whimpering noises escaping through the tape across her mouth.

The irony of the situation wasn't lost on me. Here I was telling a woman whom we had tied to a chair and gagged that I wasn't responsible for the string of violent offences that had turned me into a wanted criminal. Until this point, I hadn't done anything illegal, barring the minor misdemeanour of using another person's account details to log into the dark website. Now, I was at the very least an accessory to kidnapping and car theft. How could I possibly expect her to believe me?

"Anyway, I've got to go. I'm sure the police will find you soon."

I turned away from her, blowing out a long breath through my mouth. The torn muscle sent shooting pains up my calf as I hobbled towards the entrance, holding the black bag in my hand. As I reached out for the handle, a faint rattling sound penetrated from the other side. Without thinking, I twisted the latch.

The door slammed into my face, sending me sprawling against the wall. Before I had time to react, a man strode through the doorway. He dropped the rucksack he had been holding on the floor, grabbed me by the collar and hauled me across the carpet into the lounge. There, he released his grip, crouched on one knee and smashed a fist into the bridge of my nose. Instinctively, I raised my hands to protect the injury. Another blow crashed into my jaw. Still dazed from the first two punches, I didn't even see the third as it crunched into my cheekbone.

Everything disappeared into a haze of pain. I closed my eyes and slumped backwards, choking on the blood that poured from my nostrils. Coughing, I rolled onto my side. The man was no longer standing over me. Moments later, I sensed movement and a change in the light level. I eased an eyelid open.

The black denim of his trouser legs occupied my vision. The assailant prodded me with his workman's boot. "Who's the woman?"

"Uh ..."

He launched a vicious kick at my stomach. "I asked you a question. Who is she?"

"Neighbour," I gasped, the air wheezing in my chest.

Through half-open eyes, I watched in horror as he reached into his bag and withdrew a long-bladed knife. He strode over the carpet until he stood behind the woman. She tried to twist her head to see what he was doing. In a flurry of movement, he grabbed her hair with one hand. With the other, he drew the blade across her throat.

Blood spurted from the wound, pumping rhythmically as her heart concluded its final beats. She juddered in the chair, fighting her bonds. Within ten seconds, she lay with her head lolling backwards, staring sightlessly at the ceiling. The man released his grip, stepped around the crimson stain and resumed his position standing over me.

"We can't have any witnesses now, can we?" he said.

"You didn't have to kill her," I croaked through swollen lips.

"Oh, it wasn't me who killed her. It was you." He grinned at my confusion. "And then you felt so bad about this murder and all the others, you jumped from the balcony."

"Who's paying you to do this?"

The man chuckled. "I've no idea. I'm just the hired help." He bent down and once again seized me by the collar, effortlessly hauling me to my feet. Despite his wiry physique, he seemed to possess immense strength. Standing beside him, I could see he was a good few inches shorter than me. An inch-long scar on his scalp showed through the dark stubble of his buzz cut. His grey eyes displayed a total lack of emotion. He saw me as the rubbish to be thrown out—literally.

"What about my blood on the carpet?" I said, pointing at the stain where I had been lying. "How will the police explain that?" I was stalling for time, and we both knew it.

He jutted his face into mine. "She defended herself and injured you in the process." The reek of onions and garlic washed over me. "Anyway, that's enough chitchat. I've got a job to finish."

The sleeve of his dark grey, roll-neck sweater closed around my throat. I tried to break his grip, but he ignored my feeble attempts and frogmarched me to the sliding balcony door.

"Open it," he commanded.

My fingers fumbled with the latch.

He tightened his stranglehold. "Come on, I haven't got all day."

The mechanism clicked, and the pressure released slightly. He reached past me with his free hand and slid the frame across. Once again, I tried to break loose, but he maintained the choke hold with ease and directed me forwards. The cool evening air brushed over my face. My stomach lurched as I contemplated the long fall to the concrete below.

I allowed my body to go limp, saving myself for one final attempt to escape his grip. He manoeuvred me towards the wall. A foot away, I stuck out my good leg and shoved myself backwards with all my strength. The man retained his hold as he staggered into the sheet of glass. I flung back an elbow, but it glanced off his ribs.

The steel band across my neck tightened, and I found myself once again approaching the barrier between the balcony and a hundred feet of freefall. A sudden shove sent me clattering into the brickwork. Strong hands grabbed my ankles and lifted my feet from the floor, catapulting me forwards. I flung out an arm and closed my fingers around the metal rail running along the top of the wall. My momentum carried me over the edge, nearly dislocating my shoulder as the full weight of my body came to an abrupt halt.

My would-be murderer studied me, a cold smile touching his thin lips. He raised his fist and smashed it against my knuckles. My grip loosened as the pain surged through my hand. One more blow and I would plunge to my death, hitting the concrete below at over fifty miles an hour.

I closed my eyes and waited for the end. Suddenly, I sensed movement above my head. Two seconds later a dull thud reached my ears. In confusion, I stared at the concrete below me and immediately spotted a body dressed in dark clothing spread-eagled across the paving slabs. A pool of blood expanded slowly around it.

Nick's face appeared above me. He grasped my wrist and hauled me upwards. I flopped onto the safety of the balcony floor, gulping in huge lungfuls of air.

"Thanks," I muttered when I had recovered enough breath to speak.

"My pleasure," he replied, "but if you don't mind, we need to get out of here pronto. The police tend to congregate around dead bodies, and there are two of them here."

The woman's eyes stared sightlessly at the ceiling as we skirted her dead body. A dark stain, almost black in colour, spread from the gash across her throat and down over her midriff. I had never seen a corpse before that day; now I had witnessed the deaths of two people within the space of a few minutes. An immense sense of guilt washed over me; if we hadn't trussed her up, she would probably still be alive. I pushed the thought to the back of my mind and followed Nick out of the flat.

He supported the weight on the side of my injured leg as we limped along the corridor to the lifts.

"It would be better to take the stairs," he said.

"But it'll be quicker to use the lift, won't it?" I replied.

"If the police are waiting, I don't suppose it will make much difference. The lift it is."

No reception committee awaited us when the doors parted at the foyer. We headed past the potted plants and down the steps towards the parking garage. The neighbour's blue car, a Citroen Picasso, sat to one side of the roadway, its hazard lights flashing bright orange in the dim illumination of the underground car park.

"Won't the police be looking for this?" I asked.

"Eventually," Nick replied, "but by then, hopefully, we'll be a long way away. I'll swap the plates with something else if we get the chance."

"Do I have to go in the back?"

"There's not much point. They'll find out we've taken it when they do a check."

I sighed with relief and sank into the passenger seat. Nick took his place behind the wheel and navigated us through the town centre. Several police cars with flashing lights and blaring sirens flashed past travelling in the opposite direction. Each time, I winced in anticipation, expecting them to screech to a halt and block our path, but our journey continued unimpeded.

When we were on a minor road heading north, I turned sideways in my seat. "Tell me what happened."

Nick stared straight ahead as he replied. "I found the car fairly quickly. When you didn't appear, I wondered what was going on. I parked by the staircase and headed back up. The door to the flat was slightly ajar. I remember thinking it was a bit strange because I knew I had closed it behind me. As soon as I spotted the dead body, I realised you were in trouble. For a moment, I thought I was too late.

"Then I saw him leaning over the balcony. His attention was so focused on finishing you off, he failed to notice me creeping up. I grabbed him by the legs and tipped him over the edge. He didn't even scream on the way down."

"Do you feel bad about killing him?"

Nick's expression hardened. "Not in the slightest. Let's face it, he was trying to kill you. If I hadn't turned up when I did, it would have been you lying in a pool of blood on the concrete." He flashed me a grin. "And of course, I only get paid if I keep you alive."

"Well, I'm grateful for your concern," I said, "but what do we do now?"

Nick's eyes narrowed. "Renting another hotel room is out of the question. Your face is plastered all over the news. If anybody saw you, it would be game over. We need to ditch the car too. It won't be too long before the police work out we took it. It's too big a risk to keep driving this, even if I change the plates."

He glanced at the dials on the dashboard. "The tank's nearly empty too."

"Can't we fill it up?"

Nick shook his head. "If there's one thing you can guarantee at a petrol station, it's that they have cameras monitoring the forecourt. I suppose I could park some distance away, pretend I've run out of fuel and buy a spare container, but they typically only hold a gallon, and that wouldn't get us far."

I folded my arms. "You've told me a whole load of stuff we can't do. What do you propose we actually do?"

Nick shrugged. "To be perfectly honest, I don't know. I'm still thinking."

As I sat in silence pondering our situation, an idea occurred to me, but I hesitated to voice it. I was sure Nick wouldn't approve. After a few more miles, he signalled and turned into a lay-by.

I looked across expectantly. He pulled the handle and stepped out onto the kerb. Angling his head inside, he said, "Stay there. I need to stretch my legs." I watched as he strode ten yards behind the car, stopped and stood facing away from me. He stayed in the same position for two minutes. In a sudden burst of activity, he swung around and marched back to the driver's door.

He lowered himself into the seat and shifted to face me. "The only suggestion I have is to park up and wait it out. It'll be uncomfortable, but it's the lowest risk."

I twisted sideways and met his gaze. "What about your lady friend?"

Nick frowned. "What are you suggesting?"

"Couldn't we stay with her?"

"Absolutely not. I can't involve her in this."

"But isn't she already involved. Didn't you say she arranged the rooms?"

"She's very careful. She only uses stolen identities."

I drew a deep breath. "You told me you suspect she knows what you do for a living. Isn't this a chance to show her that your work has a positive side?"

Nick gave a snort of derision. "You call protecting somebody who's accused of murder positive?"

"But you know it wasn't me. I mean, you were with me the whole time."

"I couldn't do that to her. She's already lost too much."

"Why don't you at least ask her?"

He glared at me. After what seemed an age, his shoulders slumped. "Alright, I'll call her. But I'm not promising anything."

Once again, he opened the door and strode to the same spot behind the car. As I watched, he held the phone to his ear, pacing backwards and forwards. His lips moved occasionally, but he appeared to be doing more listening than talking. Every few seconds he glanced in my direction. Eventually, he returned the mobile to his pocket and stared at me. Then he strolled back to the driver's door.

"What did she say?" I asked.

"She said she'd help, but I have some conditions of my own. Firstly, you have as little contact with her as possible. Secondly, you leave without question when the contract is up. That means Thursday midnight. Thirdly and most importantly, if the police arrest you, you keep us both out of it."

"That all sounds fair enough. What happens next?"

"We sleep in the car overnight. Early tomorrow morning while it's still dark, we hide this car somewhere. My friend picks us up, and we travel back to the house hidden in her car."

"How far is it?"

"It's a few miles. Another condition is that you stay in the boot throughout the whole journey."

I groaned. "Can't I sit on a seat for once?"

"I don't want you seeing where we go. If you don't know where she lives, there's no chance you could lead anybody else there."

"But who would I tell? I already agreed to keep quiet about you both if the police get hold of me."

"It's not the police I'm worried about," Nick replied.

Twenty-five years ago: Wednesday, 8th February, 1995

*W*e arrived at the police station just before eight-thirty on the morning after the kidnapping. There had been no progress in the search for Elena. By now, the number of officers involved in the investigation exceeded fifty. My mother and father were due to record an appeal for witnesses at ten o'clock. In the meantime, I was there to meet the sketch artist.

I sat in the reception area with my parents and Cathy. At five to nine, a female officer in a uniform of black skirt and white shirt emerged from the office. A pair of dimples appeared in her cheeks as she smiled at me. I liked her immediately.

"You must be, Alex. My name is Sergeant Davies. Would you like to come with me?"

I rose to my feet, accompanied by the other members of my family.

"I think it would be best if it was just Alex," she said.

The others sat again as she led me to a small interview room containing a metal table and four plastic chairs.

"Please wait here while I fetch the sketch artist. Can I get you anything to drink?"

I shook my head. "No, thanks."

Several minutes passed before a man wearing a chequered shirt and blue jeans followed the policewoman into the room. He was in his early thirties, but his mop of frizzy hair was already receding at the temples.

"This is Doug," she said. "He's going to try to draw a picture of the person who took your sister. You need to tell him everything you can remember. He'll come and get me when you're finished."

The artist sat beside me and placed a sketch pad on the table. A faint aroma of body odour rose off him. Lacking subtlety, I wrinkled my nose, but he didn't seem to notice. He withdrew a pencil from his breast pocket. "It's Alex, isn't it?"

I nodded.

"Okay, so you saw the man from your bedroom. What can you tell me about him?"

Richard T. Burke

My pulse raced. The familiar feeling of panic built up in my chest. "I ... I can't remember his face," I stammered.

"That's alright," Doug said, speaking slowly and calmly. "What can you remember?"

"He was wearing dark clothing. My sister was lying on the grass, not moving."

Doug picked up a pencil and drew on the paper. "Like this?"

The conversation swung backwards and forwards between us as I described what I had seen from the window of my room, and Doug sketched it out. Eventually, he showed me a reasonably good resemblance of the scene. Finally, I started to relax a little.

"Right, let's focus in on the man," Doug said. "What colour was his hair?"

Tears welled up. "I don't know."

"That's alright," he said. "Try to tell me what you do remember. Maybe he was wearing a hood. Close your eyes and see if that helps."

I did as instructed and tried to recall what I had witnessed. Doug was right. Something had been covering the man's head. "It was a hat."

Doug smiled. "Now we're getting somewhere." He flipped the page and started a new sketch. "This sort of thing?"

"No, more like a woolly hat."

He turned over the pencil, erased part of the drawing and shaded in a different shape.

"That's it."

Over the course of the next few minutes, we refined the image. The outline seemed accurate, but even after several prompts, I still couldn't describe the features of the man's face.

"Don't worry about it," Doug said, standing. "I'll get a policeman to show you some photographs. That might help to jog your memory."

He stuck out a hand. When I eventually realised what he was doing, I raised my own, and we shook, his fingers dwarfing mine.

"It was nice meeting you, Alex," he said. "I hope they find your sister. If you wait here, I'll fetch sergeant Davies."

Doug sidled out of the room, throwing me a wave through the small glass window as he disappeared down the corridor. Several minutes later, the policewoman returned carrying a large file.

"Okay, Alex, Doug mentioned that you're still struggling to remember the man's features. I've brought a book of photographs. Would you mind going through them to see if any of them jog your memory?"

Sergeant Davies sat beside me and turned to the first page. A surly looking man with a wide face stared back at me. I studied the image for at least thirty seconds then shook my head.

Initially, I lingered over each mugshot, but after a while, they all seemed to blend into one another. Gradually, the pace accelerated. By the time we reached the end, we had picked out six possible suspects, although I wasn't convinced any of them was the man I had seen standing over Elena's prostrate form.

The disappointment was evident on the policewoman's face. "Don't worry, Alex. We'll look into the ones you've identified. If you remember anything else, please tell your parents immediately."

Despite lying awake for many hours over the following nights, trying to recall the kidnapper's features, I never provided any useful information. It would be another twenty-two years before I finally identified my sister's kidnapper.

Day Four:
Thursday, 30th July, 2020

Richard T. Burke

I woke with a start. I had reclined the passenger seat as far as it would go, but it wasn't wide enough to sleep comfortably. To my right, Nick occupied the driver's seat. His eyes were closed, and he breathed deeply, but I suspected he was still awake. He confirmed my suspicions when his left eye opened, glanced briefly in my direction and shut again.

I rubbed the condensation from the side window with the palm of my hand. The dashboard clock indicated just after two thirty. Despite the lateness of the hour, a small amount of light from the full moon penetrated the canopy of leaves high above us. Shortly after Nick's telephone call, we had driven along the forest track and then off the muddy route into a space between the trees.

Using his knife and my bare hands, we had covered most of the bodywork in a camouflage of branches. A substantial pile lay beside the vehicle, ready to be applied when we left for the rendezvous with his female friend in thirty minutes' time. Our efforts wouldn't conceal the car for long, but the covering only needed to last until we were well away from this site.

My stomach rumbled. We hadn't eaten anything since lunchtime. Nick told me it was too risky to buy food. His friend had promised us a large plate of bacon and eggs when we reached our destination. They had arranged to meet at three o'clock on the minor road where the track emerged from the woods.

I settled back into the fabric and adjusted my position slightly.

"Are you awake?" Nick murmured.

"Yeah, I can't get comfortable."

He sighed. "Me neither. I must be getting old. In my younger days when I was in the army, I could fall asleep almost anywhere. Although I can still block out noise, now I need a bed to sleep properly."

He fiddled with the seat mechanism until he sat upright. I glanced sideways at him.

"There's not long to go. Why don't we sort out the car?" he said.

"Alright. Tell me what to do."

"For a start, we need to get everything out."

I reached into the back and grabbed my laptop bag. I had stuffed my few belongings inside. Pulling the door handle, I emerged into the cool night air.

The sudden change in temperature after the fuggy warmth of the car interior drove away the last remnants of sleepiness.

"What next?" I asked as Nick exited from the driver's side.

"Cover the doors using the bits from the pile over there. I don't want to see any paintwork by the time we've finished."

We worked by the glow of the full moon, positioning the branches until they totally covered the vehicle.

Nick stood back to admire our handiwork. "It's like being in army training again. The instructors would have given that a seven out of ten, but it'll do for now."

To my untrained eye, there was little to identify the outline of the hatchback. "Whatever you say."

We trudged through the trees until we reached the track. When I turned to look back, the camouflage made the car invisible in the silvery moonlight. Nick scuffed fallen leaves over the faint outlines of the tyre tracks.

"That should do the trick," he said, glancing at his watch. "My friend will be here in a quarter of an hour. We may as well wait by the side of the road, but we need to hide if any cars come by."

Nick strode down the rutted lane. I limped along behind. Within five minutes, we left the cover of the trees and stepped out onto the tarmac. The dashed, white centreline glowed in the moon's reflection. The rustle of the leaves in the light wind sounded like running water. An owl hooted from somewhere in the woods.

I crossed the road and leaned against the low, stone wall. On the other side, the land rolled away in a patchwork of fields, painted grey by the dim illumination. A warm breath, stirred by the gentle breeze, washed over me, soon to be replaced again by the chill of the early morning. I inhaled deeply, savouring the clean air of the open countryside.

Nick paced backwards and forwards, stopping now and then to stare along the carriageway. After a few minutes, he called in a hushed voice and beckoned to me. "Someone's coming. We need to get out of sight."

I hobbled across the road and crouched alongside him behind a low bush at the edge of the woodland. The glare of the headlights blinded me for a second as a small car approached slowly from the right. It drew to a halt, the indicator flashing.

"It's her," Nick said, emerging from our hiding place. The driver's door opened, and a woman stepped out. From my vantage point, I could see she had blond hair tied in a short ponytail.

Nick hurried towards her, and they embraced for a moment. I hung back, not wanting to intrude on their reunion. He beckoned me forward.

"This is Alex," he said as I neared the couple. He took a pace backwards. Up close, I determined his friend was in her mid to late thirties. She was petite with an attractive face. She smiled tightly and stuck out a hand. As I reached out to accept her handshake, her eyes widened in shock.

"You're the teacher that's been on the news, the one the police are hunting for."

"He didn't do it," Nick said, placing an arm on her shoulder.

She shrugged it off angrily. "What do you mean? He's wanted for six murders. They can't have got it that wrong."

Nick sighed. "He hasn't been out of my sight for the past few days. Somebody is framing him. It'll only be for a day or two, and then he'll leave."

"When you told me you were taking a protection job, I had no idea it would be him."

"Look, I'm sorry. Maybe I should have mentioned it, but I didn't want to say anything on the phone."

"The rooms I booked were so you and this ... serial killer ... could hide from the police?"

"I haven't killed anybody," I said, raising my voice. "Somebody wants me dead, and your friend has been paid to keep me alive. Now are you going to help or not?"

The woman stood with hands on hips, her gaze alternating between Nick and me. Finally, she shrugged. "What the hell. If John says you're innocent, I believe him."

I had always suspected that Nick wasn't his real name, but this provided the confirmation. He frowned at the sudden revelation and grabbed me by the arm. "You didn't hear that. Just keep calling me Nick."

The woman shook her head. "I can't be doing with all this cloak and dagger stuff. My name's Val. Now, are we going to leave?"

Nick started to say something then thought better of it. "He can go in the boot. I'll lie across the back seat."

Val took a deep breath and blew it out through her lips. "You boys sort yourselves out. I don't suppose anybody will be up to see you at this time of day, but it's your choice." She opened the driver's door, sat and fitted the seat belt.

Nick led me around to the rear of the vehicle and pressed the release button. The space in the Vauxhall Corsa appeared even more cramped than the Ford Focus.

"I'll have a talk to her," he said. "She'll be okay."

"Glad to hear it," I replied drily and clambered inside.

The boot slammed shut, plunging me into darkness. The clunk of another door shutting infiltrated my confined enclosure. I cursed as the car jolted into movement.

The low murmur of conversation penetrated the barrier of the rear seat, but the drone of the engine masked the words. I drifted into my own thoughts, rerunning the exchange with Nick's female friend.

It was clear he hadn't discussed my identity with her beforehand. She had taken one look at me and recoiled in shock when she recognised me. The news networks had plastered my face across every newspaper and television screen over the past few days. It seemed the universal coverage had made me instantly recognisable. Was that how my life would be from now on, always assuming I survived?

She had referred to me as a serial killer. At what number did a murderer turn into a serial killer? As I rolled the question around in my head, I concluded the answer was at least three. With six murders to my name, I was well past that limit.

Wait. Six murders? A prickling sensation ran across my scalp. There were the husband and wife in the big house, my mother and the two who had died that afternoon in the flat. That made five. Who was the sixth? A deep dread unfurled its leathery wings inside me. Had the killers caught up with my sister?

I needed to know. "Hey! Stop the car," I yelled, slamming my fist against the back of the seat.

The jolting movement stopped. The sound of a door opening preceded the sudden glare of the courtesy light as the boot lifted.

Val stared at me. Concern etched her brow. "What is it?"

"Earlier you said I killed six people. At the last count, they accused me of killing five. Who was the sixth?"

She shook her head. "I'm not sure. I watched it on the news and the number stuck in my head, but I can't remember who they all were."

"Please, I need to know."

"There was the couple found murdered together and another three this afternoon."

"Three? That doesn't include my mother, does it?"

"That's right, I forgot about her. That brings it to six."

"You're saying there were four today?" I asked, my words quavering with apprehension.

"Yes. They discovered two at that flat, and you obviously already know about ..." Her voice trailed off. "I can't remember who the fourth was."

"It wasn't my sister, was it?"

Val shook her head. "No, I would have remembered that."

I heaved a sigh of relief. "Thank God."

"Oh, that's right. It was a woman who lived next door to you. Apparently, she'd been dead for a few days, but they only discovered the body today. Someone strangled her."

I wracked my brain, trying to think who it could be. Suddenly, it dawned on me. "Was she called Mrs Owens? She lives opposite. Did they say anything about a dog?"

"Yeah, now you mention it, there was something like that. I remember; they found her after a neighbour complained about the barking."

I closed my eyes and rested my head against the coarse carpet. The huge release in the pressure that had been building inside my chest left me feeling dizzy and breathless. Mrs Owens didn't deserve what happened to her, but my relief at discovering the latest victim wasn't anybody close to me trumped any sense of guilt that she was dead because of events I had set in motion.

"Can we carry on now?" she asked.

"Yes, thank you for stopping," I replied.

The boot slammed shut, once again plunging me into darkness.

We had been travelling for less than an hour when the wheels lurched over a kerb and came to rest. The sound of a door opening reverberated through the floor, followed shortly afterwards by a metallic clanking noise. Seconds later, the boot lifted. I flung an arm across my face to shield my eyes from the sudden, glaring illumination of the fluorescent strip light. As my vision adjusted to the brightness, I realised we were in a single garage. Despite the small size of the car, there was barely enough space behind the bumper for me to place my feet on the ground.

"Are you okay?" Val asked, her forehead creased in concern.

"Yeah, I'm fine," I replied, "but I can't recommend it as a way to travel."

She smiled and stood back to allow me the room to get out. "Come through, and I'll make a cup of tea."

I followed her along the side of the car to a door leading into the kitchen. She tossed the keys on the table and clicked the switch on the kettle.

I sank onto one of the wooden-backed chairs. Nick—I couldn't think of him as John—slumped down opposite me. We sat waiting, the silence broken only by the clink of teaspoon on china.

"Milk or sugar?" Val asked over her shoulder.

"Just milk, please," I replied. I had been trying to lose weight ahead of my big holiday, but that seemed like a lifetime ago now. "Actually, I'll have one sugar as well," I added.

She placed the mugs in front of us, then plonked herself down and sipped her own drink. After a brief pause, she looked up and met my gaze. "I'm sorry about what I said earlier. It must be awful to be accused of crimes you didn't commit, let alone losing your mother and being charged with her murder too."

"You have no idea," I replied.

"I just wanted to say I'll help, however I can."

"Thanks, I appreciate it."

Now I had the chance to study her under the bright ceiling lights, I could see she was extremely attractive. Her cornflower-blue irises complemented a kind and open face. The only slight blemishes were the grey half-moon crescents beneath each eye—hardly surprising given the disturbance to her sleep. The cream trousers hugged a trim, petite figure.

"I know it's still the middle of the night," she said, "but can I get you anything to eat?"

My stomach rumbled at the mention of food. "Nick—I mean John— mentioned bacon and egg earlier. I'm starving. We last ate around lunchtime."

"What sort of bodyguard are you anyway, not feeding your client?" she teased, turning to Nick. "John's used to a life in the army and thinks everybody else is the same."

"A little discomfort never hurt anybody," he replied with a grin, "but I could murder a fry up too." For the first time since I had met him, he appeared embarrassed. "I'm sorry, wrong word."

Val shook her head. "A certain person should engage his brain before he opens his mouth." She busied herself at the stove, and soon the aroma of sizzling bacon filled the kitchen.

I wolfed the food down and followed it with another cup of tea. Finally, a sense of normality seemed to be returning to my life.

"I guess you boys need to catch up on your sleep," Val said, glancing at the large dial on the wall. The time was approaching four o'clock. "I have to leave for work at eight. I'll see if I can get the afternoon off, but if not, I should be back around five. Help yourselves to whatever you want. I've made the spare bed, but one of you will have to take the sofa."

"I don't mind," Nick said. "It'll be more comfortable than a car seat."

"There's a towel on the radiator in the bedroom. You'll have to fight it out for who uses the bathroom first."

Nick gestured towards me. "You go. We've got some catching up to do." He grinned sheepishly at Val. "That is if you're okay to stay up a bit longer."

She shrugged. "I've already been up half the night. What are a few more minutes?" She turned to me. "The guest room is upstairs on the right. Sleep well."

I rose to my feet and wished them both goodnight. As I passed through the door, I glanced backwards with a slight pang of jealousy. Their heads were lowered, deep in conversation. What was the relationship between these two? They seemed so different to each other. I pushed the thought to the back of my mind. For the time being, I was in no situation to consider anything but survival.

The prospect of clean sheets drew me upstairs like a magnet. The room contained a freshly made double bed. A modern touch lamp sat on top of the bedside table. A built-in wardrobe with mirrors on the doors occupied the end wall.

I studied my reflection for a moment. Several pale stains marked the front of the blue hoodie. My hair stood up at odd angles. A layer of stubble coated my chin, and dark shadows rimmed both eyes. My appearance matched what I would expect from somebody on the run from the law.

I grabbed the towel and headed down the hall to the bathroom. The smell of perfumed soap invaded my nostrils as I entered. A single toothbrush sat on the shelf above the washbasin, accompanied by an assortment of female toiletries. All the evidence supported the hypothesis that there was no special person in Val's life.

I washed my face. The floral scent lingered on my skin even after drying. Squeezing toothpaste from the tube, I rubbed my finger over my gums and teeth. Then I stripped off and stepped into the shower cubicle. I turned up the temperature and basked in the steaming hot jets of water.

The stress of the day gradually dissipated leaving me feeling both clean and relaxed. With a towel around my waist, I scooped up my clothes and headed back to the guest bedroom. There, I dropped the bundle on the floor and clambered between the sheets. Within minutes, I was asleep.

When I eventually blinked awake, daylight streamed around the edges of the curtains. I held my wrist to my face, trying to make sense of the watch dial: eleven o'clock. I had slept for almost the whole morning. Easing back the covers, I lowered my feet to the carpet. A dull headache throbbed behind my eyes.

I padded across the carpet and edged the door open. A pile of neatly folded clothes greeted me. On top sat a note.

Help yourself to any of these. Val.

I grabbed the bundle and dumped it on the bed. The clothing must have belonged to Val's deceased husband. To my relief, the contents included several pairs of clean underwear. Amongst the items were also a couple of T-shirts, a long-sleeved shirt, a lightweight, green pullover and a pair of brightly coloured beach shorts. Finally, I could discard the stained hoodie.

After taking another shower, I dressed in a yellow T-shirt and the shorts. When I inspected myself in the mirror, I looked ready for a day at the seaside. All I needed were the sunglasses.

The sound of clanking pans carried from downstairs. I descended the stairs in bare feet and discovered Nick bent over the stove. He also wore a T-shirt and the same pair of trousers he had been wearing for the past few days.

He glanced up at my arrival. "Not before time. I was beginning to wonder whether you'd died in your sleep. If you're hungry, I've got toast and boiled eggs on the go."

"That would be great."

"I take it you slept well."

"Like a log."

Nick focused his attention on the saucepan.

"Do you think we're safe here?" I asked to his back.

He turned around slowly. "For the time being, as long as we don't do anything stupid to give away our location. That means no using the phone or the computer."

"And what happens when the contract is up?"

He narrowed his eyes. "That's your problem, not mine. My responsibility ends at midnight."

"Right."

An awkward silence developed as he continued to prepare the meal. After a few minutes, he placed a plate in front of me containing a slice of unbuttered toast and an egg in an eggcup.

I wasn't particularly hungry but downed the food anyway. When I had finished, I carried the dirty crockery to the sink and did the washing up. Nick stood beside me with a tea towel and dried the dishes. Between the two of us, we portrayed a picture of domesticity.

"Have you heard any more news?" I asked when we had cleared the draining board.

"No, but Val said it was alright to use her computer," Nick replied. "Like I mentioned earlier, don't type in anything that identifies you. That means no webmail or other sites that require a username to access them. Is that clear?"

"Sure."

"The machine is in the dining room. The password is Eddie one two three four."

"I assume Eddie was her husband."

"That's right."

"What happened to him?"

Nick hesitated for a moment. He seemed to debate with himself whether to answer my question. Finally, he shook his head slightly and sighed. "He was in my company. We were on station in Afghanistan. Reports came in of a patrol being hit by an IED. Some of the men were badly injured, so they sent us out in a helicopter to retrieve them. Everything was going well, and most of the wounded were on board when all hell broke loose.

"The insurgents had been hiding, waiting in ambush for help to arrive. Suddenly, we found ourselves tangled up in a gun battle. Eddie caught one bullet in the chest and another in the upper arm. I hauled him into the chopper, and we took off. At first, I didn't think the injury was that serious. The body armour protects the torso, so the chest shot only caused some bruising.

"He was bleeding a fair bit, but the medics were concentrating on the wounded we rescued from the vehicle. It was only when he collapsed that anybody realised how bad it was. It turned out the bullet in his arm had nicked an artery. He was dead by the time we arrived back at base.

"Before he died, he made me promise to look after Val if he didn't make it. As you might expect, his death devastated her. I did what I could to help. The army pension just about covers the cost of her mortgage but not by much. When it happened, she was studying computing at college, so had no other source of income. I tided her over until she finished the course.

Richard T. Burke

"When I left the armed forces, I got some work from friends and contacts, but it soon dried up. I could have worked for a military contractor, but I'd had enough of being shot at. Then, an opportunity arose for ... a private contract."

"That's when you became a hitman?" I asked.

"Yes. Val helped me to organise the technical side. She never knew what the work was about, although she isn't stupid, and I imagine she figured it out for herself. I paid her for the services she provided, and she's been helping me out ever since. She doesn't need the money anymore; she has a good job at an engineering company. After all the training, she's become something of an expert with computers. I don't have much of a clue about technology."

"Join the club," I said. "I wish I'd stayed clear of the damned things. That's what got me in this mess in the first place."

"But you're keen to go online now?"

I shrugged. "Needs must. I want to find out what new crimes I'm being accused of."

"Okay, but remember what I told you."

I headed into the dining room. A sleek, black laptop sat on the table. I lifted the lid and pressed the power button. Within seconds, a password prompt appeared; obviously, this machine was vastly superior in performance to my own ancient computer. I tapped in the characters and the background changed to show a man in army uniform smiling into the camera: Val's deceased husband I assumed.

I fired up a browser and typed my name into the address bar. A dozen images of my face stared back at me, including the photographs I recognised from my passport and school identity card. The *Top Stories* section at the head of the page contained three news articles ranging in age from one hour to five. I clicked the first link.

Police widen manhunt for serial killer. The article from the Daily Mail described the six murders of which I was accused, confirming the most recent victim as my former neighbour, Mrs Owens. According to the story, over two hundred detectives were now working on the case. They hadn't yet identified the man who had fallen from the balcony; a Photofit of his face accompanied an appeal to the public for information.

Law enforcement agencies were still searching for the car belonging to the woman who had died in the flat. It seemed our camouflage work had been effective. As I expected, they had traced the call to my sister and established the location from which I had placed it. Once again, the police were encouraging any witnesses to come forward.

Starting with a summary of my life history, the journalist questioned how a paedophile and future mass murderer could work undetected in a secondary school for so long. He called for a tightening of procedures to vet teachers. The piece concluded with a brief reference to my sister's abduction, proposing the hypothesis that the childhood incident had been an inciting factor in the crimes I later committed as an adult.

In a fit of despair, I placed my head in my hands. How the hell was I going to get out of this mess?

Val arrived home shortly after two o'clock. By now, I was sitting on the sofa, watching the television with the sound turned down low. Nick was busy changing a light bulb in the kitchen.

"Did you sleep well?" she asked.

The woman standing before me gave off an aura of professionalism. The white blouse and black trousers suited her.

I clicked the off button on the remote control and levered myself upright. "Yes, like a baby."

"Very trendy." She smiled, looking me up and down. "Are you planning a trip to the beach?"

"Thanks for lending me the clothes," I replied, suddenly feeling self-conscious in the garish shorts and T-shirt compared to her smart attire.

Her smile dimmed a little. "I have no use for them. I was going to take them to the charity shop but never got around to it. What have you two boys been up to while I've been away?"

Nick came through from the kitchen. "Oh, he's been depressing himself by reading the news on the Internet."

"I assume things haven't changed for the better," she said, slumping into the armchair and kicking off her shoes.

I resumed my place on the sofa. "You could say that. At least the murder count hasn't risen from six since last night."

"How could the police get it so wrong?"

I shrugged. "Your guess is as good as mine, but I suspect somebody is putting a huge amount of effort into framing me."

"And your theory is it's related to the dark web thing?"

"It's the only explanation that makes any sense, but even then …"

"John told me about the two policemen who visited your house. Do you think they're the ones behind it?"

I shook my head. "I'm not sure. According to my neighbour—the one who was murdered—they were around the back for a few minutes while I was out. A short time later, they turned up with a search warrant, suggesting I'd downloaded illegal material. The next thing I know, a policeman is carrying off my computer in an evidence bag."

"And had you?"

I felt the colour rise to my cheeks. "You mean pornographic images of children like they're saying? Of course not."

Val leaned forwards, an apologetic expression on her face. "I'm sorry; it was a question I had to ask."

I exhaled a long breath. "It's okay. I understand. Yesterday was the first time you'd met me. For all you know, it could be true."

"No, you can pick up a vibe off somebody. It's obvious you're not a paedophile ... or a murderer."

"Have you come across many murderers before?" I replied without thinking.

From the corner of my eye, I noticed Nick flinch slightly.

Val switched her focus to him. "Get real, John. I'm aware what you do. I don't approve, but I'm not about to tell you how to live your life. Still, can't you choose more of the jobs like the one you're doing now?"

It was Nick's turn to blush. "They don't appear that often, but I'll see what I can do."

The conversation stalled as we each mulled over the recent discussion.

"What are we going to do about you, Alex?" Val said, her tone brightening.

"John's arrangement expires at midnight," I replied. "I guess I have no option but to turn myself in at that point."

"I have to say, it's all a bit weird. John told me your brother-in-law is the one who placed the job. How is he involved in all this?"

I sighed. "Who knows? I went around to see him on the same morning the contract for my protection appeared on that site. Something or someone had scared him shitless. I assume they must have coerced him somehow. At first, he pretended he wasn't home. When I threatened to smash my way in, he told me he would try to help. He also warned me to stay clear of the police."

Val tugged at the loop of her earring. "There's been no mention of him in the news, at least not as far as I'm aware."

"You're right," I said. "I must have read every single story about the case on the Internet, and not one of them made any reference to him. I hope he's okay."

"They would've mentioned it if he was hurt," Nick chipped in.

"It still begs the question of how he placed the contract if he isn't involved in some way," Val said.

"The night before it all kicked off, I went around there to ask his advice about this dark web page. We tried to access it, so I showed him the piece of paper containing the username and password. Maybe the site was temporarily down and came back up again later. He could have used it to place the contract."

Val frowned. "Have you still got the website details?"

Nick and I exchanged a glance. He gave an almost imperceptible shake of the head.

"It's on my laptop."

"That's not a good idea for several reasons," Nick said, scowling at me. "First, you've seen the mess Alex has landed himself in by messing with this stuff."

"I'm a big girl," Val said. "I don't—"

"Second," Nick interrupted, "I think there may be something on the machine that can be used to trace it back to a location."

Val pushed herself out of the armchair and paced backwards and forwards in front of the sofa. "I'll turn the Wi-Fi router off. That way it can't send out any data. I just want to look at it."

"It's still an extremely bad idea," Nick said. "I told him I'd only bring him here if he didn't involve you."

Val halted her pacing and glared at him. "That's not your decision to make."

Nick's expression tightened. "Do what you like. You always do."

She stood with hands on hips, eyes narrowed. "What are you trying to say? You don't own me. You helped me out, and for that, I'm extremely grateful. But that doesn't mean you get to rule my life. I'm well aware of the risks, but it isn't right to abandon him just because it's the easy way out."

"I apologise," Nick said, forcing an unconvincing smile. "Go and fetch the laptop, Alex."

I alternated my gaze between the two, then pushed myself off the sofa and hobbled across the room, closing the door behind me. The muffled sound of raised voices followed me up the stairs. Upon reaching the bedroom, I flopped down on the covers. It was clear they needed some time in private to sort out their differences.

Eventually, the argumentative noises faded. I gave it another minute, then grabbed the laptop case and carried it downstairs. When I re-entered the lounge, the atmosphere was thick with tension. Val sat on the armchair with her arms folded. Nick had wedged himself into the corner of the sofa with a scowl on his face. Neither looked at the other.

Val jumped up at my arrival. "I'll turn off the router. Bring the laptop through to the dining room."

I followed her into the hallway.

There, she knelt and flicked a switch. "Right, that's the box turned off. I suggest we disable the Wi-Fi on your machine too, just to be doubly safe."

She grabbed a chair and shoved her own laptop to one side to make space for mine.

I rummaged in the bag for the mains adapter. "Can you plug this in, please? It only lasts a few minutes on battery." While she unravelled the cables, I opened the lid and pushed the power button.

"Here." She handed me the connector, and I slotted it into place. While the machine booted, she studied it critically. "I remember these. I think it's time for an upgrade. It must be at least ten years old."

"Nine," I replied, smiling, "and yes, it's a pile of crap. It belongs to the school."

She reached forward and flicked a switch on the side. "That's the Wi-Fi turned off too."

"I always wondered what that did. Now I know."

We sat in silence as the machine completed its laborious startup sequence. Eventually, after much whirring and clicking, the login prompt appeared.

"Bloody hell, is that Windows XP?" she asked.

"I'm afraid so. They haven't got the budget to upgrade."

"That might explain something. Microsoft hasn't been updating that operating system for years, so it wouldn't come as a great surprise to find it's infected with malware."

"My brother-in-law checked it over on Monday night and told me it was clean."

Val raised an eyebrow but said nothing.

I typed in my password. After a few seconds, the icons started to appear one by one, accompanied by more clicking noises.

Val folded her arms. "If I knew it would take this long to boot, I'd have done something useful, like writing a novel."

Finally, the laptop responded to my requests to access the file explorer. I navigated to the folder holding the screenshots I had captured at the Internet café.

Val dragged the machine closer and squinted at the image showing one of the jobs. "There isn't much detail, is there?"

Nick spoke from behind us. "The site lists the basics—otherwise somebody might identify the subject and warn them. Once the job is accepted, the person placing the contract sends through the particulars using Bitmessage. It's a program which uses Tor to send encrypted messages."

Val shook her head. "Yeah, I've heard of it. You're saying you have no idea who the target is in advance."

"Isn't that what I just said?" Nick snapped.

She swivelled in the chair and stared at him silently for a moment before turning back to the screen. Her fingers darted over the trackpad as she studied each of the images I had captured. "It's basically eBay for hitmen."

"Yeah," Nick replied, "except here the lowest price wins. And people pay using Bitcoin."

"I suppose that makes sense. Do you have the site address and login details, Alex?"

"You're not seriously going to log on, are you?" Nick spluttered. "Talk about playing with fire."

"Well, I'm not about to use this piece of crap—no offence, Alex. I've got a bootable Linux distribution on a DVD. I'll download Tor and have a look with my machine."

"I only understood about every third word," I said. "What's wrong with my laptop?"

Val sighed. "Apart from the fact your antique is probably riddled with malware, it also uses an unsupported—and that means insecure—operating system. On top of that, it's as slow as hell. By using a DVD, we can guarantee there aren't any modifications or hidden software programs installed. It's like starting from a fresh installation each time."

"Whatever you say."

"I don't think it's worth the risk," Nick said.

"How many times have you logged into this site?" Val asked. "I'm willing to bet you've never taken the precautions I've just suggested."

"That may be true, but I didn't have half the British police force and a pack of assassins hunting me at the time. What are you hoping to find out?"

"We won't know until we look, will we?"

Nick turned away. "Tell me if you discover anything interesting. I'll leave you geeks to it. If you need me, I'll be in the lounge."

Val shrugged. "Suit yourself." She rose to her feet and opened the top drawer in an oak cabinet. After rummaging around for a few seconds, she triumphantly held up a silver coloured disk marked with illegible black writing. "Here we are."

She returned to the table, carrying the DVD together with a pen and paper. Turning her attention to my laptop, she copied down the site details.

"Wouldn't it be quicker to use a USB stick?" I asked.

She laughed. "Not a chance. I don't want to transfer across whatever nasties are lurking on your hard disk." When she had finished, she shut down my computer. "Could you turn the router back on, please?"

When I returned, she opened the lid of her machine and pressed the power button. Her finger tapped the side, and a tray popped open. She inserted the DVD then pushed it home. Moments later, the screen displayed two large buttons, *Try Ubuntu* and *Install Ubuntu*. She selected the first option.

Several minutes passed as a series of boxes filled with indecipherable text. Occasionally, she clicked a button or typed in some data. Eventually, the display showed a number of icons on a colourful background.

"Right, I'll set up Tor and then we're good to go."

Val's fingers whirled over the keyboard until the stylised image of the globe signalled installation was complete. She squinted at the paper, carefully transposing the contents to the screen.

"Let's see if this works," she said, tapping the return key with a flourish. The bland dialogue box appeared. "So far, so good."

She entered the login details and clicked the OK button. I held my breath as the egg timer cursor rotated. Several seconds passed, and the display updated. To my surprise, the window displayed the by now familiar layout. The *All Jobs* tab contained two entries. Both postcodes began with RG.

My face and ears tingled. A wave of dizziness swept over me.

Val sensed my discomfort. She turned sideways and studied me. "Are you alright?"

When I didn't reply, she placed a hand on my shoulder. "I'm sorry. This must bring back bad memories. I should have been more sensitive. If you like, you can sit with John. I'll give you a shout when I've had a poke around."

"No, it's okay," I replied, forcing the words out through numb lips. "I'd rather stay here and watch."

"Well, if you're sure." She opened each of the jobs and studied the information. According to the first description, the contract required the termination of an unsuspecting target. The second indicated that the proposed victim employed protection services. That probably explained the disparity between the bid prices of six thousand and eleven thousand five hundred pounds, respectively.

As before, the tabs titled *Your Current Jobs* and *Your Completed Jobs* were empty. Val clicked the final option, *Create a Job*. Her eyes widened as she took in the meaning. "Does this mean somebody can just order a person's death at the click of a button?"

I nodded. "That's what it looks like. Add some funds and select your target. It's as easy as that."

"How do people join the site?"

"I don't know. My brother-in-law sent me the login details. You'd have to ask Nick how he received his."

"Oh, I intend to." She sat, staring at the screen. "This is incredible. I've heard stories about this sort of thing on the dark web, but I never thought they could be true."

"People can also place protection jobs. Without Nick's help, I would definitely be dead." I neglected to tell her he had originally bid on a termination contract. "How does this change anything, though?"

Val placed a hand on her cheek. "I'm not sure. Let me have a think about it. There must be a way to use this information to get you out of this mess."

I followed Val back into the lounge. Nick was sitting on the sofa watching a quiz show. He made a point of keeping his eyes fixed on the screen as we entered.

"I have a few questions," Val said.

Still, Nick refused to acknowledge us.

"How did you obtain your login to the site?" she asked.

Finally, Nick picked up the remote control and switched off the television. He turned slowly towards Val and studied her for a moment before speaking. "Are you positive you want to get involved in this?"

Her eyes narrowed. "If I didn't, I wouldn't be asking."

Nick sighed. "Just for the record, I still think it's a bad idea, but if you're sure. An old army friend introduced me. The system works on personal recommendation. The person doing the recommending is personally liable. And by that, I don't mean financially. It was made clear, if something goes wrong, they'll find themselves on the receiving end of a contract."

"How do you get the username and password to access the site?"

"After somebody puts forward your name, you create a user account on Bitmessage. The proposer sends your identity to the people who run the system. If they approve your application, they send you the page address and login details."

Val frowned in concentration as she took in the information. "From what you've just said, you have no idea who is behind it all?"

"That's the whole point. In theory, every member only knows the person who proposed them and anybody they introduced."

"Have you put forward any candidates?"

Nick scratched the back of his head. "No. I didn't want to take the risk—apart from which, I don't trust anyone enough to discuss it with … present company excepted."

"How do people get the rights to place a job?"

"I'm not sure, but I'd guess it was by the same system. My account doesn't give me that option."

A thoughtful expression settled on Val's face. After a few seconds of silence, she spoke again. "Alex can access the jobs placed by other members, but it looks like he also has the ability to post his own contracts. Why would that be?"

Nick leaned forwards. "That's a good point, but the bigger question is how his brother-in-law set that up … unless he's the one behind the site."

"He runs a web design company," I said. "If I had to hazard a guess, I reckon he designed the system. Perhaps somebody employed him to create it."

"That still doesn't explain why he sent you the details," Nick said. "What I don't understand is how he thought that would help you."

Thoughts rattled around inside my head as I wracked my brains for answers. Nick made a good point. Why did Jamie send me the information to access the site? He had already warned me that dangerous people were trying to hunt me down. He didn't need to show me details of the page to convince me. And why give me the option to place a job? Unless …

"Maybe he sent me his own username and password," I said. "If he was developing the website, he would have to test the process of both placing and accepting contracts."

"That's possible," Val agreed, "but I don't see how it helps us. You can't hide forever, Alex. We need to come up with a way of ending this."

"The protection contract ends at midnight," Nick said.

"Thanks for the reminder," she snapped. "We were already aware of that. Just as long as you get your money."

"I've got to pay the bills."

Val snorted in disgust. "Yeah, don't worry about anybody else. You might as well leave now. I'm sure we'll survive for the rest of the day."

I slumped on the sofa beside Nick. "Will you both please stop arguing? I can only see one solution; I'll hand myself in and take my chances. I'll keep you out of it as much as possible. Drop me off somewhere tomorrow morning, and I'll contact them from my mobile."

Val folded her arms. "You can't do that. You have a price on your head, and there's good evidence the police are involved."

"The deadline for the contract to kill me is midnight. Perhaps they'll call it off."

"He's got a point," Nick said.

Val's gaze alternated between the pair of us. "I'm not sure which is worse; one of you wants to give up, the other doesn't care. If you decide you want to live past tonight, Alex, I'll help you out in whatever way I can. But you have to work with me. If you change your mind, you'll find me in the kitchen."

She spun on her heel and strode through the doorway.

Nick and I sat side by side, both of us looking shamefaced. Val's tirade made me feel like a naughty schoolboy. I pushed myself out of the seat.

"Good luck," Nick muttered.

I followed the sound of clanking pans. At first, I couldn't see Val. As I moved further into the room, I spotted her crouching beside an open cupboard beneath the sink.

I spoke to her back. "I'm sorry, Val. Of course, I'd rather not give up, but there's no obvious solution to my problem. The last thing I want is to put you in danger. This is my mess, and I need to sort it out."

She straightened up, holding a pan in her hand. "Doesn't it make you angry that somebody has killed your mother and the whole world is accusing you of her murder? And what about the other people who have died? Don't they deserve justice? If you aren't going to do it for yourself, you should do it for them."

"You're right," I said, "but where do we start?"

"We can work it out together." She moved to the table and gestured to a chair. I dropped into a seat opposite her.

"Your brother-in-law told you that you couldn't trust the police, didn't he?"

I nodded. "It seems a good bet to assume the two men who paid me a visit are involved."

"The main problem as I see it is that we can't tell how far the corruption extends."

My thoughts turned to the policewoman I had spoken to at the start, Susie Mayhew. Thinking back to our initial conversation, I couldn't believe she was implicated. But was I prepared to bet my life on it? Perhaps the fact that I found her attractive was clouding my judgement. "There was a sergeant I talked to. My gut feeling is she's alright."

"We don't know how high up this goes. She could be clean, but it's possible somebody higher up is pulling the strings. A sergeant probably hasn't got the authority to keep you safe if one of her superiors is involved."

"What about MI5 or MI6?"

Val smiled. "MI6 are overseas. I guess MI5 is an option. It may be worth looking into."

"What other alternatives are there?"

"There's always the press, I suppose. Actually, that might not be a bad idea."

"How does that help me?" I asked. "I'll still have to deal with the police at some stage."

"As I see it, the biggest problem is keeping you safe while you're in custody. Once the story is out in the open, they would have to take your protection seriously. That gives us the opportunity to prove your innocence."

"Only if Nick—I mean John—testifies," I said, "and there doesn't seem to be much chance of that."

"We'll worry about that when the time comes."

"Can we trust the journalists though? What's to stop them from turning me in?"

Val steepled her fingers. "From what little I know, they have a code of conduct. If they went running to the police whenever they got wind of something illegal, nobody would ever talk to them, and they'd lose all their sources. It's definitely another option."

"How would we make contact?"

"I'm not sure. I'd have to do some research. When a big case like this comes up, I bet they're swamped with all sorts of calls from cranks and weirdos."

We both fell silent as we pondered the options.

Eventually, Val pushed her chair back and stood. "I'll look into it after we've eaten. I was only going to put some chicken in a pan and throw in a readymade sauce."

"Let me do it," I replied. "One of the benefits of being single is that I've learned to cook for myself. I think I can manage."

"Thanks. The chicken pieces are in the fridge. Fry them then add the contents of the jar. I left it by the cooker. Rice is in the cupboard. Just add water and boil for ten minutes."

I paused at the door and turned back. She flashed me a cheerful grin. "Don't worry, Alex. We'll find a way out of this."

The aroma of sweet and sour sauce permeated the kitchen. A sheen of condensation coated the windows. I drained the rice and left it steaming by the sink as I went to fetch the other two. Nick grunted from his position on the sofa where he was still watching the television. Val hunched over the laptop in the dining room.

"Have you come up with anything?" I said to her back.

She gave a slight start. "I was so engrossed I didn't hear you behind me. Yeah, I've got the outline of an idea. Why don't we talk about it while we eat?"

She lowered the screen, and I followed her through the lounge. The clink of cutlery came through the doorway. Nick had laid the small table for three. He took his seat in silence while Val and I dished out the food.

She smiled as she placed the plates before us and sat. "This is great. You two should come to stay more often."

Her good humour failed to dislodge the tension between the pair. We ate for a while without speaking.

"What's the big plan?" I asked.

Val rested her fork on the plate. "It's like we discussed. We'll call a newspaper. There's a fair chance they won't believe us. If they need proof, we could send a photograph."

"You can use my camera if you want," Nick said. They were the first words he had spoken in the last hour.

"Thanks," Val and I replied in unison.

"What happens after that?" I asked.

"We show them the website and the screenshots you took of the job to kill you," Val replied. "It would be better still if you talked to them, John. I'm sure they would guarantee your anonymity."

"Not a chance," Nick said. "Even if they keep my name out of it, it wouldn't take much for the people behind the site to put it all together. Then I'll be the one on the receiving end of a contract."

"But once the press become involved, the whole thing will come crashing down."

Nick scowled at her. "I'm sorry, but I'm not prepared to risk it."

"Alright," I said, keen to change the subject. "What happens after that?"

A frown worked its way onto Val's forehead. All of a sudden, she looked less certain of herself. "That's the part that still needs some work. Hopefully we can expose the two corrupt policemen. Until we meet the journalists, I'm not sure how we'd do that."

"Wait. Did you say *meet* them?"

"I don't see any alternative. However this goes down, I'm guessing the press will want to talk to you face to face."

"Okay," I said, drawing out the last syllable. "At some stage of all this, I'm still going to have to hand myself in to the police."

"That's unavoidable," Val replied, "but we need to ensure they keep you protected. Once everything is out in the open, they'll be forced to take your protection seriously."

"I'm not sure. A lot of things might yet go wrong. What if they arrest me before the story comes out? What if the journalists don't believe me? There are too many unknowns."

"Look, Alex, however you dress it up, this is a bad situation. There are risks whatever we do. We can't change that. All we can do is to try to give you the best chance of getting through this in one piece. The more people who know about what's going on, the greater your odds are of surviving."

Her words rattled around inside my skull, but my brain refused to cooperate. I couldn't hold on to any thought long enough to make sense of it. Maybe I was too close to the whole thing. At least somebody was fighting my corner.

"Alright," I said. "I'll go along with whatever you think is best. When are we going to do this?"

"I'll phone in sick to work tomorrow. We'll contact them in the morning."

Nick folded his arms and leaned forwards. "Drive somewhere else with the mobile before dialling the number. You don't know who could be tracking the call."

Val gave a slight shake of the head. "Didn't you tell us it was a burner?"

"Just because it's never been used, it doesn't mean somebody isn't listening in. Given the circumstances, a bit of paranoia might keep you alive for longer."

"Whatever you say."

We finished the meal without further argument. After loading the crockery into the dishwasher, we retired to the lounge. Now we'd come to a decision and everybody seemed to have accepted it, the tension eased a little. Nick was still adamant he would leave in the morning. It was clear Val resented his lack of support, but there was nothing we could do about it.

Nick sat in the armchair while Val and I occupied opposite ends of the sofa.

"Have you got any other family?" she asked me.

"Only the one sister," I replied.

"And she's separated from your brother-in-law?"

"Yeah, she was staying at my mother's house with her two daughters ..."

A flush rose in Val's cheeks. "I'm sorry, that was insensitive of me. I didn't mean to bring up painful memories. Just ignore my stupid questions."

"No, it's okay. The worst part is knowing her murderer is out there, and the police aren't even looking for him."

"I'm sure they'll catch the person who did it. After we contact—"

She stopped talking in mid-sentence. Her words had triggered an intense feeling of déjà vu. She must have noticed a change in my expression because she leant sideways and placed her hand over my own. Her palm felt cool against my skin. Suddenly, the memories came flooding back.

"Are you alright?" she asked. "You look like you've seen a ghost."

"Ah ... what you just said. It reminded me of something from my childhood."

"Let's change the subject—unless you want to talk about it."

I hesitated for a moment. Other than the investigating police officers, I had never discussed the night of my sister's abduction with anybody outside my immediate family, and I had only known the other two people in the room for a matter of hours. Nick would not have been my first choice as a confidante, but Val was a sympathetic listener. Given that I might not survive the following day, perhaps it was time to share my story.

"My mother isn't the only member of our family to have been murdered."

Val's hand shot to her mouth. Even Nick sat forward in his chair.

"When I was nine, somebody abducted my sister, Elena. She was six years old. The police kept telling us they'd find her and catch the kidnapper. They failed on both counts. Actually, that may not be strictly true, but it is accurate to say they never prosecuted anybody for her abduction."

Val shook her head. "That's awful. But what do you mean, they didn't prosecute?"

"They arrested the man who took her for other offences against children, but they chose not to charge him with my sister's murder."

"Why not?"

Richard T. Burke

"The main reason is that they considered me an unreliable witness."

Three years ago: Saturday, 20th May, 2017

*O*ver the course of the year following my sister's abduction, life gradually returned to something resembling normality. After six months with no significant results, the police scaled back the investigation.

Every so often, an enthusiastic journalist would resurrect the story, throwing a new hypothesis into the mix. My parents tried to buffer Cathy and me from the rumours that cropped up in the more salacious newspapers although they couldn't prevent us from overhearing other people discussing those articles.

For years after the crime, they turned off the television whenever the news came on. On one occasion, I questioned my mother about it. She said we had been through enough pain ourselves without needing to hear about the suffering of others. In those days, the Internet was still in its infancy, so there was little opportunity for the conspiracy theorists to air their views.

We no longer discussed the events of that night as a family. The subject was taboo at the dinner table. My parents put on a brave face, but beneath the veneer, the loss of their youngest daughter sucked all the joy out of their lives. They argued more, mostly about insignificant issues, and my father's health began to deteriorate. Soon after, they moved into separate beds. Both drank heavily; it was not unusual to find them in the evening slumped on the sofa asleep, empty glasses resting on the carpet beside them.

Despite my parents' reluctance to go over old ground, every year on the anniversary of Elena's abduction, Cathy would ask me whether I had remembered any more details about the kidnapper. The answer was always no.

Three years after my sister went missing, my father suffered a massive heart attack and died. The endowment policy paid off the mortgage, and his company's life assurance scheme added four times his annual salary. In the terms of his will, both Cathy and I became beneficiaries of a trust fund. My mother approached a stockbroker and invested the majority in dot-com stock during the height of the boom in the nineties. After taking further advice, she transferred most into property weeks before the crash of two thousand. By the time I reached the age of twenty-one and gained access, I was fortunate to have sufficient funds in my account to buy a good-sized house in a decent area.

As we grew older, my surviving sister took a more proactive approach to prevent other families from having to go through the same heartbreak we experienced. At first, she raised money for children's charities and volunteered her services at weekends. In subsequent years, Cathy donated a large proportion of her income to the same charitable causes.

The day I finally identified the man who had taken Elena, I popped into a convenience store to buy a pint of milk. On the way to the counter, I passed a newspaper rack. While I waited for the customer in front to pay, my gaze roamed over the headlines. My eye settled on the red top of The Mirror.

Notorious paedophile released from prison.

The upper half of a man's face appeared in a grainy photograph above the fold. He wore a dark woollen hat above thick, bushy eyebrows. His nose was long with a slight bump at the bridge. His eyes stared at a point to the left of the camera. The mouth was not visible, but I had seen enough already.

In my shock, I dropped the milk on the tiled floor. The carton split, splashing the legs of the woman in front. She whipped around. "Hey, watch out."

"Sorry," I mumbled, snatching up the paper.

"You'll have to pay for that," the shopkeeper chipped in.

I fumbled the wallet out of my back pocket, withdrew a ten-pound note and slapped it on the counter.

"I'm sorry," I repeated. "Keep the change."

I hurried out of the shop, oblivious to the stares of the other customers. My car clunked as I jabbed the unlock button on the remote control. The handle slipped in my haste to haul the door open.

I sank into the seat, the breath wheezing in my throat. I have never suffered from asthma, but at that moment I felt my airways constricting. My heart pounded as if I had just covered a mile rather than the ten yards from the shop entrance. With trembling hands, I unfolded the newspaper.

I hadn't seen the face staring from the page for well over twenty years, but the time dropped away in an instant. Memories surged back into my mind as if it was yesterday: standing at the window, the figure looking up at me, my sister lying on the frozen grass.

I shook my head in a vain attempt to steady my thoughts. My eyes tried to scan the words, but I found them involuntarily returning to the photograph. There was no question; this was the same man I had seen in the garden that night.

I forced myself to concentrate and read the article. His name was Donald Cox. Prior to his conviction, he worked as a caretaker at a primary school. He had been sent to prison for the rape of two young children.

It turned out he had recorded his crimes from cameras hidden inside the school's toilet cubicles. To make matters worse, he shared the material with other paedophiles. That was his undoing. An undercover officer infiltrated the group and traced the identity of one of his victims. Following Cox's arrest, police discovered thousands of incriminating photographs on his computer involving both girls and boys.

In his summing up, the judge called Cox a dangerous criminal who had coerced innocent children into performing unspeakable acts. The nature of the crime and the fact he shared the images online resulted in a twenty-year sentence.

The newspaper revealed that Cox had become a free man two months earlier after serving the majority of his term. The article disclosed that the parole board had declined his application several times over the years before eventually deciding he no longer posed a risk to the public.

A reporter discovered that the notorious paedophile was living under a different name after an eagle-eyed reader recognised him while out jogging. The paper was calling for the ruling to be reversed and for action to be taken against those who had supported the decision to release him. One of the victims, now an adult, had waived anonymity and come forward to back the campaign.

Why had I not seen the man's photograph during the trial? The answer came to me quickly. Seventeen years ago, I would have been fourteen-years-old. That was two years after my father died. At the time, we were still turning off the television whenever the news started. My mother banned newspapers from the house too. It was only when I reached my mid-teens that she relented. By then, my sister's kidnapping was no longer considered newsworthy.

What was I going to do with the information? The thought of telling my mother and sister overcame me with the familiar, deep sense of guilt. My mother had never given up hope, and I was reluctant to shatter her illusions.

My concerns over Cathy were different. If I told her, would it change the way she felt about me? Since my mid-twenties, she had finally stopped asking me whether I remembered anything about that night. Even though she no longer asked the question, I still sensed that deep down she held me partially responsible for the failure to apprehend Elena's abductor. I resolved to keep the news to myself for the time being.

Richard T. Burke

But should I go to the police? Or perhaps the newspaper? I quickly rejected the latter; it was already hard enough to live with myself for my inability to identify the kidnapper without the additional burden of bringing the whole story and my sorry part in it to light.

The law had punished Cox for his original offences, but the court never heard evidence of the more serious crime he had committed. I decided that I owed it to myself and my family to report this new information to the authorities. Once I gauged their reaction, I would determine how much to share with my mother and sister.

Having made up my mind, I turned on the engine and headed for the multi-story carpark in the centre of Basingstoke. Half-an-hour later, I pushed through the entrance to the police station. A bored-looking officer occupied the front desk. He kept me waiting for several seconds, typing away at a computer keyboard, then looked up.

"May I help you, sir?"

"I have some information about a murder."

Any sense of boredom dropped from his face. "Okay. Can I take your name?"

"Parrott. Alex Parrott. Two Rs and two Ts."

"Your address and phone number?"

I provided him with the details.

"Have you got any proof of identity?"

I pulled my driving license from my wallet.

"And what is this information, Mr Parrott?"

Up to that point, I had given no thought to exactly what I would say. "Ah ... my sister was abducted twenty-two years ago. We never saw her again."

He raised an eyebrow. "Twenty-two years, you're saying? Is that what this is about?"

"Yes. The man who took her—at the time, I was unable to recall his face. Today, I spotted a photograph of him in the newspaper."

"Let me get this straight. You witnessed your sister being taken, but you couldn't remember what the person looked like?"

"That's right."

"What was your sister's name?"

"Elena."

"And how old was she?"

"She was six, and I was nine."

"Elena Parrott. Now you mention it, that does ring a bell. It must have been in the nineties. I vaguely recollect hearing about the case although it was before my time. So, all of a sudden, you have a burst of memory?"

"That's right. I saw the man's photograph in the newspaper." I placed the paper on the counter. "He's the one who kidnapped my sister."

"Oh, the delightful Norman Cox. So why are you only now remembering what your sister's kidnapper looked like?"

I had been expecting the question, but I still didn't have a good answer. "Um ... at the time, they thought it was some sort of amnesia brought about by stress. When I saw his picture today, it jogged the memories loose."

The policeman tugged at his earlobe and inspected me without speaking. Finally, he broke the silence. "You're telling me that for more than twenty years you can't remember a thing, and suddenly, out of the blue, you recognise the man who took your sister? If that's true, why didn't your memory return during the court case? That photograph—or ones like it—would have been all over the press back then."

I tried to explain how my parents banned television news programmes and papers from the house after the abduction, but my explanation sounded lame even to me.

"Are you sure this isn't about trying to punish a person who committed other crimes against children?" he asked.

I opened my mouth to speak, but nothing came out. Eventually, a strangled "no" escaped.

"Okay, Mr Parrott, here's what I'm going to do. I'll pass this information on to my superiors. Somebody will contact you in the next few days to inform you how we decide to proceed. How does that sound?"

I didn't know how to reply. "Alright, I suppose."

"Thanks for bringing this to our attention. We'll be in touch."

I left the police station in a daze. I hadn't known what to expect, but the officer's reaction surprised me. However, the more I thought about it, the more sense it made. How could they trust a statement from somebody who claimed to have recovered a lost memory from twenty-two years earlier? If I was being honest with myself, I would have been just as sceptical.

It didn't come as a great shock when two days later a policeman visited me and told me there was insufficient new evidence for them to take the case any further.

I stopped talking. Nick and Val stayed locked in position as if I had pulled the pin from a grenade.

"What did you do after that?" Val asked, breaking the silence. She and Nick had sat through the whole story without commenting until this moment.

"What could I do?" I replied. "I didn't tell my mother or sister for the reasons I mentioned earlier."

She drew her legs up onto the sofa. "Isn't there somebody you can complain to?"

"What would be the point? After more than twenty years, there won't be any evidence. And like I said, given my inability to describe him at the time, a court of law would hardly consider my testimony reliable."

Nick cracked his knuckles. "This bastard abducted your sister, then in all probability killed her, and nobody wants to do anything about it?"

Blood rushed to my face. "It's not that I don't want to."

"What would you do if you could get hold of him and do whatever you liked, just assuming there would be no comeback?"

"I'd kill him." The words were out of my mouth before I had time to engage my thought processes. The question had set loose all the feelings of guilt and anger I struggled so hard over the years to suppress. Would I really do it? Was I capable of ending the life of another human being?

"There's been enough talk of killing," Val said, shaking me from my internal debate. "Let's change the subject."

"What about you, Val?" Nick persisted. "What would you do?"

"I don't have a sister."

"Alright then, a different close family member. If somebody murdered your parents, for example, would you just let it go?"

Val shuddered. "I would want that person to be punished, but I'd leave it to the law."

"But what if the police weren't interested? That's what happened to Alex. He knows the identity of his sister's kidnapper with one hundred per cent certainty, but the authorities won't do anything about it. Assuming you could kill the murderer without being caught, would you do it? Or would you let them get away with it?"

"If we went around killing criminals, society would regress back to the dark ages. I mean, where would it end? What about rape, for example? Should we execute rapists?"

Nick met her gaze full on. "Yes."

"And what about people framed for a crime they didn't commit, or when the police arrest the wrong suspect? You can't exonerate them once they've been executed."

"Acceptable collateral damage to coin a phrase from my army days."

Val shook her head. "That's why you and I could never be together. You've become accustomed to killing. You think it's the solution to every problem."

"In that case, why did you marry a soldier?" Nick said, raising his voice. "Do you seriously believe Eddie never killed anybody? I saw him kill several men with my own eyes."

Val's face drained of colour. "Don't bring my husband into this."

I glanced at my watch: a quarter to midnight. The room simmered with tension. I tried to change the subject. "About tomorrow; assuming the newspaper are happy to talk to me, how do we meet without anybody else seeing me?"

Val and Nick continued to glare at each other in silence.

Eventually, Nick levered himself out of the armchair. "I'm going to pack my bag."

Val's eyes followed him to the doorway. "God, that man drives me nuts. Whenever he leaves, I keep forgetting how annoying he can be. Sorry, Alex, what did you say?"

I repeated my question.

"I'm not sure I understand," she said.

"My face is plastered across every television screen and newspaper in the country. If I turn up in public, somebody is bound to recognise me."

"We need to arrange the meeting somewhere where nobody will see you."

"Exactly."

Val and I sat at opposite ends of the sofa, deep in thought, although I suspected her mind was on other things.

"We don't need an answer until tomorrow," I said, pushing myself out of the cushions. "I'm going to bed. Thanks again for all your help."

"Goodnight."

Before I reached the door, it swung open. Nick entered the room, a compact camera dangling by a cord from his hand. Behind him, I spotted his rucksack lying in the hallway.

"One more thing," he said. "I need evidence that you're alive."

"So you can get paid?" I asked.

He shrugged. "No proof, no payment; that's the way it works."

"How are we going to do this?"

"If you stand to the side of the television, I'll put the news on and record a short video clip. As long as the time is on the screen, that should be enough."

"Don't mind me," Val said. "It's only my house. I'll leave you two to it. Goodbye, John. I'll see you in the morning, Alex."

Nick stepped back awkwardly as Val passed through the doorway. He watched her until she started up the staircase and disappeared from view. Blowing out his cheeks, he grabbed the remote control and navigated to the BBC twenty-four-hour news channel. The time in the top right corner signalled a minute before midnight. "Just there," he said, pointing.

I moved into position. "Is this okay?"

Nick nodded and fiddled with the camera controls.

The introductory music played. "Welcome to the BBC news at the start of Friday, the thirty-first of July, two thousand and twenty," the presenter announced. "In our top story, police are intensifying the hunt for schoolteacher turned murderer, Alex Parrott, as the search enters its third day."

I glanced sideways and saw a photograph of my face staring out from the screen.

"Later in the programme, we have an interview with the Secretary of State for Education where we ask how safeguards put in place to protect children have allowed a serial-killer to slip through the checks and work in a classroom. We'll also—"

The picture turned to black as Nick pressed the off button. "Thanks," he said, lowering his head to watch the playback on the tiny viewscreen. "That's all I need."

"What happens next?"

"When I get back to my house, I'll transfer it to my computer and send it via Bitmessage."

"You're leaving now?"

"I'm not Val's favourite person at the moment. It's probably best for all of us if I leave right away."

I wanted to defend her but was unable to think of an appropriate response. "How are you going to get home?"

"Don't worry about me. I'll find a way. As we discussed, I'd appreciate it if you would keep my name out of it, if and when you talk to the police."

"No problem. Thanks for keeping me alive."

Nick grinned. "I'd like to say it was a pleasure, but it wasn't. Good luck tomorrow. I'll be watching the news carefully. And sorry about your sister— and your mother."

He crossed to the front door and grabbed his rucksack. He slipped the camera inside and pulled out a pair of mobile phones together with their detached batteries. "One of these is yours. The other is the burner I bought the other day. You may as well keep them. I don't need to tell you they can be traced when the battery is fitted."

I stuck out my hand. Nick shook it, crushing my fingers in his powerful grip.

"I hope you have a long and successful life," he said. "Good luck and stay safe."

Day Five:
Friday, 31st July, 2020

Richard T. Burke

I spent much of the night awake, my brain continually running over my predicament. Even during the short spells when I found a restless sleep, I dreamt I was being pursued by faceless assailants. By six o'clock, the light was already creeping through the edges of the curtains. I decided there was little point in staying in bed any longer.

I rose and showered in the small bathroom. As I emerged afterwards, the sounds of movement ascended from the kitchen. I dressed quickly in jeans and a T-shirt and limped down the stairs. Even three days after the initial injury, the muscle still ached whenever I put weight on my leg.

I pushed through the door to discover Val sitting at the small table in her dressing gown with a half-eaten bowl of cereal before her. Judging by the dark shadows under her eyes, she had slept as little as I had.

"Good morning," I said, trying to inject a note of cheeriness into my voice.

"Morning," she mumbled in reply and shovelled in another mouthful.

"I take it you couldn't sleep either."

She shook her head. When she had finished crunching, she pointed with the spoon to the cupboard to the left of the cooker. "Cereals are in there. Milk is in the fridge. You'll find a bowl in the dishwasher. Help yourself."

"Look," I began. "About last night. I wasn't—"

"Don't worry about it. I think that's the main reason I didn't get much sleep. If I'm being totally honest about it, despite what I said, I would want to kill somebody who'd murdered a loved one. It's just that John was so sure of himself. That's what annoyed me. It's all very well talking in hypothetical terms until it happens to you. I remember after John told me how my husband, Eddie, died; I wanted the men who killed him to suffer."

"And did they?"

"Suffer, you mean? John said they traced the ringleaders and blew them up with a drone. After hearing that, it didn't make me feel any better though. I can't imagine what it must have been like for you, not being able to remember the face of your sister's kidnapper."

"For years, I blamed myself, despite all the counselling. What made it worse was the fact that the police took no action when I finally brought the information to them."

"Perhaps you were right. Maybe he does deserve to die."

We both ate in silence. When the bowl was empty, I put down my spoon. "Which newspaper should we approach?" I asked.

"I've been giving it some thought. My recommendation would be The Sun. Their website made a big thing of wanting to receive information from the public. It was only a first impression, but some of the others seemed less interested in receiving direct contact. The Sun also said they pay for stories."

I frowned. "This isn't about the money. All I want is for this to go away."

Val reached across the table and placed her fingers over mine. "I know that, but you have to consider the future. If you need a lawyer, they don't come cheap. And even when you do clear your name, the chances of resuming your job as if nothing had happened are pretty slim. If a newspaper is prepared to pay for your story—and I'm sure they will when they hear it—you shouldn't reject the idea out of hand."

"Yeah, you're right, I suppose. Did you have any more thoughts about where to get together with the journalists, always assuming they agree to meet?"

"I was hoping they might suggest somewhere," Val replied, sitting back.

"Actually, I did have a moment of inspiration while I was tossing and turning last night."

"Go on."

I explained my idea. Val asked a few more questions, then she said, "Yeah, I like it. It's still risky, but it doesn't expose us until we know we can trust them."

"How are we going to make contact? Actually, now I think about it, Nick left a pair of burner phones behind."

"You should definitely stay here. We can't risk somebody spotting you and calling the police. I'll take a phone and drive somewhere a few miles away before using it."

"Okay. We'll need to make sure it's charged."

"It isn't possible to tell without reconnecting the battery, and that's not a good idea until we're ready. It's alright, though; I've got a car charger that will fit."

"Remember, only turn it on for long enough to make the call."

A half smile touched Val's lips. "Yeah, I know that."

"I'm sorry. Just ignore me. This whole thing is making me really nervous. What if the newspaper people don't believe you?"

"We'll worry about that if it happens. Personally, I think they'll jump at the chance to talk to you."

"I certainly hope so."

With the details settled, I moved to the lounge while Val went upstairs to dress. She appeared twenty minutes later wearing a pale blue blouse over beige trousers. It was clear she had also applied makeup; the grey shadows beneath her eyes were no longer in evidence.

She smiled at me. "Today's the day we get your life back on track."

"I hope so. What time are you planning to go?"

Val glanced at her watch. "I don't want to call too early in case there's nobody on the switchboard. If I leave at nine o'clock and drive for twenty minutes, that should be alright."

We still had a little over an hour to wait. Val was easy to talk to. The conversation steered clear of the subjects sensitive for both of us, ranging over a variety of topics including jobs and holidays. We discovered we had a mutual interest in water sports.

"I was planning a windsurfing holiday in Greece or somewhere like that," I said. "You could come with me." The words just tumbled out. I felt myself redden. We had only known each other a matter of hours, and here I was asking her to spend time away with me. I silently cursed myself for my stupidity.

Val sensed my embarrassment and flashed a sympathetic smile at me. "I'd love to, but money's still a bit tight at the moment."

We sat in an awkward silence for a few seconds. Val consulted her watch again. "It's a quarter to nine. I can't stand all this waiting around. I'm going to leave now."

"Do you have everything you need?"

She pointed to her bag on the low coffee table. "I've got the phone and its battery. The number's written on a piece of paper. Am I missing anything?"

I thought for a moment. "What about a pen? You may want to take notes."

"Good point. There's one in my handbag though."

"Right. I hope it goes well."

We stood awkwardly at arm's length. Then Val stepped in and gave me a quick hug. "I'll see you in an hour or two."

I followed her to the front door and closed it behind her. With a sense of deflation, I sank back onto the sofa and turned on the television. It was still set to the BBC twenty-four-hour news programme. I was in no mood to hear any more people talking about my case, so I flicked through the channels until I came across a re-run of the classic British sitcom, Only Fools and Horses.

Under normal circumstances, I could easily have wasted time watching Rodney and Del Boy's antics, but I found it impossible to concentrate. In frustration, I poked the off button. I pushed myself upright, limped over to the bookshelf and perused the titles. The books were a mix of fiction and computer manuals. I pulled a Dan Brown hardback out and read the blurb. Exactly what I didn't need—a story about kidnapping and murder. Returning the book, I wandered restlessly from room to room.

The first suggestion of a headache nudged at the region behind my eyes. I grabbed a glass of water from the kitchen and took it with me upstairs. After draining half the contents, I lay on the bed, fully clothed. I stared at the ceiling for a few minutes then turned on my side.

To my surprise, my eyelids began to feel heavy. I woke two hours later to the sound of the front door opening.

I leapt off the bed and rushed downstairs. Val stood in the open doorway, a broad grin spread across her face.

"I take it the call went well," I said.

Val pulled the door closed behind her. "You could say that. I told you they'd be interested, and they were. They should be here in about half an hour."

"Who did you speak to?"

"To start with a receptionist. When I explained what it was about, she asked me where I was calling from then put me straight through to a journalist. He was sceptical at first, but when I described what had happened, he was champing at the bit and wanted to meet straight away. He gave me his mobile number."

"How many are coming?"

"Just him and his assistant initially. He told me they'll want to bring in a photographer after the initial interview."

"And you're sure we can trust them?"

"Yes, I think so. Why would they give up a lead like this?"

"To claim they trapped a serial killer?"

Some of the shine left Val's face. "We'll take the precautions we discussed this morning. It'll be okay. By the way, he said if everything I described was true and we gave them exclusive access, they'd pay well into six figures for the story, perhaps even seven."

I did a quick calculation in my head. "Seven figures? That's at least a million quid."

"Correct. Then there's the book deal and the film rights."

"Aren't we getting ahead of ourselves? The first priority is to clear my name. Anything after that is a bonus."

"I know. But with that sort of money, you could do whatever you want. You'd never have to work again."

"I'd rather have my old life back." I inhaled a deep breath then blew out through my mouth. "But thanks for arranging everything," I added, keen not to seem ungrateful.

Val's mood deflated slightly at my lack of enthusiasm. She glanced at her watch. "They'll be here soon." She took a pace backwards and studied me. "In the meantime, we need to make you look more like a schoolteacher and less like a criminal."

I looked at my reflection in the hall mirror. My hair needed brushing, and I badly needed a shave.

A wry smile tugged at her lips. "There's a comb in the bathroom cabinet. You can borrow my razor to scrape the fluff off your face."

I followed her up the stairs. She grabbed a pink, lady razor from the side of the bath and rummaged in the cupboard above the sink.

"Here you are," she said, handing me an unopened pack of razor blades and a plastic comb. "Try to make yourself a bit more presentable."

"Thanks, Mum," I replied.

She laughed and stepped out, closing the door behind her.

Ten minutes later, I emerged shaven and groomed. I returned to my room and selected a chequered long-sleeved shirt from the pile Val had left for me. Still doing up the last of the buttons, I headed towards the staircase.

"In here," Val called from the master bedroom. I followed the sound of her voice and found her looking out of the window. On the double bed lay the burner phone and its battery.

"Any sign of them yet?" I asked.

She shook her head and glanced at her watch. "There's still ten minutes to go until the agreed time—oh hang on, this could be them."

I shuffled closer and inhaled the faint scent of her perfume. Looking over her shoulder, I watched a black BMW glide to a halt beside a semi-detached house diagonally opposite on the other side of the road. A large, red and white *For-Sale* sign stood outside. Two men emerged. The driver withdrew a scrap of paper from the pocket of the dark jacket he wore above a pair of blue jeans. He studied the contents before conversing with his colleague. Together, they walked past the estate agent's board towards the front door of the property.

"Are you going to call them?" I whispered.

Val waved a hand to shush me.

We watched from across the quiet residential street as the man in the jacket pressed the doorbell. Seconds later, he repeated the action and peered through the door's frosted glass panel.

"Are they alone?" Val asked.

I moved forward half a step and inspected the vehicles parked alongside the pavement. "As far as I can tell, yes."

"Right, I'll make the call. Keep an eye out for anything unusual."

I rested my elbows on the window sill and studied the two men. The driver pressed the doorbell once again, shuffling from one foot to the other as he waited impatiently for somebody to let them in. While I watched, the man placed his hand inside his jacket.

"He's answering," I said.

Behind me, Val spoke into the handset. "Is that Josh Nixon?"

"… No, we're still planning to meet you. We just wanted to make sure you'd come alone. I hope you understand given the circumstances."

"… Of course. You can leave your car where it is; it's on the other side of the road. The house is number fifty-four."

"… Right. See you in a minute."

From my vantage point, I saw the man return the phone to his jacket and stare in my direction. I stepped back behind the cover of the curtain. When I peeked around the edge moments later, the pair were already halfway across the street, striding towards our location.

"Any other sign of movement?" Val asked, her voice rigid with tension.

My gaze ran along the parked cars. All seemed empty. "No, only those two."

Even though I was expecting it, the chime of the doorbell sounded incredibly loud.

"I'll let them in," Val said. "You go into the kitchen and stand by the back door. If anything looks wrong, I'll shout and you can make a run for it."

"Alright," I replied, although I had no intention of leaving her alone if things took a turn for the worse.

"After you."

I hurried down the stairs as fast as my injured leg would allow and headed along the hall into the kitchen. As I entered the room, my eye caught sight of a knife rack with half a dozen handles sticking out. I grabbed the largest I could see and moved towards the door leading into the small back garden.

"Are you ready?" Val called from the hallway.

"Yes," I replied, my voice squeaking under the strain. I repeated my answer, this time at my normal pitch.

The clunk of the latch opening reached my ears. The sound of muffled voices travelled through the open doorway, but I couldn't make out the words above the pounding of my pulse. Footsteps approached along the hallway. I tightened my grip on the knife.

"It's okay, Alex," Val said as she stuck her head around the door. Her eyes widened as she took in the shiny blade clamped in my hand. "Ah … you should probably leave that in here."

I locked my gaze on her face. She gave me a smile of encouragement as I deposited the makeshift weapon on the kitchen table. Val stood back to allow me to pass.

"They're in the dining room," she said.

I ran my tongue over dry lips. Suddenly, the house seemed far too hot. I wiped a bead of sweat from my forehead as I followed the corridor towards the open doorway. Drawing nearer, I picked up a whispered conversation. Whoever had been speaking stopped at the sound of my feet shuffling on the carpet.

When I entered the room, I was met by the astonished gaze of the two men I had observed from across the street.

"Mr Parrott," the man in the jacket said, failing to hide his surprise.

"Were you expecting somebody else?" I asked.

"No, it's just … In our line of business, we receive a lot of false leads, so we weren't too hopeful you'd actually be here. Let me introduce myself; I'm Josh Nixon. This is my assistant, Andy Parker."

Both men shook my hand.

"Shall we get on with this?" Val said from behind me. The journalists moved around to the opposite side of the table and sat. Val took a seat beside me.

"Do you mind if we record this?" Nixon asked, pulling a compact recorder from his jacket pocket.

I looked sideways at Val. She shrugged.

"I suppose that's okay," I replied.

"Mrs Devine told me somebody set you up, and you're not responsible for any of the recent murders which the police are claiming you committed. Can you tell us what really happened?"

Up to that point, I hadn't known Val's surname. The new information threw me off my stride for a moment. "Um … well, like you said, I didn't kill anybody."

I started by telling them about the note I had found and the visit by the two policemen. I omitted my brother-in-law, Jamie, from the start of the story, but when it came to the part where Nick turned up at the Internet café, Nixon stopped me.

"You're saying somebody hired a hitman to protect you? Who placed the protection contract?"

"Ah … I'd rather not say at the moment."

The journalist studied me for a few seconds, his forehead creased in a frown. "Is there any proof that this dark website exists?"

"We've got screenshots on my laptop," Val said. "We copied them across yesterday. If you want, we should be able to log in."

Nixon exchanged a glance with his assistant then turned back to me. "We'd like to have a look, but I'd prefer you to finish the story first."

I went on to describe how Nick had chased me and subsequently convinced me he was there to help. Nixon halted my account again when I came to the killing of the woman in the flat.

"You witnessed this man committing the murder?"

"That's right. After that he tried to kill me by throwing me off the balcony. If Nick hadn't turned up when he did, I'd have been the one they discovered dead on the pavement."

"This Nick person—can we have a chat with him?"

I shook my head. "He was adamant he wouldn't talk to anybody."

"But you know who he is, don't you?" he said, turning to Val.

She hesitated before replying. "Yes. He's a friend, and he definitely won't do any press interviews."

"How do you happen to be acquainted with a hitman?" Nixon asked. "Is he your partner, or maybe one of his friends from the army?"

The journalist studied Val's shocked face with a hint of amusement. "I couldn't help but notice the photographs around the room of a man in military uniform," he explained.

"My husband died in Afghanistan," Val replied, frowning, "and I'm not going to tell you who my friend is."

Nixon held up his hands in a placatory gesture. "Never mind. So, Alex—can I call you that?—a mystery hitman turned bodyguard brought you here, and you had nothing to do with any of the murders."

I nodded. "That's correct."

The journalist scratched his chin. "I believe you, but the big problem is there's no proof. You won't tell me who placed the protection contract, and the one person who can corroborate some of your story isn't prepared to talk to the press. I don't understand why you haven't just turned yourself in to the police."

"Two of them framed me, and my brother-in-law told me I couldn't trust them." The words were out of my mouth before I realised what I had done.

Nixon sat back triumphantly. "Let me guess; your brother-in-law is the one who placed the contract to protect you."

I inhaled deeply and met his smug gaze. This man was an expert at getting answers. I needed to be more careful when answering his questions. "Like I said earlier, I'd rather not say. The two policemen who came to my house knew exactly where to look. They're definitely involved."

"But you don't know their names?"

"No."

"And you're not a paedophile?"

My breathing quickened, and my ears glowed with heat. "Absolutely not. Until a week ago, I was a schoolteacher, happy in my job. Now, I'm the most wanted man in Britain, accused of murdering half a dozen people including my own mother. Doesn't that sound a bit strange to you?"

Nixon's expression softened. "You may be right. It does seem peculiar, but I've seen a lot of weird cases over the years. My team have done their research on you, and there's nothing in your past to suggest you're capable of committing these crimes. The problem I have is that you have no alibi."

"What about the website screenshots?" Val asked.

"We'll have a peek at those in a minute," Nixon replied. "But let's face it, for all we know, you could have created the site yourself."

I slumped forward, resting my chin on my hands. All the optimism had drained from my body. "Look, if you're not interested, I may as well hand myself in to the police and be done with it."

"Hang on a sec; I never said I wasn't interested. I already told you I believe you. This is the biggest news story of the year, maybe even the decade. We just need to work out how to tell it."

Val reached out an arm and gently rubbed my back.

I raised my head in renewed hope. "Okay, but where do we go from here?"

"Let's see this website," Nixon replied.

Val opened the lid of the laptop. The two journalists came around the table. I rose to my feet and offered Nixon my chair. Parker stood behind him, peering over his shoulder. First, she took them through the screenshots.

"Can we take copies?" Nixon asked.

Val glanced back at me. "I don't see why not," I replied, "but only when we've agreed a contract."

I noted a slight stiffening of the journalist's posture. After Val had run through the captured pages, she suggested we connect to the live site. She retrieved the shiny disk from the drawer and slotted it into the tray on the side of the laptop as she had done the previous day.

"What are you doing?" Nixon asked.

"I'm booting from a Linux DVD," she replied. "It's a way to make sure there's no unwanted software running."

The journalists watched as she downloaded the Tor browser and installed it. When the startup sequence completed, she transposed the page address from the scrap of paper she had removed from her purse. The cursor rotated … and carried on rotating. Eventually, an error box popped up: "Unable to connect".

Frowning, Val typed in the letters a second time. Once again, the same message appeared.

"Is it connected to the Internet?" I asked.

"Yes," she snapped. "The site's down."

"But it was—"

"I know, but it isn't working now."

The two journalists exchanged a glance. They said nothing; they didn't need to.

"That went okay," I said.

"Hmm. It could have gone better," Val replied, sitting next to me.

While she was seeing off the journalists, I had made another attempt to access the website again with no luck.

"Why do you think the page is down?"

"Who knows? Maybe the person running it has cold feet. By the way, why were you reluctant to tell them about your brother-in-law?"

I hesitated as I tried to rationalise my feelings. "I guess it's because Jamie helped me. He saved my life, so I didn't want to drop him in it."

Val raised an eyebrow. "Call it a hunch, but I'm not sure you fooled them."

I gave a short laugh. "You might be right. But they did agree to leave him alone for the time being."

"I liked your idea about how to provide proof you're telling the truth," she said.

"I'm going to look pretty stupid if it doesn't work. On the positive side, this whole thing will be over by the end of tonight."

My eyes tracked the fingers of Val's left hand as she twisted her wedding ring. She looked up and met my gaze as she spoke. "Are you sure you want to go through with this plan? You'll be putting yourself in a lot of danger."

"What's the alternative? I could always turn myself in. Let's face it, it'll be dangerous either way. At least doing it like this, there's a chance to prove my innocence."

"That won't do you much good if you die though, will it?"

"You're right, but I could wind up dead whatever I do. We're still dependent on Mr Nixon and his friends holding up their side of the bargain. But can we trust them?"

Val stared at me for a second before answering. "We have little choice."

"At least they agreed to pay for a legal team."

"I think they would have paid more, but it's your decision."

Josh Nixon had made a brief telephone call at the end of our meeting and confirmed that the newspaper would fund the cost of lawyers for my defence if the case came to court. In exchange, I consented to an exclusivity deal for my story over the next three days. The photographer would shoot his photos before the main event that evening.

For the rest of the morning, Val and I loitered around the house. We talked about everything under the sun from films to favourite foods. At three o'clock exactly, she replaced the battery in the back of the mobile phone. It may have been a pointless precaution to leave it unpowered until then, but Nick's words of warning still rung in our ears.

At two minutes past the hour, the electronic trill of the ringtone broke the silence. Val snatched up the handset and tapped the answer icon.

"Oh, hi Josh," she said.

"Josh?" I mouthed silently, raising my shoulders in question.

Val scowled at me. "… Yes, he's here." She listened for several seconds.

"… Okay. We'll be there at eight thirty. And you're sure you can keep him safe?" Her eyes locked on mine.

"… Right. No, we won't forget. I'll see you there. 'Bye."

She ended the call and removed the battery.

"I take it from that, it's on," I said.

She nodded. "I assume you heard the time."

"Yes. And the location is as we suggested?"

"Yeah, but we could have set it up here," Val said.

"No, that wouldn't have worked. There has to be no doubt about where I am. They don't know about your house, at least I hope not. We're in trouble if they do."

"I just pray we've made the right decision."

"You're not the only one," I replied.

The rest of the day seemed to tick by incredibly slowly. Val prepared an omelette for our evening meal, but I had no appetite. Tendrils of fear wormed their way through my stomach, replacing any sense of hunger as the deadline drew nearer. I became conscious of my laboured breathing, the acrid scent of my own sweat. This must be how a condemned man felt, waiting out the last few hours before his execution.

Despite my dread of what lay ahead, it came as something of a relief when Val announced it was time to leave.

"Do I need to go in the boot again?" I asked, my heart dropping. The prospect of spending an hour in cramped, pitch black confinement filled me with gloom.

"No, I think it'll be fine if you lie across the back seat."

I sighed in gratitude. "Thank God for small mercies."

216

"Have you got everything?"

I lifted the laptop bag. "It's all in here. Do you have the postcode?"

She showed me her mobile. "Let's go."

I followed Val through the door into the garage and let myself into the rear of the Corsa while she raised the metallic door. The suspension rocked slightly as she sank into the driver's seat.

"Are you alright back there?" she asked over her shoulder.

"Never better," I replied.

She twisted the key in the ignition, and the engine rumbled into life. Moments later, we were zipping along the road. The journey passed uneventfully. We spoke little as I contemplated what lay ahead. The satnav application gave clues to our progress, but after a while, I stopped listening, lost in my thoughts. Eventually, Val stated we were five minutes away.

"Go down the drive and park as close as you can to the back door," I said.

We drove in silence until the female voice emanating from Val's mobile announced we had arrived at our destination. The car turned and slowed. Gravel crunched beneath the wheels as we drew to a halt.

"We're here," Val said.

"Is anybody around?"

"Not that I can see."

I reached for the handle and scrambled across the seat. Once my feet were on the ground, I pulled the bunch of keys from my pocket. A gust of wind ruffled my hair as I fiddled with the lock. Seconds later, I was standing in my dead mother's kitchen.

"I think you should move the car," I said as Val followed me inside. "The neighbours will be suspicious if they see a strange vehicle outside. Go up the road and park it somewhere near the end."

Val retraced her steps. I watched as the Corsa reversed past the window. The tyres crackled on the small stones covering the drive. It was a dull, blustery day, and dark clouds scudded across the sky. Dusk was falling, but I didn't want to alert anybody to our presence, so I resisted the urge to turn on the lights. I checked my watch; we were fifteen minutes early.

I waited by the sink until Val's windswept figure returned. She let herself in through the back door and joined me in the poorly illuminated room.

"There's a bad smell in here," she said, wrinkling her nose.

Now she had mentioned it, I too detected the sickly-sweet odour of decomposition. The foulness increased in strength as I raised the lid of the cylindrical, steel pedal bin.

She held her hand in front of her face. "That'll be it."

Normally, I would have dumped the contents in the outside wheelie bin, but an attentive neighbour might notice if I left the confines of the house. Instead, I removed the plastic liner and tied a knot before dropping it by the back door. The foul miasma still lingered afterwards.

"Why don't we wait in the lounge?" I said, eager to escape the assault on my nostrils.

Val folded her arms tightly across her chest. "Okay," she replied, following me down the hallway. My hand automatically reached for the light switch as we entered the room, but I stopped myself just in time.

We sat at opposite ends of the beige, high-backed sofa. In the deepening gloom, the branches of the large oak tree in the corner of the garden swayed under the force of the wind. We waited in silence, ears straining for any sound of movement above the hiss of the leaves. As the seconds ticked slowly by, I allowed my mind to wander. Had my mother been sitting here when her murderer arrived? Did she open the door to him, or did he sneak up on her? Would I suffer a similar fate at the hands of the same killer?

The crunch of footsteps on gravel shook me out of my morbid thoughts. I peered into the gloomy twilight. The journalists were here.

Half an hour later, we were all set.

The handle turned, and the door moved inwards. A tremor ran through me. I was the tethered goat, and the tiger had arrived to collect its prey. The room flooded with light. I blinked in the sudden glare.

"Hello, Percy. Fancy seeing you here."

My vision gradually adjusted to the increase in brightness. I immediately recognised the man who had spoken. He clutched a pack of cigarettes in his right hand. I studied him from my position on the sofa as he tapped a cigarette out and lit it. He blew out a cloud of smoke and stepped into the room to make space for his taller partner. The two men were dressed similarly in jeans and long-sleeved shirt. Each carried a rucksack on his back.

"Little and large," I said. "You never did tell me your names. Are you really policemen?"

"You've led us quite a merry dance," the smoker said, ignoring my question. "I have to admit this is one of the least likely places I expected to find you. Come to pay our last respects, have we?"

An influx of anger surged through my body. "Are you the ones who killed my mother?"

"If you'd handed yourself in like a good little boy, nothing would have happened to her."

My eyes followed the taller man as he strolled towards the window. "Let's keep this private," he said, dragging the curtains together. "After all, we don't want the neighbours looking in, do we?"

The smoker moved a step closer, shrugged off his backpack and dropped it on the carpet. "To answer your earlier question, yes, we are both policemen. I'm D.S. Wickford, and he's D.S. Bowman. We work in Vice, and I have to say you've made our lives considerably harder over the past few days."

"You still haven't told me if you were responsible for my mother's death."

Bowman, the taller of the two, sighed theatrically. He spoke with a slight, northern twang. "Does that really matter now? You'll be able to ask her yourself in a few minutes."

"Come on. It's the least you owe me after what you've put me through."

"It was me," Wickford said, his face widening in a slow grin. "She was only too keen to let us in when we told her we had information that might clear your name. Don't worry though; she died quickly."

I propelled myself off the sofa and lunged for his throat. Bowman had anticipated my move and met me with his shoulder, sending me sprawling back into the cushions.

"Settle down. Let's not get over-excited. We've still got some questions for you."

"Go screw yourself," I growled through clenched teeth as I tried to regain my breath.

Any hint of cheeriness left his voice, replaced by a threatening coldness. "You will answer our questions one way or another. You can make it quick and easy or slow and painful. It's your choice."

I glared at the two men in silence.

"Who's been protecting you?"

"His name is Nick."

Wickford rolled his eyes. "Not terribly useful, that. What's his surname?"

"I have no idea. He never told me. Like most of the people who accept jobs from that site on the dark web, he's keen to remain anonymous. I expect it's bad for business in his line of work if you give away your real name."

I could tell by the way they exchanged glances that my answer had surprised them.

"And you didn't know him beforehand?"

"No," I replied. "Somebody paid him to protect me."

"Who?"

"I never found out."

"A mystery benefactor placed a contract to keep you alive, but you have no idea who. Seriously?"

I flashed a grin of my own. "That's right."

The first flicker of uneasiness sparked between the two detectives. I could only suppose they had been expecting me to be cowering in terror by this stage.

"Anyway," I said, "if you're policemen, aren't you supposed to be stopping criminals?"

"There's more than one way to prevent crime," Wickford replied, recovering his composure.

"How did you find me?"

"The laptop has software installed to report its location. Whenever you turned it on, it told us where you were."

I raised my eyebrows in a feigned look of surprise. "I wondered how you tracked me. Why did it take you so long to locate me at the hotel?"

"We were busy tidying up other loose ends," Bowman said with a grin. "The silly cow who lives opposite you won't be recording any more number plates. It all worked out well in the end, especially when an *anonymous caller*"—he waggled his fingers in invisible quote marks—"saw you fleeing the scene."

"How did you get the software on the computer?" I asked. "Was it during the search when you loaded those pictures onto my PC? I take it you left the laptop behind on purpose."

Wickford narrowed his eyes and scowled at me. "We're the ones asking the questions. Where else have you been hiding the last two days? Obviously, we know about the hotel and the flat."

"I haven't got a clue. We stayed in an empty house. The guy who was protecting me blindfolded me during the journey."

"If that's the case, how did you end up here?"

"The contract ended. He asked me where I wanted to go. I told him my mother's place, so he dropped me off half an hour ago. Guess what? He used a blindfold again."

The policemen exchanged a glance, clearly unsure whether I was telling the truth. I was starting to enjoy the way my answers were unsettling them. But something was still nagging at my subconscious.

"So, you decided to sit here in the dark, surfing the Internet?"

"That's right. I wanted to catch up on my email. A few people have been trying to get in touch with me over the last few days."

The two men locked eyes. Wickford, the smoker, shrugged. "I think we've heard enough." He took one final drag from the cigarette, stubbed it out on the back of the packet and placed the stub inside. "We don't want to leave any evidence behind, do we?"

Reaching down, he unzipped the rucksack he'd dropped earlier. If he came out with a gun, I was in trouble. His hand emerged holding a pair of leather gloves. He slipped them on and delved into the bag once again. This time, he pulled out a nylon rope, tied in a noose.

Bowman moved a pace closer while Wickford uncoiled the blue cord and slung the end over the top of the door. "It seems your little crime spree is about to come to a conclusion," he said. "All they'll find is a hastily scrawled note saying sorry. An anonymous call in the morning reporting a prowler seen near your mother's house should be enough."

"Please, …" I hesitated before completing the sentence. My brain finally latched onto what had been teasing away at the edge of my conscious mind.

"I've got another question. You called me Percy when you arrived. There's only one person who calls me that. What have you done to him?"

Wickford frowned in confusion. Then his face lit up in delight. "Oh, your dear brother-in-law, Jamie Saunders. I thought you'd figured it out."

"Is he still alive?" I asked.

The smoker gave a laugh that morphed into a coughing fit. When he had recovered enough to speak, he looked me in the eye. "I'm sorry to disappoint you, but it was Jamie Saunders who told us where to find you."

Suddenly, all the pieces fell into place. I laid my head back against the blue cushion and stared at the ceiling.

"Jamie?" I said, still reeling from the unexpected revelation.

Bowman seized me by the arm and hauled me upright. "Time's up."

In my stunned confusion, the code phrase slipped my mind. I was halfway across the room before the words, "Please, no more," escaped my lips.

The two men stopped, frozen in place by the sudden sound of running feet. Susie Mayhew was first through the door. "Armed police! Get down on the floor!" Despite her diminutive frame, she slammed Wickford against the wall and cuffed him before he realised what was happening. With the warning still ringing in my ears, I turned around but saw no guns.

Bowman must also have noticed the absence of firearms because he glanced towards the window as if deciding whether to attempt an escape. In his moment of indecision, two unarmed constables surged into the room past the female sergeant and slammed him face down onto the carpet. One man hauled back his arms as the other expertly applied the handcuffs.

A cameraman was next to enter, followed closely by a beaming Josh Nixon. The journalist put an arm around my shoulders and took me aside while the camera panned across my would-be murderers.

"That was amazing," he said. "The video quality wasn't great, but we caught it all." He strode towards the mantelpiece and snatched up the two golf-ball-sized cameras he had planted earlier. "I was surprised when you hung on so long. We all thought you'd forgotten the phrase. The police wanted to burst in and arrest them as soon as they admitted to killing your mother, but I persuaded them to wait."

"Look, if you'll excuse me, I need a little space."

"Sure, no problem." He re-joined the cameraman. The pair followed the prisoners as the policemen escorted them out to the waiting cars.

A hand touched me on the shoulder. I turned to see Val, smiling at me. "It's over," she whispered. She moved in and enveloped me in a hug. The fresh smell of her hair broke down my barriers. Tears streaked my cheeks as I wrapped my arms around her.

I'm not sure how long we held onto each other, but we only broke apart at the sound of somebody clearing their throat. Susie Mayhew stood to one side. "They're on the way back to the station with my two officers," she replied to my unasked question. She looked away, unable to meet my gaze. "Look, I'm aware you've been through a lot, but I'm going to have to arrest you and take you in as well."

She must have detected my shocked expression because she added, "Don't worry, it'll be a different location to those two. I know you're worried about your safety, so I'll make sure somebody I trust stays with you at all times. It's just routine, and you should be able to go home tonight."

"Thanks," I said, dabbing at my eyes with a handkerchief. "What will happen to my brother-in-law?"

"A couple of cars are heading to his house as we speak."

A sudden thought occurred to me. "That's why he told me it wasn't safe to contact the police. My guess is he was trying to protect himself. He was worried your lot might believe me and ask him some awkward questions. What better way to prevent me from talking than by telling me it was too dangerous?"

The policewoman crossed her arms. "I'm inclined to agree with you, but we're not about to take any more chances. What we did tonight was risky enough. Of course, somebody will interrogate him at length as soon as we get our hands on him. I don't anticipate much resistance from those two either. We've got them on tape admitting to your mother's murder. If anybody else is involved, I expect we'll pick them up pretty quickly."

"By the way, when you charged in, you yelled 'armed police'. I didn't see any guns."

Her mouth twisted into a wry smile. "I wanted to throw them off their stride and not give them time to think. There weren't enough people here, really, with just the three officers. If they had resisted arrest, we would have been in trouble. But after what your journalist friend told us, I didn't know who I could trust."

"Well, thanks for believing me."

"To be perfectly honest, I'm not sure I did. All the evidence indicated you were guilty. I figured if nobody showed up, at the very least I would have you in the bag. Everything after that was a bonus."

"You're not going to use those, are you?" I asked, pointing to the strap by her waist.

"What? The handcuffs? I don't think that will be necessary. As soon as some more officers arrive, we can leave. Ah, here they are."

A blue flashing light illuminated the edge of the beige, patterned curtains. Moments later, a group of four uniformed men entered the room. Their eyes widened in surprise as they identified me. That would happen a lot over the next few weeks.

The policewoman left me and took her colleagues into the hall. After a few seconds, she returned holding a set of car keys. "Shall we go?"

"Can my friend join me?" I asked. "That is, if you want to," I added hastily, turning to Val.

Val patted me on the arm. "Yeah, of course."

The police sergeant studied us for a moment then shrugged. "Under normal circumstances, I'd have said no, but there's nothing normal about tonight. I don't see why not." She led us through the house towards the front door.

Josh Nixon was sheltering in the porch, talking loudly into a mobile. He glanced up at our approach. "You're not leaving, are you?"

"I'm under arrest," I replied.

He stepped back in shock. "What?"

"It's just routine," Val said. "I've got your number. We'll give you a call tomorrow."

"Remember our arrangement. I'll be banging at your door if I don't hear from you."

"I won't forget."

"Bloody parasites," Mayhew muttered under her breath as we emerged into the stormy night.

I smiled to myself at the contradiction; less than an hour earlier she had been all too grateful to accept the journalist's information. The wind blew a strand of hair into her face. She brushed it away with one hand and unlocked the police car with the other. She opened the rear door and held it open. Val entered, and I followed, glad to escape the wild weather.

For the first time in several days, I travelled upright in the back seat.

Epilogue:
Friday, 7th August, 2020

One week later

I removed my sunglasses as I pushed open the door. Despite the disguise, I had received several curious glances from passers-by as I made my way from the car park to The Corner Café. It shouldn't have come as too much of a surprise; I had become something of a celebrity. For the past fortnight, my face had been front and centre on every newspaper and television screen, initially as a villain and subsequently as a hero.

Val had returned to work after taking the first part of the week as holiday. I stayed at her house in Newbury while the police investigated the case. So far, her name had remained out of the press. Despite only knowing each other for a matter of days, we had become close friends. I still held out hope that our relationship might develop into something more meaningful.

The bell clanged as I passed through the doorway. Molly was working behind the counter. She glanced up at my entrance and performed a double take. A worried expression flashed across her face, and I saw her glance towards the kitchen as I approached.

"Hi, Molly," I said, smiling. "I only came in to apologise."

She studied me for a second and seemed to relax a little. "Hello, Mr Parrott. You've become quite famous over the last week or so."

"Look, can we talk for a minute?"

Molly glanced around the café. At this time of the morning, customers occupied only two of the tables. "Alright," she said.

I followed her to the nearest table. She pulled out a chair and sat. I crossed to the opposite side and did the same.

Placing my elbows on the polished surface, I leaned forwards. "I guess you know by now what I was mixed up in."

Molly nodded. "It's been hard to avoid it."

"When I came here the last time, I'd recently discovered somebody was trying to kill me. My head was all over the place. When you mentioned your boyfriend used the dark web, I assumed he was the one sent after me and that you helped him. I just wanted to say sorry."

Her expression softened. "After that night, I asked him about it. As you probably noticed, he visits the gym a lot. Apparently, he buys this high protein powder off the Internet to build up his muscles. He gets it off a dark web page. I've told him he can't guarantee he's getting the genuine article, but he swears by it. Anyway, it doesn't matter anymore because we've split up."

"Oh, I'm sorry to hear that."

"Don't be. It hasn't been great for a while. That was one of many things we argued about. What are you going to do now?"

"I'm not sure. There are still four weeks until the start of next term—if they agree to have me back. I plan to take a holiday. After that, we'll see what happens. I've received several offers for book and magazine deals, but I haven't decided what to do yet."

"Well, good luck, Alex."

We both stood. I held out my hand, but she dragged me into a hug. "Look after yourself," she said.

I glanced at my watch: forty minutes until my scheduled meeting with Cathy. My sister had been answering police questions about her husband for most of the last week, and today was the first opportunity for us to meet face to face. I left the café and headed back to the car.

~

"It's a peaceful spot, isn't it?" I said, glancing sideways at my sister.

Cathy nodded without looking at me, her eyes focused on the trunk of a large oak.

We stood behind the yellow crime scene tape. Sunlight cut through the branches of the surrounding trees and lit the morning air with golden shafts of brightness. Patchy grass and low shrubs covered the floor of the clearing located a few yards off the rutted track leading through the woods. The muted drone of insects produced a background hum in keeping with the sombre mood. The scent of warm, damp earth assaulted my nostrils.

"In some ways, it would be good if she could stay here."

Cathy swung to face me. "You know that's not possible. Anyway, I want her final resting place to have a marker."

"They could always put a gravestone here." I knew she was right, but it was a spot I might have picked for myself given the choice.

"Until they perform the excavation, we can't be sure she's here at all," Cathy said, shivering despite the warmth of the summer day.

I pulled the printed sheet of paper from the back pocket of my trousers. It wasn't the original—the police had taken that—but a photocopy. The letter was undated with no sender's address or date. It contained only three lines of typewritten text and a name.

I am sorry for what I did. Every time I close my eyes I see her face. I cannot live like this any longer so I am going to end it.

I buried her beneath the large oak tree at this location: 51.308290, - 0.97280234

Norman Cox

The envelope had arrived two days earlier bearing a first-class stamp, addressed to me in typed letters. The police were in possession of that too. What they didn't have was the yellow, handwritten post-it note I found stuck in between the folded sheet. For the hundredth time, I read the scruffy handwriting.

Hi Alex, I felt bad about leaving you and Val to sort everything out. Hopefully this goes some way towards paying you back. I'm almost certain the information is correct but I can't be absolutely sure. I suggest you hand the letter to the police but I'd appreciate it if you kept this part to yourself. Best wishes, Nick

I had adhered to his request by removing the post-it note before handing the rest over to the two policemen who paid me a visit a few hours later. When they investigated the property that Cox had inherited from his mother, they discovered him hanging from a rope tied to a beam in the garage. The investigators confirmed the paper and the ink used in the letter matched those found in the printer inside the house. They drew the obvious conclusion and classified the death as a suicide; only Cathy, Nick and I knew differently.

In a few minutes, a forensic team would arrive to commence the excavation that would validate the information. From the short time I had known Nick, I suspected it was genuine. I allowed my mind to wander, imagining the paedophile's last moments. Had he been genuinely remorseful, or had he resisted until the end? If I ever saw Nick again, I would have to ask him.

Cathy glanced down at the letter. "You should have told me you found out who had taken her."

We had held this conversation several times by phone over the past two days. I repeated what I had said previously. "What difference would it have made? The police informed me they couldn't use it to prosecute him. I didn't want you and Mum to suffer any more."

Cathy's frown deepened. "You thought you'd play the martyr and keep it to yourself to protect us?"

"What good would have come from telling you?"

My sister shook her head and turned her back on me. A tremor ran through her body. "I could have done something about it."

"What? Like arranging a hitman to pay him a visit?"

Cathy froze as if I had slapped her. I apologised immediately. She remained frozen in place for several seconds then shuffled around to face me. At first, I thought my thoughtless response had angered her. As I studied her expression, I recognised a different emotion. Rather than the fury I expected, I detected resignation in her eyes.

"So, you know?" she said, her voice barely above a whisper.

"Know what?"

The question lay unanswered between us. My brain whirled in a frenzy, trying to make sense of what I had heard. Then it all fell into place. I opened my mouth to speak, but the words failed to materialise.

She lowered her gaze. "I thought you'd worked it out."

In the aftermath of my brother-in-law, Jamie's arrest, we had barely found the opportunity to discuss my ordeal, and I was still none the wiser as to the identity of my mystery benefactor. Under police questioning, Cathy denied all knowledge of her husband's activities. What she had just said revealed that to be a lie.

Finally, I forced my vocal cords into action. "It was you who placed the contract to protect me."

"Yes."

"But ..." I faltered, unable to say more.

Cathy raised her head. "Jamie created the site, but it was all my idea."

"I don't ... Why did you do it? Was it for the money?"

Cathy scowled at me. "You seriously think we set everything up for financial gain? Is that how little you understand me?"

"Well—"

My sister cut me off. "Twenty-five years ago, somebody abducted and killed Elena. The police gave up on the case and stopped searching for the man who did it. I came to the conclusion I couldn't sit back and do nothing, so I persuaded Jamie to create the website. Then I started my research. I decided if I was unable to identify the bastard who took our sister, I would at least try to prevent others from suffering the same fate.

"The targets I selected were paedophiles, particularly those involved in creating child pornography or worse. I paid the fees, and the hitmen we signed up did the dirty work. In most cases, it was made to appear like suicide, but for the worst offenders, I wanted to send a message."

"Are you saying you arranged the murder of the first couple they accused me of killing?" I asked.

Cathy nodded. "Indirectly, yes. He ran several legitimate businesses, but I learned he was also bringing underage girls into the country and selling them into prostitution."

"What about his wife?"

"She wasn't supposed to die. She must have disturbed the killer. Either that or she saw his face."

"And you managed to find out about this man all by yourself?"

Cathy sighed. "No. When we started out, I did my own research. I learned a lot talking to the victims I came across during my charity work. But then those two policemen, Bowman and Wickford, became involved. They worked in Vice and it turned out they were investigating some of the same people on my list. Somehow, they discovered a link between the targets, and eventually, they tracked us—or should I say Jamie—down. But rather than arresting him, they made him work for them. They never realised the site was my idea."

She must have seen the confusion on my face because she continued to explain. "Where they were investigating a case with insufficient evidence or little chance of a conviction, they instructed Jamie to create a job to target the suspect. As long as he placed the contracts, they agreed not to arrest him.

"They paid all the fees, but they were careful to distance themselves from the site and always used Bitcoin to transfer the money. When Jamie asked them where it came from, they refused to answer. My guess is they siphoned off some of the proceeds from the crimes they investigated.

"For a while, our objectives aligned, but then they started targeting a different group of people. I suspect most were still criminals, but I can't be sure. By then, we couldn't back out without implicating ourselves. Jamie and I argued about what to do, and that was one of the reasons we split up.

"Despite our quarrels, we did agree that neither would give evidence against the other if they ever arrested one of us; it meant the girls would always have at least one parent to look after them. Then, by sheer chance, you found a note with the login details to the site."

I dreaded the answer to my next question, but I had to ask. "Who placed the contract on me?"

"After you visited him, Jamie panicked, and told Bowman and Wickford. At first, they attempted to discredit you by planting the material on your computer. When you contacted that policewoman, they threatened to kill him and the girls if he didn't place a hit on you. As I said earlier, they weren't aware of my involvement, so I created a job to protect you. I arranged for the man to pick up my old mobile so he could find you. I left the house with Sophia and Zoe, and tried to persuade Mum to join us. She had no idea about any of this stuff, and I certainly couldn't tell her. In the end, she refused to leave. I never thought they would do anything to her."

"Who sent the username and password?"

"That was me. I wanted you and your protector to be aware that somebody was out there trying to kill you. But I also needed to keep it anonymous in case the police got hold of the phone."

"I'm guessing one of you took the money from my bank account."

"Jamie did that. He needed the cash quickly to place the job. Bowman and Wickford said it was his problem to sort out and refused to pay for it. As you figured out, he put the software on your laptop to tell him your location whenever you turned it on. Once it was installed, he also gained access to all your data."

"Why did they target Mum?" I asked.

"Jamie was getting cold feet. He was about to confess. They did it to demonstrate how far they were prepared to go if he went against them."

"Christ," I said, "what a mess. What happens next?"

Cathy's eyes locked onto mine. "That depends on you. If you tell the police what I've just told you, both Jamie and I will end up behind bars, and your nieces will grow up in foster care."

"And if I don't?"

"Bowman and Wickford have no knowledge of my involvement, and Jamie will keep me out of it. He'll spend a long time in prison either way, but at least the girls will still have their mother to look after them."

I raised my hands to my face. Despite the warmth of the air in the clearing, my fingers felt cold against my cheeks.

Cathy played her final card. "The thing is, it was totally unnecessary. Yesterday, I found out you identified that sick bastard over three years ago but didn't tell anybody. Had I known, it would all have ended with him, and we wouldn't be in this situation today."

The sound of vehicles disturbed the stillness. Through the trees, I picked up the approach of two dark-coloured vans and a white police car. The engines died one by one. The clunk of shutting doors reached my ears, followed by raised voices.

I turned to my sister and examined her face. She stared back at me. The decision was easy to make. Two decades ago, I had lost one sister. I wasn't about to lose the other.

Richard T. Burke

THE END

Author's Notes

Dear Reader,

I'm flattered that out of all the books on the market, you chose this one. I sincerely hope you enjoyed reading it. If you did, I would be extremely grateful if you could tell your friends and leave a review on Amazon or Goodreads (or preferably both). Reviews are an important factor in helping to sell books and are especially important for independent authors. I pay particular attention to all comments and use them to try to make my books better.

If you would like to receive news of forthcoming books and a free short story, please sign up to my mailing list at www.rjne.uk.

I would like to express my gratitude to my early reviewers and readers, including Marika and the members of my Facebook launch team. Thanks also to fellow authors, Ross Greenwood and Andrew Maclure, who provided loads of useful advice and encouragement.

All the above gave their time freely to help me with this book, and I am eternally grateful for their support.

This book has undergone thorough review, but those typos are pesky beggars and sometimes sneak through undetected. Please let me know if you find one so that other readers will benefit from your sharp-eyed attention. The best way is to leave a comment on my website.

The Dark Web is a fascinating subject, and there are numerous articles on the Internet. There have been several stories over the years about sites for hitmen, but these days, there's a good chance any such website has been set up by law enforcement officers as a honeypot to catch criminals.

The software tools I mention in the book (TOR and Bitmessage) are freely available. I can't confirm whether Internet Service Providers track their usage; all I can say is that nobody has contacted me about my occasional access during the research for this book!

I have some ideas for a sequel but whether I write one or not will depend to some extent on the reaction to this volume. I am always interested to hear from readers and would welcome any feedback via the comments feature on my website at www.rjne.uk. I try to read and respond to every comment I receive.

Richard T. Burke

If you enjoyed this book, you might like to try one of my other novels such as Decimation: The Girl Who Survived (http://mybook.to/Decimation) or The Colour of the Soul (http://mybook.to/COTS).

Thanks for reading.

Richard T. Burke   August 2019

To read the author's blog and to see news of upcoming books, please visit www.rjne.uk or follow him on Twitter @RTBurkeAuthor.

Printed in Great Britain
by Amazon